A DETECTIVE SASHA FRANK MYSTERY

COLD CONSEQUENCES

DAVID ROHLFING

RIVER GROVE
BOOKS

Published by River Grove Books
Austin, TX
www.rivergrovebooks.com

Distributed by River Grove Books

Design and composition by Greenleaf Book Group
Cover design by Greenleaf Book Group
Cover Images: ©David Rohlfing and ©iStockphoto.com/Subodh Agnihotri

Publisher's Cataloging-in-Publication data is available.

Print ISBN: 978-1-63299-388-5

eBook ISBN: 978-1-63299-389-2

First Edition

To my wife, whom I owe my life.

When you endeavour to decipher the mind of a killer, you willingly and consciously enter the world they exist and will, without taking extreme measures and caution, become who they became. You must therefore be of strong enough mind to ensure that you do not succumb as we all possess an inner madness.

—Doctor Ephraim H. Kahn (1832–1911)

ACKNOWLEDGMENTS

In March of 2019, my wife, along with a 911 dispatcher, a police officer, paramedics, and an amazing group of medical personnel at Carle BroMenn Medial Center, brought me back to life after fifteen minutes without a pulse when I suffered sudden cardiac arrest. If it were not for the heroes listed above, I would not have been alive to write *Cold Consequences*. I thank God for the miracle that I survived.

I would like to thank my editors and publisher at Greenleaf Book Group. They helped me learn while writing and editing this book that less is often more. I have greatly appreciated their help in my journey as a writer.

I also want to thank the team of publicists and marketers at Books Forward who've been invaluable in building momentum for the Detective Sasha Frank Mystery Series.

1

I t had been almost two years since Ashley Cummins had graduated from college and returned to live with her father in his home. She'd played NCAA Division I soccer and had been selected to first-team all-conference before suffering a concussion, along with neck and upper back injuries, when she'd been blocked hard into an unpadded goal post during a regional semi-final game her senior year. Ashley had recovered quickly from the concussion, but the other injuries had ended her childhood dream of making the Olympic team and going pro.

Ashley's doctors had prescribed her pain killers, but after she'd been on the meds for a number of weeks, they had become concerned she was developing an addiction and refused to write additional prescriptions. Instead, they told her she would require long-term pain management protocols. They tried to convince her to go to physical rehab and a pain clinic to help her find long-term solutions to control her constant agony, but she preferred the immediate relief drugs provided. She tried getting them from other doctors but found buying them on the street a much easier way to keep her growing addiction secret from both family and friends. A new friend she'd met when she returned home had introduced her to Danny Williams, known as D, who had become a reliable source for Ashley's opioids.

It was almost 1 a.m. on a Saturday morning when Ashley drove down the dark street on Bloomington's west side in the BMW 3-series convertible her father had given her as a college graduation gift. She was on her way to meet D to buy an opioid known on the street as "beans." She parked near the intersection where the dealer had instructed her to wait.

A few hours earlier, she'd texted D that her need was desperate. He let her know he couldn't meet her then at the Uptown Normal bar, their usual meeting spot, but he could the following night. Ashley texted back that she needed her pills now, so he agreed to meet her at a street corner near his home.

She'd never been to this part of the city, and she hoped D wouldn't be late. As she waited, she turned down her radio, lit a cigarette, turned up the heater, and cracked the driver's side window. Besides being addicted to pain killers, she'd also developed a pack-a-day habit and drank too much vodka every night. Not a good combination, and it was beginning to take a toll on her mind and body.

Because of her increased drug use the past few months, she'd been arriving late to work several times a week and sometimes missing it entirely, but she wasn't too concerned because her father owned the company. Charlie Cummins Luxury Home Builders had a reputation throughout Illinois for the exceptional quality of their work building residences exclusively for the well-to-do. Ashley was supposed to be learning the business so she could take over as president of the company when her father retired.

She'd been waiting about five minutes when, out of the corner of her eye, she saw D angling across the street toward her car. He was wearing a heavy overcoat with a hood and leather gloves. As he walked toward her, Ashley hit the down button on the driver's side window and tossed out her cigarette. "Come on, D," she said.

D nodded, walked past the front of the convertible, and opened the passenger door.

Across the street, two men standing in the shadows watched as the drug dealer got into the late-model BMW. Big G whispered to Sticks, "Who's that?"

"Danny." Sticks didn't like Danny because the dealer was always flaunting his success, making sure everyone else in the neighborhood knew how much money he had. Sticks and Big G supplied most of the dealers in the area, but Danny got his from someone in Chicago, bypassing the two of them. "It's either a booty call, or he's pushin' his beans," Sticks said. Danny had a reputation as a big-time player in the college bars in Bloomington and Normal, selling high-end drugs to rich students. Sticks hadn't really seen him on the streets much since Danny's girlfriend, Hallie, had given birth to his daughter a couple of years ago.

D slid into the front seat and closed the door. "Hey, little girl. Sorry I couldn't get to the club tonight. Kayla is sick."

"Sorry to hear that, D. I hope she feels better soon."

"Thanks. She'll be fine. I just needed to stay home tonight to help Hallie take care of her." D knew Ashley didn't care how his two-year-old daughter was feeling. He reached into his right front coat pocket and pulled out a plastic vial containing ten beans.

Ashley opened her purse and took out seven hundred dollars in cash.

D handed her the vial and took the seven bills from her. He'd never used drugs, and he couldn't understand her addiction to the little, round, green, 80 mg pill that cost her several hundred per day, but she never offered to trade him sex for drugs like some of his customers did. Ashley had money, and that was the type of customer he preferred.

She popped the top off the vial and took one of the pills, quickly washing it down with water from the light blue aluminum bottle she always carried. "Thanks, D. We done?"

He smiled to himself. "Yes, we are, Ashley. Have a nice night." As he started to get out of the car, a man shoved a pistol into his chest and started pushing him to the ground. D dropped to his knees immediately.

Sticks then pointed his SIG Sauer 9mm in Danny's face. "Don't say nothin'." He tapped the barrel on the bridge of Danny's nose. "Understand?"

Danny nodded.

Sticks found nothing in Danny's pants pockets other than some keys and a billfold, but then he found the cash from the deal in his right front coat pocket.

Another man crammed himself into the front seat and closed the door. Inside the car, Big G smiled at Ashley as he waved his Glock back and forth over the center console. The big man pointed his gun at her chest. "What you got for me, girl?"

Ashley had never been held at gunpoint, and she was unsure what she should do next. "What do you want?"

Big G laughed. "Now, what do ya think?" He grabbed her purse as Ashley pushed back up against the driver's side door.

Ashley screamed and swung her fists at him as she tried keep ahold of her purse, but she was no match for Big G, who easily shoved her away. Inside her purse were a few hundred dollars, credit cards, her driver's license, and the remaining pills she'd just bought, which were her main concern. She tried scratching him, but he was wearing leather gloves and a winter coat. He laughed at her as she tried to fight back. He reached across the console with the Glock in his right hand and tried hitting her with the pistol's barrel. "Bitch!" he shouted.

Sticks turned to see what was going on inside the car, and Danny took the opportunity to shove him backward into the side of the car. Sticks hit his head on the passenger door window and fell to the ground, dropping his gun. Danny got up quickly and started running back toward the safety of his house.

Momentarily stunned, Sticks reached for his gun and started to get up just as he saw a bright flash and heard the sound of a muffled gunshot. He turned to see Big G pushing open the car door, saying, "We outta here."

Sticks peered inside the car and saw that Big G had shot the girl in the face, just below her right eye. She stared blankly back at him, and he knew she was dead. He slammed the door shut and ran after Big G.

It took Danny less than a minute to run the few blocks back to the house he and Hallie rented on West MacArthur Avenue. He realized his keys had been stolen and knocked on the front door. As he waited for Hallie to let him in, he found that he also didn't have his billfold or the cash Ashley had paid him for the drugs. "Crap!" He knocked again. Whoever had robbed him now had his ID. They probably already knew who he was, even though he hadn't been selling in the neighborhood since Kayla was born. He didn't want to contribute to the drug problem where his daughter would be growing up.

Hallie flicked on the porch light, looked out, and opened the door. "What are you doing? You're going to wake the baby."

Danny stepped inside and quickly closed and locked the door. He turned off the porch light and the lights in the front room of the house. He crossed to the window and looked out to see if anyone followed him. It didn't seem anyone had. He'd just started telling Hallie what had happened when they heard the first police siren.

———

Sticks and Big G entered through the back door of Sticks's mother's house, nine blocks from the crime scene. Sticks reached into the refrigerator in the kitchen and pulled out two cold cans of beer and tossed one to his partner. "Damn it, G!"

"That bitch wouldn't stop trying to scratch the hell outta me." Big G took a drink of beer, "I kept trying to hit her, but she wouldn't stop coming at me."

"You certainly paid her back, big time. That girl is stone-cold dead." Sticks reached into his jacket pocket and pulled out the bills, billfold, and keys he'd taken from Danny. "But look what we got."

"At least we jacked the pusher," Big G said. "How much is that?"

Sticks counted out the money.

"Cool. Do you think he knew who we were?"

"Maybe," Sticks sneered, "but I think mostly all he saw was my SIG Sauer. Scared the crap outta him, man."

Big G laughed. "No doubt."

"What did you get from the girl?"

Big G tossed over the purse. "Check it out."

Inside, Sticks found a cell phone, which he immediately turned off. Next, he pulled out a vial of pills, the girl's ID, a debit card, and couple of credit cards. He counted out over three hundred in cash and smiled. "Not bad, G. Not bad."

"Plastic is useless with her dead."

"True. We'll dump anything with her name on it. Still a good night. We're not gonna see Danny sellin' on our turf again."

They heard sirens in the distance, and the two stopped talking and looked at each other. Big G took another drink. "We need to stay low for a while."

Sticks nodded, and they clinked their beer bottles.

2

Sasha Frank had been with the Bloomington Police Department since 1984 and was promoted to senior detective almost four years ago. He was home asleep in bed with Janet, his partner of nearly five years, when his cell phone started chirping at 1:40 a.m., the distinctive ring signaling a call from the Bloomington Police duty sergeant.

The senior detective listened intently as he was told the scant details of a shooting that had taken place a short time ago on the west side of the city. After hanging up, Sasha quickly got out of bed and walked to the bathroom.

Janet sat up. "What's up?"

Sasha stepped back out of the bathroom. "There was a shooting southwest of downtown. Officers on the scene found a female DB in a parked vehicle."

"How do you do that?"

Sasha looked back through the door at Janet, unsure of what she meant. "Do what?"

"Get up so fast. I hit the snooze button, then lay in bed for ten minutes after I wake up, and I still don't feel like getting up."

"Years of practice." Sasha walked into the closet and started getting dressed.

Janet got out of bed. "Who shoots somebody sitting in their car?"

"Not that hard to figure." He smiled at her. "My guess is, it was a bad guy."

"Smartass." She headed to the bathroom.

He quickly dressed in blue jeans and a sweatshirt, then slipped into a pair of insulated boots. Snow was forecasted for later in the day. He followed Janet into the bathroom to quickly shave and brush his teeth.

From her seat on the toilet, Janet watched Sasha. "You know that electric shaver makes you look like you shaved last night and not this morning, right?"

"I don't care, and I don't think anyone else will either."

"If you're going to be doing a television interview sometime today, don't you want to look your best?"

He turned and winked at her. "Like you care." Sasha finished shaving and did a quick check to make sure he hadn't missed a spot before brushing his teeth.

Janet rose from the toilet. "I'm going to make you some coffee to take with you."

"Thanks, sweetie," Sasha said as he finished brushing his teeth. "I'll be there in a minute." He walked back to the closet and retrieved his Bloomington PD winter jacket.

Sasha walked into the kitchen as Janet was pouring coffee into a large insulated to-go mug. "Thanks for the coffee." He gave her a quick hug. The senior detective clipped on his holster and gun, then picked up a pair of leather gloves and a watch cap before heading out to the garage. He stopped and turned back to Janet. "It'll be a long day. Talk to you later."

She smiled and shouted out to him, "Stay safe! Good luck catching the bad guys."

———

Sasha was less than a minute out from the crime scene when he radioed dispatch to let them know he was arriving. As he approached from the east on Oakland Avenue, he saw blue lights flashing four blocks ahead at the crime scene. He turned on his grill-mounted police lights to signal the officers manning the blocked intersection of his arrival.

There was just enough room for him to maneuver the car past the police cruiser partially blocking the road. He rolled down the driver's window and slowed down. "Morning, officer," Sasha said as he rolled past the cruiser and parked on Lee Street behind another one.

The senior detective saw that his partner, Darcie Lyman, was already on scene. Darcie had joined the department as a police officer in 2005 after graduating from the University of Illinois and had been a detective for two years. She was intelligent and intuitive, compassionate and inquisitive, all traits of a good detective. Sasha expected Darcie to replace him after he retired and take over the title of senior detective with the Bloomington PD, unless she pulled the trigger and decided to move to Denver to realize her dream of living in the Rockies. Selfishly, he hoped she would stay until he retired. Darcie was a solid detective.

Sasha climbed out of his vehicle and walked to where Darcie was standing. "It's freezing out here. How'd you get here so fast?"

Darcie nodded, agreeing about the temperature. "I was up watching a movie when I got the call from dispatch. I live five minutes from here. I had a date, but that went south when the guy started talking politics."

"He doesn't sound like a very perceptive guy. Surely you signaled him that that was a bad idea?"

"No, I didn't. One of my cousins thought the dude was perfect for me, but I knew right away I wasn't going to see him again. I also found out he's a Cubs fan. The date was doomed from the start." Darcie smiled. "I'll set her up with some loser as payback."

Sasha laughed, then focused his attention on the white convertible a few feet away. "So what we got?"

"Female DB. Sounds like a single shot to the head, based on the chatter. Dispatch said you'd be here ASAP, so I waited until we could both talk with Bill Watkins and the two officers." Darcie got out her notepad for the names of the other responding officers. "O'Malley and Cruz." She turned and looked toward the house where the white convertible was parked. "Cruz has evidently talked with the lady in the white house over there who called 911."

"Okay. Let's talk with Bill and the other officers to see what they've found." Sasha and Darcie walked over to where the three were standing. "Morning, Bill." Sasha reached out and shook hands with the police captain.

"Morning, Detective."

Sasha nodded to the other two officers, then looked back at Bill. "Can you fill us in on what you found when you arrived?"

Bill nodded. "I was first on scene at 1:23 a.m. The white convertible was parked with the engine running. Cruz and O'Malley arrived shortly after I did." The captain turned and briefly looked at the vehicle, which was still idling. "We left it as we found it." He looked back at Sasha and Darcie. "I used the bullhorn, but I got no response from the occupant. So we approached the vehicle, and there was still no movement from the occupant. I shined my flashlight through the passenger side window and could see the wound under her right eye. I opened the passenger door to check for a pulse, and there was none. She was obviously DRT."

Sasha nodded. "Anything else?"

"Cruz talked with the lady who called 911, Jasmine Warren. She called in the shots fired at 1:18."

"What did she have to say?"

Bill looked at Officer Cruz. "Josey?"

Officer Josey Cruz stepped forward, holding a notepad. "Jasmine Warren was awake in bed and heard a vehicle running out front of her house shortly after 1 a.m. She got up and was watching from her bedroom window when someone got into the vehicle a few minutes later. The only light was from the streetlight at the corner and her front porch, so she's not positive, but she believes the person getting into the passenger side was a male wearing a heavy winter coat and a hoodie." She looked up from her notes. "Lady's daughter is sick, so she steps away from the window for a couple of minutes to take care of her. When she next looks out, she sees what she thought were two males standing outside the vehicle's passenger door. She says one was a big guy, and the other one was much smaller. A few seconds later, she sees the first person she'd watched get into the vehicle open the door and start to get out. The smaller man puts the guy on the ground and starts waving a gun in his face, then starts going through his pockets. The bigger guy gets into the vehicle. The man with the gun turns and looks at the vehicle, and that's when the guy on the ground pushes or kicks the man with the gun down and then gets up and starts running. He runs to the corner of Lee and Oakland, then heads east on Oakland. A few seconds later, there was a flash of light inside the car, and she heard the sound of a muffled gunshot. The bigger guy gets out of the vehicle and takes off running toward the same intersection, but she thinks he may have headed west on Oakland. She loses sight of him. The smaller man quickly looked inside the car, then took off after the bigger guy. She then called 911."

"Thank you for that update, officer." Sasha turned to Darcie. "Any questions, Detective?"

Darcie nodded. "Did she recognize any of them?"

"I asked, and she said no." Josey looked down at her notes. "All of them were wearing coats, hoodies, or sock hats. Her front porch light was on, like I said." Officer Cruz turned and looked toward the house. "But as you can see, it's not providing much light."

"And the car?" Darcie asked. "Did she say if she recognized it?"

"Sorry. Yes. I asked that too. She said she'd never seen it before." Josey looked over at the car. "She said she doesn't see many BMW convertibles in this neighborhood."

"Dispatch called with the registration, Sasha." Captain Watkins pulled out his notepad. "The registered owner is CCLHB LLC d/b/a Charlie Cummins Luxury Home Builders. The address listed is on Hershey Road, south of Route 9."

"Besides checking the DB's pulse, did you touch anything else inside the vehicle, Bill?" Darcie asked.

"No, Detective. Dispatch told me you guys were on your way. I didn't see any urgency to do a search under the circumstances."

"We appreciate that." Sasha and Darcie briefly talked with the officers about securing the area around the car with crime scene tape before the two detectives turned their attention to the car. They took off their leather gloves and pulled on latex gloves before starting their search of the white convertible.

Sasha pointed the beam of his flashlight into the window of the driver's side door. It was intact, which meant the bullet fired at the victim should be found either inside the car, or more likely, inside the victim's skull based on what Captain Watkins had told them. He slowly walked around the front of the convertible, keeping the beam of his flashlight on the body. Darcie followed close behind.

Sasha stopped at the front right fender of the car and called out to Captain Watkins. "Was the passenger door closed when you arrived?"

"Yes."

"Thanks." The senior detective wondered why they had taken the time to close it, especially if the men the witness saw at the scene had all run once there was gunfire. Sasha turned to Darcie. "I'm going to open the door and do a cursory inspection." She nodded.

Warm air poured out as he opened the door. He shined his flashlight onto the passenger side floorboard. The carpet looked wet. Probably from melted snow from the shoes of one or both of the perps who had been inside the vehicle. He squatted down and shined his flashlight into the face of the victim. He turned toward Darcie, who was standing behind him. "Beautiful girl."

"Except for the bullet wound under her right eye."

"Really?" The senior detective shook his head.

"Sorry." Darcie realized she shouldn't have said that out loud. "Insensitive, I know."

A small amount of blood had coagulated on her cheek. Sasha followed a trickle of blood that continued down onto her white fur coat. He searched the floorboard on the driver's side with his flashlight, hoping to find the victim's purse, but he didn't see one.

Sasha refocused his attention to the back of the passenger side bucket seat, which was reclined at about a fifty- to fifty-five degree angle. It didn't look normal. He pushed the back of the seat and easily rocked it back and forth. Without using the seat adjustment lever, he was able to pull the back of the seat forward to where it almost touched the dashboard. That couldn't be how the German engineer designed the seat to function. He made a mental note to talk to someone who knew the victim to see if the seat was already broken.

He shined his light into the back seat, which was a mess. There were coffee and soft drink cups and fast-food wrappers strewn everywhere. Odd, he thought. The front seats and floorboards were immaculate.

"You going to turn off the engine, Sasha?" Darcie asked.

"I don't think so. I'll let the ME decide when to turn it off. It's been running for a while. Best not to change anything." He opened the center console and rummaged through it. He handed Darcie a clear plastic pouch with papers inside. "Take a look at what's inside. See if you can find a name."

Darcie untied the string on the flap and pulled out the first piece of paper. "Registration is in here." The registration inside the car matched what Captain Watkins had told them a few minutes ago. "There's a business card too." Darcie shined the beam of the flashlight onto the card. "Name on it is Ashley Cummins. Director of Marketing at Charlie Cummins Luxury Home Builders."

"Check the Secretary of State's database for a driver's license picture for an Ashley Cummins," Sasha said. "I didn't find a purse or billfold with ID in here." Darcie nodded and walked to her car. Sasha spent a couple of minutes searching the floorboards and under the passenger seat for spent bullet casings. Finding nothing, he gave up.

As he approached his partner's vehicle, she rolled down the driver's side front window and turned her onboard computer screen toward Sasha so he could see. "The photo looks like it could have been taken a few years ago, but it looks like our vic. Ashley Brittany Cummins. Long, dark hair with brown eyes."

"That's her," he said.

Captain Watkins walked over to tell Sasha that the ME had arrived.

"Roger that. Thanks." Sasha turned back to Darcie. "Showtime."

Darcie got out of her vehicle, and the two headed to the intersection where the ME's vehicles were parked.

Sasha stopped short of the intersection. "We'll talk to the 911 caller Jasmine Warren as soon as the ME and her team get started. There's really nothing more for us to do here until the ME updates us."

An extended Ford Econoline van driven by Medical Examiner Juanita Gordon was parked in the middle of the intersection of Lee and Oakland. She gave a small wave to Sasha and Darcie as they walked around the front of her van. A Medical Examiner box truck was parked behind her.

"Juanita is really good," Sasha said to Darcie. "With Beff Turner out on maternity leave, I'm glad she took over as acting ME."

Juanita got out of her van. "Morning, Sasha." She looked at Darcie and said, "Detective." She opened the back doors, reached into a compartment inside and pulled out a CSI investigation kit. Juanita began donning the coveralls, booties, and latex gloves from the kit as Sasha told her everything they'd learned about the crime scene, along with the name of the victim.

Juanita looked up when she heard the name of the girl found in the vehicle. "Ashley Cummins? Oh, my god! Are you sure? You know who she is, right?" she asked as she pulled on a hair cover.

Darcie quickly answered, "The business card said she worked for Charlie Cummins Luxury Home Builders. How's she related?"

Juanita shook her head. "She's Charlie Cummins's daughter. Only child. One of my daughters was in the same class as Ashley in school. They weren't close friends, but they hung out some. Her mother died when she was in junior high. Ashley's grandfather is Judge Cummins."

Sasha glanced at Darcie. "I don't know why we didn't already put all that together."

"Maybe because it's just after two in the morning," Juanita said. "You two are working on a couple of hours of sleep."

"I knew Charlie Cummins built homes," Sasha said, "but I didn't put his name together with Judge Cummins."

"Ashley is twenty-three or twenty-four years old." Juanita stood up and shook her head. "Sad."

Darcie looked at her notes. "She would have been twenty-four in May."

"What a loss." She picked up a flashlight and her gloves. "Okay. Thanks to you both. I'm going to talk to my team, then I'll be moving over to the vehicle."

As Juanita left to join her team, Captain Watkins walked up to Darcie and Sasha with two cups of hot, black coffee. "I thought you could use this."

"Thank you, Captain." Darcie hadn't had coffee yet this morning, and she took a quick gulp. It certainly wasn't as strong as her preferred brew, but it was nice and hot.

Sasha took the other cup. "Did everyone get some?"

"Yes. I sent out for coffee for everyone. There are a couple of containers sitting in O'Malley's cruiser if you want more."

"Great. Thanks, Bill." Sasha took a sip as Bill walked back to join the officers watching over the crime scene.

Sasha looked over at the white BMW convertible. "What was Ashley Cummins doing here so late at night?"

"Good question," Darcie said. "She's not from this neighborhood."

"Do you recall her home address from the driver's license database?"

"I wrote it down." Darcie checked her notes. "Stonebrook Court in Bloomington."

"Fancy."

Darcie took a sip of the coffee. "I'm not familiar with it."

"It's a very nice street with expensive homes. Maybe Ashley's dad built it for her, or maybe it's his home?" Sasha looked over at his partner. "We'll need to check that out."

The two detectives went over the details as they stood at the back of the ME's van and discussed what questions they'd ask the witness. When Sasha felt they were ready to interview the witness, he looked at his partner and said, "Darcie, you take the lead." Darcie nodded, and the two headed for Jasmine Warren's house.

———

It had been almost an hour and a half since Jasmine Warren had spoken with Officer Cruz, and she'd gone to sleep on her couch. The detectives apologized for taking so long to get back to her. Darcie asked her to re-tell what she'd witnessed, and it took Jasmine about ten minutes to recount all that she'd seen after first hearing the white convertible in front of her house until her call to 911. Officer Cruz had done a great job relaying what the lady had told her in the earlier interview. The facts hadn't changed one iota. Sasha thought Jasmine would make a fine witness on the stand when the district attorney prosecuted those responsible for Ashley's death.

The two detectives stood on the sidewalk in front of Jasmine's home, watching Juanita and her ME team gather evidence from the car. Portable light units had been set up around the perimeter of the BMW convertible, allowing the ME to conduct a more thorough investigation. Several members of Juanita's team had positioned a gurney and appeared ready to remove Ashley Cummins's body from the car.

Juanita was sitting in the passenger seat when she saw Sasha and shouted through the open car door, "Sasha! Come here. I'd like to show you something."

Sasha and Darcie walked over to the opened door. "What is it?" he asked.

"The victim was shot at close range. Typically, stippling on the skin is present when the barrel of the gun is within three feet when a shot's fired." She shined her light on the entrance wound. "You can clearly see the skin is burned several inches around the entrance wound. I think the barrel was less than two feet from the victim."

"Got it."

Juanita turned back to Sasha. "Aside from that, I found nothing special. Once I get her on the table, I'm sure I'll find something."

"Any evidence suggesting why she was here at this hour?"

"Not really. Ashley was a smoker. The car smells of cigarette smoke, and the ashtray is full of butts and ashes. We found a water bottle filled with what I assume is water, but I'll confirm that and let you know." She got out of the car and turned to the two team members standing by the gurney. "Let's move her now, please."

The team members spread out a large vinyl sheet on the pavement outside the open driver's side door, then lifted the gurney onto the sheet before moving it closer to the victim. Another assistant placed an open body bag on the gurney and stood ready to help the other two. Juanita got back inside the car to help maneuver the victim's legs out from under the steering wheel as the assistants on the outside pulled her from the front seat. The body bag easily held the small frame of Ashley Cummins, even fully clothed and wearing a fur coat.

After zipping the bag closed, the three moved the gurney away from the car and methodically folded the large sheet that had been beneath it. They put the sheet into a large evidence bag. Two of the assistants slowly rolled the gurney toward the ME box van. The remaining assistant turned off the car's engine, closed the door, and followed the two pushing the gurney.

"We're going to head back now," Juanita said. "I should be ready to start the autopsy by five."

"Sounds good. We should both be able to be there."

They waved to Juanita as she departed.

"What's next?" Darcie asked.

"I'm going to call dispatch to have a flatbed sent out to transport the car to the barn for a more thorough search." Sasha glanced at his partner and said, "Also, text me Charlie Cummins's home address."

"You read my mind." Darcie headed for her car. "Will do."

Sasha called the dispatcher and arranged for the convertible to be picked up and taken to the CSI barn, then he walked over to where Bill Watkins was standing. "Dispatch is sending a flatbed to remove the vehicle," he said. "Once they depart the scene, can you knock on doors to see if anyone else saw anything?"

"No problem, Sasha."

"Thanks, Bill."

Darcie walked over to where her partner was standing and said, "I told the crime scene guys that you were having the vehicle transported back to the barn. They're returning now to get ready for it to arrive."

Sasha's text alert went off, and he saw that Scott's Towing and Recovery would be arriving in about fifteen minutes. As he was reading the text, another text came through. "I just saw the address for Ashley's father you sent," he said. "Same address on Stonebrook Court?"

"Yes. I'm guessing that she probably doesn't still live there," Darcie said. "Almost nobody changes their address on their driver's license when they move. They wait until renewal time to change it."

"As soon as Scott's heads out with the car, we'll go over to notify Mr. Cummins." He looked at his watch, then quickly sent Juanita a text to let her know they might be running late for the autopsy.

Sasha leaned back against Captain Watkins's cruiser and sipped the fresh coffee. He needed to start talking with his partner about the key crime scene questions—the who, what, when, where, how, and why of this murder that had to all be answered to solve the case. "What's your theory on why Ms. Cummins found her way to this spot today, Detective?"

Darcie knew that questions would be coming since the minute she'd gotten the call from dispatch. She also knew the senior detective was an incredibly thorough investigator who would doggedly sift through every scrap of evidence along with any information they could dig up to solve the crime. She suspected that Sasha already had a working theory, so the questions were just part of his process of talking things through.

"There can't be many reasons why Ashley Cummins would be here this late on a Friday night," she said. "Why did she park in front of this house? If we can pull her car GPS navigation logs, we can see if she's ever been here before or has ever stopped anywhere close. I bet a dollar she hasn't." Darcie had heard Sasha tell stories of him and Janet making one-dollar bets.

Sasha smiled. "Funny." He couldn't begin to remember how many bets he'd lost to Janet over the years, both serious and silly. "Okay. You're on. So if this was the first time she'd been in this neighborhood, was she here to meet perp number one? If yes, then why?"

"Maybe a booty call? Or a drug buy?" Darcie took a sip of coffee. "Let's face it, Sasha, there can't be many reasons she was out here so late."

"I know I'm old-fashioned, but it doesn't seem reasonable to me that she'd respond to a booty call in her car in February, especially when the temperatures are below freezing."

"She and I are close to the same age, and I agree. So she's here to buy drugs?" Darcie looked up and down the street. "If she was, whomever she was meeting likely lives nearby."

"After the autopsy, we need to talk with the vice unit to start looking for known drug dealers within a few blocks of here."

"Sounds good." Darcie turned to see a large flatbed truck stop at the intersection across from them. "Scott's here."

It took several minutes for the police cruisers to relocate so the large flatbed could get into position to roll Ashley's car onto the back of the truck.

A few residents were standing on their front porches or sidewalks watching the car being moved from the scene. Sasha called out to Captain Watkins. "Bill!" He motioned up and down the street. "It looks like you've got a few people to interview."

The captain nodded. "Will do, Sasha."

For ten minutes, they watched the truck driver secure the convertible onto the flatbed. As soon as he was ready, the driver slowly began maneuvering through the parked police vehicles. There was a police cruiser leading in front and one trailing behind. "Let's hope they find something for us to go on," Sasha said.

Darcie nodded and looked down at her watch. "If we leave now, we'll be knocking on Mr. Cummins's door a few minutes after five."

"Yes. Notifications are never easy, but to wake someone to tell them that their twenty-three-year-old daughter was murdered—" Sasha shook his head.

3

The homes on Charlie Cummins's street were new, large, and on huge lots. Considering that Cummins built luxury homes, it made sense that he'd live in one himself. The two detectives got out of their cars and walked up to the well-lit double front doors and pressed the ornate doorbell. It took about a minute before a voice sounded from a speaker mounted below. "Who is it?"

"It's the Bloomington Police Department. My name is Senior Detective Sasha Frank. Am I speaking with Mr. Cummins?"

"Yes."

Sasha looked at Darcie. He waited a few seconds for Mr. Cummins to continue, but when he didn't, Sasha began again. "Do you mind if we come in and talk with you?"

There was a short pause. "Okay," Charlie Cummins replied. "Give me a minute."

It took several minutes until one of the front doors opened. Standing just inside was Charlie Cummins, who looked to be in his early fifties. He was of average height and weight. There was no question that he'd been asleep. "How can I help you?"

"As I said, my name is Senior Detective Sasha Frank. My partner is Detective Darcie Lyman. Would it be possible for us to step inside to talk with you?"

Charlie Cummins stepped back, letting the two detectives into his home. He closed the door behind them and led them into a library off to the side of the two-story foyer. Beyond the entrance was a large open area that led out to a patio.

Built-in shelves filled with books, mementos, and countless pictures lined the walls. In the middle of the room were two large leather sofas with a coffee table between them. Just past the sofas was one of the biggest desks Sasha had ever seen. Both Sasha and Darcie sat down on the couch across from Charlie Cummins.

"What is this all about, Detectives?"

Sasha began slowly. "You're the father of Ashley Brittany Cummins, correct?"

Cummins sat up straight. "Yes. Why?"

"There's no easy way to tell you this, sir, but I'm sorry to inform you that your daughter was found dead in her car shortly after 1 a.m. this morning."

The look on Charlie Cummins's face showed the pain of the news immediately. It was a combination of disbelief and horror. He shook his head. "That's impossible."

"Why do you say that, sir?" Sasha asked.

"It's just not possible."

"We're very sorry, Mr. Cummins. She was found in a car near the corner of South Lee Street and West Oakland in Bloomington. Your daughter's body has been taken to the medical examiner's office."

"How do you know it's her?"

"Our initial identification is based on her driver's license photo on file with the Illinois Secretary of State. She was found in a white 2011 BMW 3 Series convertible registered to your company." Sasha waited for Charlie Cummins to respond, but he didn't. "Sir? Sir."

"Yes."

"Later this morning, we're going to need you or another family member to come over to the office to positively identify Ashley."

Charlie stood up and took his cell from his pocket. He opened his favorites and punched his daughter's name. The phone call went immediately to voicemail. "Ashley, it's your father," he said. "Please call me as soon as you get this." He ended the call and typed out a text: "PLEASE CALL!" He walked over to his desk and picked up a picture of his daughter. "This isn't happening."

"I'm very sorry, sir. Could you please give us her cell number so we can trace her phone? We didn't find it with her or in her car."

"Certainly." Charlie pulled up his daughter's cell number on his phone screen and handed the phone over to Sasha. The detective nodded and wrote down the number.

"Detective." Sasha handed his notepad to Darcie, and she immediately rose and walked into the foyer to call dispatch so they could start the process of tracing Ashley's phone.

"Thank you, Mr. Cummins."

Charlie Cummins was tearing up. "Thank you, Detective. Can you tell me what happened?"

Sasha wanted to ask Charlie Cummins a few questions regarding his daughter's movements yesterday, so he quickly restated when and where she had been found. He didn't feel he should provide the distraught father all the details related to her murder. As Sasha relayed the information, Charlie slumped back and leaned against the top of the desk, shaking his head.

"I don't understand."

Sasha doubted that anyone in Charlie Cummins's shoes could understand the murder of their child. "We will do everything we can to find the person or persons responsible for this senseless act, Mr. Cummins."

Darcie entered the library and asked if Sasha could step into the foyer for a minute.

He excused himself and left the room with her. "What do you have?"

"Dispatch put a trace on the telephone number. It's currently turned off."

"Damn. Okay. Thanks, Darcie." They returned to the library.

Charlie Cummins looked up at Sasha. "Anything new, Detective?"

"No, sir. Do you mind if I ask you a few questions?"

Ashley's father nodded. "Go ahead."

"When was the last time you spoke with your daughter?"

"Ashley left the office around 5:30 yesterday evening. She told me she was going out with friends."

"Did Ashley live with you here, sir?" Sasha was beginning to think that maybe the address on her license was correct.

"Yes. Ever since she graduated from college and moved back to Bloomington, she's lived here at home with me. We've been planning to build a home for her here in town." He looked down at the floor. "We were going to break ground later this year." He shook his head and cried softly.

Sasha gave him a moment to compose himself. "So you said she told you she was going out with friends last night?"

"Yes. Ashley said she was planning on staying over at a friend's house after they went to a concert in Peoria." Charlie crossed over to the sofa and sat down.

After Sasha nudged her, Darcie asked the next question. "Did Ashley say who she was going to the concert with?"

Charlie looked up at Darcie. "Mindy Sinclair was one. Ashley may have mentioned another name, but I don't recall. I can give you Mindy's number."

"We'd appreciate that very much."

"So you didn't hear from your daughter after you last talked with her at your office yesterday evening?" Sasha asked.

"No, Detective."

"No phone calls or texts?"

Charlie quickly checked his phone. "No, sir. Nothing."

"I'm sorry that we have to ask you these questions."

"I'm sorry too." Charlie looked up at Sasha again. "Why was she killed?"

"We don't know that at this time, sir. We've got very little information so far, but we have her car at the police garage, and CSI investigators will be looking for anything that could provide a motive."

"How was she killed?" Charlie stood back up.

"We're going to be releasing very few details on what took place as it could hamper our investigation, so anything I tell you I'd like you to keep confidential. Do you understand?"

"Yes."

"Ashley died from a single gunshot."

Charlie Cummins sat back down on the sofa and put his head in his hands.

"I'm sorry, sir. I'd like to ask you a few more questions if I may?"

"Certainly."

"You said Ashley lived here with you, correct?"

"Yes."

"And she worked with you at your company?"

"Yes, she did. Ashley is my only child, Detective." Charlie paused. "*Was* my only child. After my wife passed away almost ten years ago, Ashley worked at the business when she wasn't in school or playing soccer. When I retired, she would have taken over running the company. That was the plan anyway."

"Do you know of any reason why she would have been at the corner of South Lee and Oakland last night at 1 a.m.?"

Charlie Cummins stood back up. "No, Detective, I don't."

"Do you know if she had a friend who lived in that area?"

"I have no idea. I know some of Ashley's friends, but I don't know where they all live."

"You said that your daughter played soccer?" Darcie asked.

"Yes, she did. She'd been playing soccer since she was four years old. She helped lead her high school team to state, then got a college scholarship to go out to California to play Division I. But in the final game at regionals, she suffered an injury that brought an end to her career."

"What happened?"

"She was blocked into a goal post and suffered a concussion along with neck and back injuries." Charlie walked over to the desk and picked up another framed photograph. "Here's a picture of her. She was a co-captain. That's her in the front row. Number 5."

Darcie took the picture and recognized the young lady she'd seen a few hours ago in the car. "She's beautiful, sir." She handed the frame to Sasha.

"Thank you, Detective. Yes, she was." Charlie turned away from them as tears streamed down his cheeks. "I just don't understand how this could happen."

Darcie took a moment to formulate another question. "Did she require surgery after the injury?"

Charlie wiped away his tears and turned back to the two detectives. "No, she didn't. She recovered from the concussion quickly, but the neck and back injuries lingered and remained a problem. Ashley was often in a lot of pain." He shook his head. "Because of the pain, she initially saw doctors in California while she was in college. After graduation, she returned home, and she saw doctors here in Bloomington and Chicago over the last couple of years for the pain."

Sasha lightly tapped Darcie in the back as a signal for her to stop questioning Mr. Cummins. He walked around her and stood in front of Ashley's father. "I have one additional question, and then we'll be leaving."

"Go ahead, Detective."

"Do you have someone you can call to come over and be with you at this time?"

"I'm going over to my parents to let them know. I'll be with them until I head over to the medical examiner's office. I assume you'll give me a call when you'd like me to come over?"

"Yes, sir. I understand." Sasha couldn't imagine telling his parents that one of their grandchildren was dead. "I'd like to trade telephone numbers with you. You can call me anytime, Mr. Cummins."

"Thank you, Detective." Charlie reached for a business card holder on his desk and removed two cards and handed one to each detective. "You can reach me on my cell number anytime. I want to help find whoever did this."

"I don't have any more questions at this time, Mr. Cummins." Sasha paused. "We would like to search Ashley's room later today. We may also need to check any electronic devices for potential clues both here and at the office."

"You have my complete cooperation and access to anything you need."

"Thank you, sir. We'll let ourselves out." Sasha shook hands with Charlie Cummins. "We want to offer you our sincerest condolences and tell you that we will work tirelessly to find who did this to Ashley."

As soon as Charlie Cummins had shut the door behind them, Darcie said, "That was tough."

"I can't imagine being on the receiving end of news like that." Sasha looked back at the house. "We can talk after the autopsy, but Ashley's college injury sounded bad. We'll need to check out her room and office to see if we can find anything related to that."

"You mean pain medications?"

Sasha nodded.

"Understood."

4

Sasha and Darcie walked into Juanita Gordon's office at the County Medical Examiner's Office almost an hour later than they'd planned. Juanita looked up from her desk. "Do you want to be in the room while I perform the autopsy, or do you want to watch from the side room?"

"We'll both suit up," Darcie said.

"Have you seen an autopsy?" Juanita asked her.

"Not directly, but I've watched training videos."

"If at any time during the examination you need to step out, please do so," Sasha said. "Understand?"

"Got it."

"Let's get started." Juanita led them out the back door of her office and down a hallway. Outside the suite where Ashley's body was lying, she pointed to a pile of plastic-wrapped bags on a table. "Pick out the right size and put them on. Once you're set, knock on the door, and I'll give you a signal to come in."

They each picked out a bag, tore it open, and quickly put on the throwaway jumpsuits and booties. The kit also contained a headcover and a mask.

The two detectives walked over to the door and looked through the window at Juanita and one of her assistants talking next to the examination table. Ashley's body lay partially covered on the table. Sasha knocked on the window, and Juanita waved them in. As the detectives entered, the assistant walked over and stood next to an adjacent table as she waited for Juanita to start the autopsy.

Juanita wore a lab coat over her navy scrubs, booties, and gloves. She put on a mask and dropped the plastic face shield to further protect her from body fluids or fragments. She removed the sheet and instructed her assistant to begin recording. "This is the body of Ashley Brittany Cummins, a twenty-three-year-old Caucasian female. She is 5' 2" tall and weighs 89 pounds, about ten pounds under ideal body weight for a woman her size. Scars are visible on both knees. We need to check with previous medical records, but they look like old injuries from childhood play or possibly from sports injuries."

"Her father just told us she'd played soccer from age four," Sasha said.

"Most kids suffer bumps and bruises. Nothing out of the norm here." Juanita rolled the body over and examined Ashley's backside. "There is a tattoo of a pine tree on her right shoulder." She looked over at her assistant, who was taking notes, and the assistant nodded.

"Unusual tattoo for a twenty-three-year-old," Sasha said.

Juanita nodded. "Stanford University logo. There are no other identifying marks on the body." She rolled the body back over, then reached for a scalpel on the tray beside the examination table. Juanita began making a Y-cut starting at the shoulders and ending at the top of her pubic bone. Over the next hour and a half, Juanita took blood and fluid samples and methodically removed organs for examination and weighing. She also took Ashley's stomach contents and put them into a container before placing the removed organs back into the body cavity.

During the autopsy, Sasha kept glancing toward Darcie to make sure she was doing okay. The young detective seemed fine and was fully engaged in the entire process.

"I'm going to explore the wound on her upper right cheek and recover bullet fragments." Juanita used another scalpel to make an incision from one ear to the other on the back of her skull. Slowly, the pathologist separated the skin from the back of Ashley's head, pulling it forward over her forehead. She used a skull saw to remove a large portion of the back and top of the skull. "Since there wasn't an exit wound, I assume the bullet ricocheted inside her skull, perhaps severing her brainstem. You can already see the massive damage to her brain." She removed the young woman's brain and placed it on a scale.

"Did she die instantly?" Sasha asked.

"That's difficult to say with absolute certainty. With a severed brain stem, the brain and heart generally cease functioning immediately and death results almost instantaneously. Brain cells die within six minutes of oxygen loss. I'm sure she was rendered unconscious due to the severity of the damage the bullet did to her brain."

Juanita turned Ashley's head around and placed a small trajectory rod directly through the entry wound, then continued to gently work the rod through the small opening. "Amazing." The pathologist turned to speak to her assistant. "The bullet appears to have entered the skull slightly below the right eye socket through the infraorbital foramen."

"What's so amazing about that?" Sasha asked.

"The infraorbital foramen is a small opening in the maxillary bone. Blood and nerves travel through that opening." Juanita looked up at Sasha. "That was a straightforward explanation, but I just find it interesting that the bullet entered the skull at that exact point."

"Gotcha."

As Juanita pushed the rod through the opening, she slightly turned Ashley's head. The pathologist was inspecting the inside of the skull when she noticed lying on the table a full metal jacket 9mm bullet. The bullet appeared to be in pristine condition. "Looky what we've got here." She gently laid Ashley's head on the table and grabbed a pair of forceps to pick up the bullet.

"Wow." Sasha looked closely at the bullet. "It's as if it were new."

Juanita placed the bullet in a small plastic bag that her assistant had at the ready. The assistant closed the bag, marked the outside with a marker, and asked, "Would you like to see it, Sasha?"

He took the bag and looked at the bullet. "It looks in better shape than a bullet fired at the range. Truly amazing."

"Did you push the bullet out?" Darcie asked.

"No, I don't think so." Juanita asked if the assistant had written down the weight of the brain on the scale. The assistant nodded. "Thanks. I'm going to put her back together now, then ask my assistant to complete any sewing and cleanup to make her presentable for identification." She turned to her assistant. "Let's get pictures of the entry wound and the surrounding skin. Please also take additional swabs of the skin around the entry wound."

Sasha handed the evidence bag back to the assistant. "Is that it?"

"I think we've got everything we need," Juanita answered. "We'll analyze her stomach contents. From just a visual inspection, it didn't appear as though she'd eaten solid food since maybe late afternoon yesterday. There's no question she'd been drinking. We should have the blood test back by Monday." Juanita looked at her assistant. "How long do you think, Jillian?"

"I think Monday is possible if there are no backups in the lab."

"Can you move the test to the top of the list?" Sasha asked.

"Any problem with that request?" Juanita asked her assistant. Jillian shook her head.

Juanita motioned to Sasha and Darcie to follow her. They walked back into the side room and removed their protective clothing and gear before heading to Juanita's office. She poured them each a cup of coffee, and the detectives sat down in the chairs in front of her desk.

Sasha asked, "Any further thoughts?"

The pathologist sat down and leaned back in her chair. "I was surprised to see the condition of the bullet." Juanita took a sip of the coffee. "You've got to admit we've got great coffee here."

"No argument there." Sasha took another drink of coffee. "So—"

"So, as I mentioned earlier, based on her height, she's well under the weight you'd expect. The reasons for her being underweight could be from disease, poor eating habits, alcoholism, and/or drug use. We'll know more once we start getting test results, along with the report on stomach contents."

Darcie leaned forward in her chair. "Did she look unhealthy to you?"

"I'm not necessarily saying she is unhealthy, but there is a reason for her being ten pounds or so under normal weight. Her body frame type isn't slight. She was an athlete for the majority of her life." Juanita jotted a couple of notes on a pad. "Ashley had a very muscular frame. I would have estimated that she would have weighed perhaps up to ten to fifteen percent more or an even greater amount based on her physical conditioning."

"Her father talked about her college injury and the pain she'd experienced. Maybe she wouldn't have been able to work out as she had during college, which resulted in her weight loss. What do you think?" Darcie asked.

Juanita poured another cup of coffee and offered more to the detectives. "I had heard that she wasn't able to work out due to the injury and on-going pain." She sat back down in her chair. "Confidentially, I overheard my daughter and one of her friends talking about Ashley's drinking. I didn't hear anything about drugs, though. I'd ask that you look elsewhere for confirmation of that before talking to my daughter. Ashley had close friends who'd be much more familiar with her drinking or drug use. Maybe one of them would even know why she was there."

"I appreciate your desire to keep your daughter out of this." Sasha looked at Darcie. "We would only speak to her as a last resort." Darcie nodded.

"Thank you for the courtesy." Juanita took another sip of coffee. "There weren't any signs that she was injecting herself with drugs, but I predict we're going to find traces of drugs in her body. What kind, I don't know."

"The questions are, why was Ashley parked on South Lee, and who was she there to meet at that hour?" Darcie said. "That will be the key to finding the killer or killers."

"I agree with Darcie," Sasha said. "And I think we're going to find out drugs were involved. With what little we now know, that makes the most sense."

"I also agree." Juanita leaned back in her chair.

Darcie's phone made a chirping sound signaling she'd received a text. She quickly read the text and turned to Sasha. "It's from CSI. They've found a lot of fingerprints both inside and outside the vehicle. They will need fingerprints from Ashley's family and friends so they can eliminate them as possible suspects.

"Cold weather tends to preserve fingerprints longer than warmer temperatures." Juanita said. "At least you've got that going for you."

Sasha nodded. "Juanita's right. Warmer temperatures tend to cause deterioration of all sorts of evidence. My bigger concern is that due to how cold it was last night, the three men at the scene were likely to have been wearing gloves."

Juanita added, "You also need to consider that the prints inside the car may have deteriorated somewhat due to the heater having been on at a high temperature for several hours."

Darcie nodded. "That all makes sense."

"If there's nothing further for us to learn now, Juanita, I think we'll head back to the station." Sasha stood up.

"I won't have anything until Monday at the earliest." Juanita looked at her computer screen. "I've got an update from Jillian. The bullet is confirmed to be a 9mm. We will be comparing the striation pattern to the digitized database of the Bureau of Alcohol, Tobacco, and Firearms NIBIN."

"Let us know if you get a hit. We'll be working this today and tomorrow. Thanks, Juanita." Sasha took a last sip. "And thanks for the coffee."

Juanita smiled. "It keeps people coming back." She walked the detectives to her office door. "I'll be in touch."

The detectives quickly walked out of the ME's facility and back to their cars. "I'll see you back at the garage in a few minutes," Sasha said. "I need to make a couple of calls."

"Sounds good. See you." Darcie got into her car and backed out of the parking space to head to the police garage, where the CSI team was investigating Ashley's convertible.

Sasha watched Darcie drive away, then called Janet. She answered on the first ring. "How's it going?" she asked.

"Slowly. The victim is the daughter of Charlie Cummins. You know the guy who builds high-end homes?"

"You're kidding. His father is Judge Cummins, right?"

"Yes, I know." Sasha opened the door on his car and got in. "There's bound to be some pressure to solve this ASAP."

"Well, the judge and his family have been here as long as anyone, Sasha. They're big community supporters and big philanthropists, too."

"Got it." Sasha started the car and backed out.

"I'm just saying that when a member of one of the most wealthy and influential families in the area is murdered, it's going to be a high-profile case, Sasha. Deal with it."

Sasha always appreciated Janet's unique way of pointing out the obvious. "I understand. Gotta go. Talk to you later, sweetie." The senior detective drove to the police garage to get an update on potential evidence in Ashley's BMW. He was hoping for a treasure trove that would allow them to quickly find those responsible for murdering Ashley.

5

Charlie Cummins sat in his car in his parents' driveway, trying to decide how best to break the news of Ashley's murder. The two-story house stood on a tree-lined street filled with stately homes mostly owned by local doctors and attorneys. Judge Cummins and his wife, Marjorie, had lived in the house for over fifty years. Charlie and his three younger siblings had grown up in the well-to-do area of Bloomington. The two were sitting in the back sunroom reading the paper and having coffee when the doorbell rang. "Seems early for a visitor," the judge said. He got up, walked to the front door, and peered through one of the windowpanes in the door to see his son standing on the front porch. The judge opened the door. "Morning, Charlie. We're having coffee; would you like some?"

Charlie nodded. "That would be great, Dad." He stepped inside, and the judge closed the door behind him.

Charlie followed his father into the large kitchen in the back of the house. After pouring the coffee, the judge asked, "What's up this morning?" He sensed something was wrong by the look on Charlie's face.

"Where's Mom?"

"In the sunroom."

"Let's go see her. I've got something I have to tell you both."

"Maybe you better tell me first, Charlie."

"No, I need to tell you both at the same time."

Judge Cummins studied his son's somber expression, trying to understand. "Alright. Let's go."

In the sunroom, Charlie sat across from his parents and immediately began sharing the dreadful news. "There's no easy way to tell you this." Charlie lowered his head, took a breath, and looked at his parents. "Ashley's dead. She was shot and killed shortly after one this morning."

His parents were slow to react. "I don't understand," his father said. As soon as the judge had spoken, Charlie saw his mother's head drop.

"I know it's inconceivable," Charlie said, focusing on his mother, "that I could be sitting here delivering this horrible news. But Ashley was shot in her car near Oakland, a few blocks west of Main Street." Charlie glanced at his dad. "She died at the scene."

"This can't be," Marjorie said. "I just talked to her yesterday afternoon about coming to visit us while we're in Paris in April." She shook her head. "No. This can't be right."

"Why, Charlie? Why?" his father asked.

"The police don't have any idea why Ashley was there. I can't imagine why she was there, either." His mom began to cry, and Charlie quickly went to her and knelt beside her. "I know, Mom. It's a lot to absorb."

"When did you last see her?" his father asked.

"She left the office around 5:30 p.m. last night. She said she was going to a concert in Peoria with some friends and would stay with one of them last night."

"Was she by herself?"

"Evidently she was, Dad."

The judge stood up. "What the hell was she doing there?"

"I don't know."

"I'm going to call somebody to find out what the hell is going on." The judge turned to find his cell phone.

"Don't call anyone, please." His father stopped and turned around. "I'm very confident the police will do everything they can to find who did this."

"It won't hurt if I make some calls."

"Can we just grieve together?" He looked at his father, then his mother. "Mom needs us right now."

Judge Cummins was used to having his way. Like most judges, he had ruled his courtroom with absolute authority from the bench he'd occupied for twenty years. He was always able to bend the will of others to do what he wanted.

The three of them held each other, trying to comfort one another the best they could. "Mom, I'm going to call Tina and Deb to come over," Charlie said. His brother lived in Chicago, but his sisters lived nearby, and they could help comfort their mother.

Charlie went into the kitchen to call his sisters. Both said they'd be right over. Calling David could wait until his sisters arrived to help take care of their mom.

After making the calls, Charlie returned to the sunroom and saw that his parents were holding each other and crying. He put his arms around them both. "Tina and Deb will be right over."

"I'm heartbroken, Charlie," his mother said. "Who could have done this to my grandbaby?"

"I don't know, Mom, but the detectives who came to the house earlier promised me that they'd find the person or persons responsible." Charlie looked from his mother to his father. "I'd like you to let the police do their jobs, Dad, and stay out of this."

Judge Cummins nodded. "I will, son. I will."

6

Sasha walked into the police garage just off Main Street, where the CSI team was searching Ashley's BMW. Darcie was leaning against a workbench that ran the length of the garage bay, drinking a cup of coffee. "Did you save one of those for me?"

"There's plenty more where this came from." She took another sip. "It's not as good the ME's, but it's hot."

Sasha poured a cup and walked over to where the three CSI techs were standing beside the BMW convertible. "How's it going, guys?"

The lead tech was Andy Simon, who had been with the department for the past twelve years. "It's going slow. We've cataloged over fifty-five finger and palm prints off the outside of the car and at least that many inside."

"Seriously?"

"It will take us days to identify the prints and eliminate those not directly connected to the murder."

"Have you found anything interesting yet?"

Andy looked at Alan Jonas, a tech that had been with the department for three years. "Alan can tell you what he found."

"I found a prescription drug vial under the driver's seat. It was a standard eight-dram vial, 2.4 inches high with a one-inch diameter. The childproof cap was on the vial. I took swabs of the inside as it appeared to contain a white, powdery residue."

"Was there a prescription label?"

"There was not. We'll try to determine if there was ever a label on the inside or outside of the vial."

"Sasha, this is Eli Mack," Andy said. "Eli has been with us for just under a year. He joined us after graduating from your alma mater, Illinois State."

Sasha smiled. "Congratulations, Eli."

"Thank you, sir."

"Eli also found something you'll be interested in," Andy said.

Eli smiled. "I was working on the passenger side of the vehicle. After Alan and I collected fingerprints, Andy told us to start taking swabs of surfaces throughout the vehicle. We methodically started working on the front seats before moving to the back-seat areas and the inside of the convertible top, and lastly the dash."

It had been a long night, and Sasha was impatient. "What did you find, Eli?"

"Sorry. As I was taking swabs of the passenger side dash, I also decided to take swabs of the inside surface of the front windshield. I could see a spent cartridge lying in the crevice where the windshield and dashboard meet."

Sasha smiled. "Excellent."

"It's a 9mm shell casing."

"That matches the type of bullet recovered from the victim during the autopsy. Find any fingerprints?"

"I immediately placed it into an evidence bag. We haven't checked it for prints yet."

"Andy?"

"We'll get right on that, Detective."

"Anything else?"

"The victim was shot sitting in the driver's seat, right?" Andy asked.

"Correct."

Andy shook his head. "I don't have your experience, Detective, but I was surprised by the limited amount of blood inside the vehicle."

"It's possible," Sasha said, "that the victim had blood on her coat and clothing."

"I was surprised that there was virtually no blood on the seat."

Sasha nodded. He understood why Andy was interested in learning more about the crime scene, but as with any crime, the CSI team's role was to collect evidence, then analyze that evidence to help detectives solve the case. Specific crime scene details were on a need-to-know basis, and Andy didn't need to know.

Darcie stepped up to Sasha. "I think we need to head to the station so we can start going over what we've learned while Andy and his team start working on the evidence they've collected."

"Agreed. Please give me a call as soon as you've got fingerprint information and analysis of the residue in the vial." Sasha looked at Andy. "And whatever you find regarding the shell casing."

"Sure thing," Andy said. "As you know, it will take a couple of hours for us to run the latent prints that we've collected through the FBI IAFIS database for any matches. Then we have to analyze both the full and partial prints to potential matches."

Sasha nodded, then he and Darcie walked out of the garage and got into their unmarked cars for the short drive through the lot to their parking places at the station.

When they stepped out of their cars, Darcie quickly caught up with Sasha as he was opening the front door. "You okay?"

"I'm fine. I'm just tired."

"Well, we're all tired."

Sasha stopped just inside the double-entry doors at the back of the station. "You're right, and I'm sorry, Detective."

"Yes, sir." Darcie had made her point.

"Let's go to the conference room and talk over what we know and what we need to learn." Sasha started walking to the conference room where the two could begin piecing together evidence, which he hoped would ultimately solve the murder of Ashley Cummins.

The detective picked up a piece of chalk and started listing on a blackboard the critical facts of the murder. He began at the top, left corner with "Ashley Brittany Cummins." Then he wrote "3 unidentified males" with three blanks labeled A, B, and C immediately below, followed by "9mm," "Ashley's purse, ID & credit cards," "Prescription vial," and "Fingerprint evidence." He looked at Darcie. "What else should go up here?"

"We need to find out her specific movements after she left work."

"Correct." Sasha wrote and said out loud, "Whereabouts – 5:30 p.m. – 1:00 am." He also wrote down "Peoria concert" and turned back toward

Darcie. "We need to find out who went to that concert with her and what she did for the rest of the night."

"I'll focus on that if you'd like, Sasha."

He nodded. "Yes, please. We didn't find her cell phone, so we'll have to get a warrant to get her call history from her carrier."

"I can start that, too."

"Can you give Juanita a quick call to confirm when she'll be ready for a family member to ID Ashley's body?"

Darcie punched the number into her cell phone as Sasha watched, then turned back to examine the blackboard. Juanita answered her call, and Darcie thanked her. "The ME's office is ready, Sasha."

"Okay. Thanks." Sasha pulled out his cell phone and punched in Charlie Cummins's cell number to arrange a time that would work for him to meet to identify his daughter's body. Charlie answered on the first ring.

"Mr. Cummins, this is Detective Frank."

"Yes, Detective."

"I wanted to ask when you'd be available to identify your daughter?" It was never easy to ask a family member this question, but it's something that happened in every murder investigation.

"I'm available now. Let's get this over with. I can be there in five minutes."

"I'll meet you in the parking lot of the ME's office, then I'll accompany you for the identification."

"Okay, Detective. I'll see you in the parking lot shortly."

Sasha ended the call and put his phone on the conference table. "He's heading over now, Darcie. While I'm gone, get a warrant for Ashley's call data so we can start piecing together the timeline."

As Sasha pulled out of the parking lot for the quick drive to the ME's office, he called Janet. "Nine hours in and getting nowhere fast," he said when she answered.

"Well, it is early."

"True. If we don't get a hit on a print of a viable suspect, well, you know, it's going to be much harder since the witness didn't get a good look at anyone at the scene."

Sasha sounded like this at the start of every case. "You'll figure it out," Janet said. "You always do."

"You have to say that."

"Yes, but it's true. You'll work like a dog to catch whoever's responsible for this murder. That's who you are."

"Thanks." Sasha pulled in and parked in front of the ME's office. "Gotta go. Talk to you later."

"Okay. I'll be thinking of you." Janet disconnected the call. She knew she wouldn't see him until late that evening.

Sasha kept his car running until he saw a Mercedes sedan pull into the ME's lot and park next to him. Charlie Cummins was alone in the car.

Charlie got out of the car and started walking toward the door. He stopped when he noticed Sasha getting out of his unmarked car. "Have you learned anything you can share with me, Detective?"

The two shook hands. "When we're finished, I can answer your question. I'd also like to ask you a couple of questions, if that'd be okay."

"Certainly, Detective."

They walked inside and were greeted by Jillian. She led them down the hallway to a door that opened into a small, dark room with a large window. On the other side of the window was an even darker room. "I need to ask you a question, sir." Jillian lifted a notepad.

"Yes, ma'am."

"Could you please tell me your name and relationship?"

"My name is Charles H. Cummins. I'm Ashley's father." Charlie lowered his head.

Sasha moved in close. "Thank you, sir. I'm going to gradually increase the light in the adjacent room, which will allow you to provide us with identification. Do you understand, sir?"

"Yes." Charlie stepped closer to the glass window, and Sasha moved with him.

Jillian stepped to the side of the window and started to slowly increase the light in the room where Ashley's body was covered with a sheet, only her head exposed. The body was positioned so that the left side of her face and profile was facing the window, and the right side of her face where the bullet entered was less visible.

As the light level in the room increased, Charlie lifted his right hand and placed it against the window. After a few seconds, he lowered his head. "Yes, that's my daughter. That's Ashley." Charlie turned around, looking away from his daughter's body.

"Thank you, Mr. Cummins." Sasha put his hand on Charlie's left shoulder. "I'm so sorry, sir." The detective looked over at Jillian, who was already darkening the room holding the body.

"If you'd like to stay in this room, you're welcome to do so for as long as you'd like." Jillian looked at Sasha. "Will you be able to stay with Mr. Cummins and provide him an escort out of the building when he's ready to leave, Detective?"

"Yes, Jillian. Thank you."

"Your daughter will be available this afternoon, Mr. Cummins." Charlie nodded, and Jillian turned and left the room.

"When you're ready, Mr. Cummins, we can sit in the lobby to talk."

Without lifting his head, Charlie whispered, "Can you tell me what you've learned since we spoke this morning?"

"At this point, I don't have much more I can share with you. We moved your daughter's convertible to the police garage, and CSI has been processing it for evidence."

"You haven't found anything?"

"We have the witness calling 911 after she heard a gunshot. It was very dark out, and she was unable to identify anyone at the scene."

"How many people were there?"

"I'm afraid I can't share that with you at this time."

Charlie nodded. He understood, but he was doubtful his father would. "Is there nothing more you can give me?"

"The ME believes your daughter died instantly." Sasha thought this might be comforting. Reassuring, at the very least. He knew that if, God forbid, his own daughter, Emily, were killed and didn't suffer, he would feel better knowing that.

"Thank you for telling me, Detective." Charlie looked at the floor and wiped tears from his eyes. "You said outside that you had a few questions."

"Yes, sir. Do you know if your daughter was taking any prescription drugs?"

"I don't know if she was still taking drugs related to her injury or not. I'd assume she'd be taking something considering she still suffered pain."

"Earlier, we asked if we could search your daughter's room."

"Certainly, Detective. I can give you access to my entire home."

"Thank you. I'd also like to ask if you've noticed any recent changes in Ashley's behavior."

Charlie looked at Sasha. "Nothing unusual. What are you suggesting?"

"I wasn't suggesting anything. I was just asking if you had noticed anything out of the ordinary with your daughter recently."

"Nothing I can think of."

"Thank you. CSI found an empty prescription drug vial under the driver's seat of her BMW. The vial didn't have a label."

"I'm sorry, but I wouldn't know anything about that."

"I understand. I have one last question. Can you get us a list of her closest friends so we could speak with them?"

"Certainly, as soon as I can. If there isn't anything else, I'm going to head back to my parents' house. Please call if you have further questions or updates on what you've found."

"Can we arrange a good time to search your home, Mr. Cummins?"

"You tell me what time works best for you, and I'll make it happen. I'll make sure someone is there to let you in."

"I'll check with CSI and let you know shortly." Sasha led Ashley's father down the hallway and through the lobby to the entrance of the building.

———

As Sasha walked back into the conference room at the station, Darcie was working on the timeline of Ashley's last night.

"What concert did she and her friends go to last night?"

"The only concert last night in Peoria was at a place called Park's Music Theatre."

"Have you confirmed she attended?"

"Not yet. I'm waiting for the okay for the warrant for Ashley's phone so we can access the GPS data."

Sasha nodded. "Have you heard from Andy?"

"Not yet." Darcie looked at the clock on the wall. "The earliest we're probably going to get anything back from him will be around lunchtime."

"Sounds good. Once Andy and his team are available, we will search the Cummins' home."

"Do we need a warrant?"

Sasha shook his head. "He gave his verbal authorization, and he'll arrange for someone to be there to open the house for investigators."

Darcie called Andy and arranged to meet at the Cummins' house at 1 p.m. When she hung up, Sasha said, "Let's order lunch in. Your choice. Mr. Cummins will be sending us contact info for Ashley's friends, and you can start reaching out to them."

"Has Ashley's name been released?"

"I don't know for sure, but I doubt it. I'm going to guess that the chief will want to do that himself." He headed toward his office and called his superior. He then returned to the conference room. "The chief says he's planning on a 2 p.m. news conference today in his office. There's a possibility that Ashley's father will show."

Darcie nodded.

"I'll go over with you to start the search, but as of now, the chief wants me here when he talks with the media."

"That's understandable." Darcie tossed Sasha one of the menus lying on the conference table. "I'm thinking of ordering subs from Kiva's Place. Sausage and peppers okay with you?"

"Good choice." Sasha stood up. "I'm going to take a few minutes to think in my office. Let me know when lunch arrives." As Sasha sat down at his desk, he thought Janet was right, the pressure was building. He rubbed his temples, hoping the headache he was feeling coming on wouldn't get worse.

7

I t was midmorning when Sticks rolled out of bed and texted Big G. "Chicago?"

Big G quickly replied. "Yes."

Sticks sent a thumbs-up. When Big G had left Sticks's mom's kitchen almost eight hours earlier to head back to his place, the two had agreed that he would dump his 9mm in Chicago first thing in the morning. Other than Danny, the gun was the only thing that they thought tied them to the murder. And Big G was going to throw the clothes they were wearing last night into a dumpster at a gas station somewhere along Interstate 55 on his way north.

Sticks and Big G knew enough about evidence gathering that the steps they were taking would blunt Danny ratting on them. Regardless, the two were convinced that Danny wouldn't rat. To survive dealing drugs, there was a code of silence that people like the three of them followed. They thought Danny would adhere to that code. There was no way he'd put his baby or his baby momma in danger, unless his back was up against a wall.

After dropping the bag of clothes in a gas station dumpster fifty miles north of Bloomington in Gardner, Big G exited the interstate again at a fast-food joint to get a couple of burgers, some fries, and a shake in a far west suburb of Chicago. When he finished the meal, he reached under the seat and pulled out the purse he had taken from the girl last night. He put it into the fast-food bag, then added the food wrappers. He stepped out of the car and walked over to a garbage can and dropped the bag in, followed by what was left of his shake.

Arrangements had been made to trade the Glock he'd hidden under the tire in the trunk of the Chevrolet Impala he'd borrowed from his grandmother, to Rattler, the Chicago-area gang leader who supplied them drugs. Earlier, as he sat in the parking lot eating, he had texted Rattler to let him know he'd meet him in their usual place just south of downtown Chicago in the Fuller Park neighborhood, near the tennis courts.

He parked the car on Princeton Avenue across from the empty tennis courts just before noon. It was twenty-eight degrees out, so it wasn't surprising that the park was empty. A few minutes later, Rattler pulled up behind him in a big SUV. Big G got out of the car, walked back to the SUV, and sat down in the passenger seat. "What's up, man?" The two bumped fists.

Rattler scanned the area around them. "Not much."

Sensing that Rattler wanted to move things along, Big G pulled cash out of his jacket and handed it over. "Thanks for meeting with me."

"No problem." Rattler tossed the bundle into the back seat without counting it. Big G knew what would happen if they were short on the six-thousand-dollar payment for the drugs they were buying. Rattler reached around the back of the passenger seat and grabbed a grocery bag that contained the drugs. He placed the bag on the SUV's console. Big G didn't look inside. That would have been disrespectful.

"How about the gun?" Big G asked.

Rattler reached under his front seat and pulled out the towel-wrapped gun and laid it on the console beside the bag of drugs. "Glock 19. It's brand new. Never been fired."

Big G smiled. "Mine is in my trunk." He grabbed the bag of drugs, opened the door of the SUV, got out, and stopped at the rear of his Impala. Big G quickly looked around to make sure no one was watching, then he opened the trunk and placed the bag inside. He'd wrapped the Glock 17, the gun he'd shot the girl with last night, in a towel and placed it under the spare tire. He looked around again before retrieving it, then closed the trunk and walked back to the SUV. Big G climbed back in and tried to hand the towel-wrapped gun to Rattler.

Rattler shook his head. "Back seat."

"Okay." Big G put it in the seat directly behind Rattler. He then pulled out ten hundred-dollar bills from his jacket pocket. Rattler had told Big G that he would make the gun trade but asked for a thousand dollars to make sure that the gun wouldn't be traceable back to him. Big G laughed to himself. With any luck, whoever bought the gun would be caught carrying it and have to explain why he was in possession of a weapon used to kill a girl in Bloomington. Just as good would be for someone to get shot with it in Chicago. That would lead Bloomington police to Chicago to look for the girl's killer. Either way, police would be forced to consider whether someone from Chicago might be responsible for the murder.

The thousand dollars Big G handed over went straight into Rattler's jacket pocket. "We're done."

Big G nodded. The two bumped fists again, and Big G got out of the SUV with the new Glock wrapped in the towel. Rattler immediately drove away. Big G spotted a couple of kids throwing a football in the park. After quickly hiding the new gun under the spare tire, he got back into the Impala for the short drive to the northbound Dan Ryan. Before getting on the expressway, he pulled the car into an empty lot across from Sticks's favorite restaurant. Ten minutes later, he carried out a five-pound bag of ribs. He put them out of reach in the back seat, got in the car, and started the drive home.

8

At the agreed-upon time, Darcie rang the doorbell of Charlie Cummins's home. The door opened, and one of Cummins's employees stepped aside as Sasha and the team walked in to begin their search. Darcie closed the door behind them and stopped to ask the employee a few questions, beginning with whether she knew Ashley.

"Yes, I did. I saw Ashley in the office almost every workday. My name is Laura Gill."

"Were you friends with Ashley?"

The employee was watching the remaining team members begin their search. "We were friendly, but she wasn't a friend."

"I understand. You worked together and didn't socialize outside of work?"

"As I said, we worked together, but we weren't friends. We didn't see each other outside of work. Not once."

"Got it. Do you know any of Ashley's friends?"

"There were a couple of friends that would drop by the office."

"Can you tell me their names?"

She nodded. "One was Mindy Sinclair. Mindy stopped by more than anyone else. Before I forget, Mr. Cummins gave me a list of Ashley's friends for Detective Frank. It's in an envelope on the kitchen island."

"Thanks, but before we take a look at that, could you tell me the other names you remember?"

"There was Sheila Arken."

Darcie wrote down the name. "Anyone else?"

"Cindy Murdock and Jamie Shunk. Those were people I remember stopping by to see Ashley. There could be others, but those girls stopped by a lot."

"Any friends who were men?"

"Not that I recall stopping by the office."

"Okay. Now can you show me the envelope?" Darcie followed the employee past a large living room and formal dining room. The kitchen was part of a cavernous family room with a stone fireplace that must have risen twenty feet from the floor. The back wall of the house was a bank of sliding doors that led out to an expansive outdoor patio and a pool. This house was the biggest she'd ever been inside.

Laura handed her the envelope. There was a company logo on the back of the envelope and on the front, "Charlie Cummins Luxury Home Builders" was emblazoned in the upper left corner, along with the business's address. Across the front of the envelope was handwritten "Sasha Frank." Inside the sealed envelope was a folded, lined yellow page torn from a note pad. "Best Friends" was written across the top and underlined, followed by eight names and telephone numbers.

The list included the names of Sheila Arken, Jamie Shunk, Cindy Murdock, and Mindy Sinclair. "Do you know a Courtney Daniels?" she asked.

"No, I don't think so."

"How about Heather Hancock?"

"Sorry. No."

"Rebecca Berens or Danielle Stone?"

"I think there was a girl named Becca who stopped by the office. Just a few times, though. That could be the Rebecca you mentioned."

Darcie nodded. "Did any of those five people stop by yesterday or around the time Ashley was leaving work?"

"Not that I remember."

"How was Ashley around the office?"

"What do you mean?"

"Was she easy to work with? Was she nice to others in the office?"

"Ashley was like a boss around the place. She was Mr. Cummins's daughter. She didn't talk to me all that much. Only if she wanted something from me or if she wanted me to do something for her."

"Whatever you tell me is confidential and will help us learn about Ashley and her life. Nothing more."

"I know she was in trouble for showing up late for work some mornings. Maybe too much partying or something."

"On those days she came in late, did she seem okay?"

"Okay?"

"You know. Did she have a hangover, or maybe seem a bit out of it?"

"I can tell you I've got friends who do drugs, and sometimes she acted like them." After Laura said that, she shook her head. "I've already told you more than I should."

Darcie pressed her. "So you think she may have used or was using drugs regularly?"

"I can't say. I can tell you that I don't ever remember Ashley smelling like she'd been drinking."

"You've been very helpful. I promise you that what you've told me will be confidential. Mr. Cummins won't know that we spoke." Darcie put her hand on Laura's shoulder and looked her in the eyes. "I promise. He won't know."

"Thank you, Detective. Please understand I'm happy to help in any way I can. I just don't think I know anything else."

"I understand." Darcie reached into an inside pocket of her jacket. "Please take my card. If you remember or hear anything else you think would be helpful to our investigation, please give me a call. Will you do that for me?"

Laura took the card from Darcie. "I will."

"Thank you. Now, could you please sit here while we finish our search?" Darcie pulled out one of the leather stools lined up against the island. "We'll try to finish up quickly."

When she reached the staircase, which led up as well as down to the basement, she called out for Sasha. He replied from upstairs. She found him in a large bedroom she assumed had been Ashley's.

"What did you learn from the girl?" Sasha asked.

She handed the list to Sasha. "Mindy Sinclair was the friend who stopped by most often."

"There's a couple of local doctors' and lawyers' last names I recognize on this list."

"You do know that other people have those last names, too, right?"

"Funny." Sasha gave Darcie the sheet of paper back. "When we get back to the office, we can start contacting them."

Darcie looked around the bedroom. The walls were grey except for one, which had been painted cardinal red. "Nice room. Nice house."

"I did a quick walk around the second floor. There are five bedrooms, and each has a full bath. The main bedroom is at the other end of the hall from this room. The vaulted ceiling of the family room downstairs is between the main bedroom and Ashley's room. Both have big balconies that overlook the pool and backyard. There are three bedrooms across the front of the house. This place is huge."

"Find anything yet?"

"Andy is going through the bathroom in here now. Eli is looking through the three front bedrooms." Sasha looked over at the open door of the walk-in closet. "Alan, as you can see, is going through her closet."

"Wow! That closet is as big as my apartment bedroom!"

Sasha laughed. "Wait until you see the bathroom. Did you learn anything else?"

"Laura said Ashley came in late for work sometimes and had gotten in trouble for it. Well, as much trouble you can get into as the boss's daughter."

"Did she say why she was late for work?"

"She said she never smelled alcohol on Ashley, but—" Darcie checked her notepad. "Let me make sure I get what she said right." The detective read from her note pad. "She said, 'I can tell you I've got friends who do drugs, and sometimes she acted like them.'"

"So we've got Ashley showing up late for work often enough to get into some kind of trouble, and she acted like other people the girl knows who do drugs?"

"When you repeated that back to me, it somehow didn't seem as bad as when she said it."

"Sorry. That wasn't my intent. It sounds bad to me. When you consider multiple pieces of evidence together, you begin to see the relevance. The empty vial in Ashley's car combined with the witness's statement paints a pretty clear picture."

"That's what I thought, too." Darcie looked into the closet where Alan was going through shoeboxes. "I'm going to help Alan in here."

Sasha turned and walked to the bathroom. "How's it going, Andy?"

"I don't think I've ever seen so much makeup."

The senior detective smiled, thinking of Janet who didn't use very much makeup and was absolutely beautiful. "Have you found anything?"

"Nothing of interest. I'm examining each item closely, so it's going to take some time."

"Can I help?"

"Why don't you go through the linen closet?"

Sasha started in the upper right cubicle containing pillows of different sizes and shapes. He unzipped the ones with zippers to look inside, but he didn't find anything. The next cubicle was filled with bed linen. There was nothing of interest in that cubicle, either. Three folded blankets were neatly stacked one on top of the other in the next cubicle. He shook out each, refolded it, and placed it back in the stack. When he shook the last blanket, a plastic bag dropped on the floor of the bathroom.

"What you got there, Sasha?" Andy asked.

"Cigarette wrapping paper, a roach clip, a lighter, and a small baggie of marijuana." He placed the zippered bag into the evidence bag.

"That's not really what you were looking for, was it?"

"Marijuana is easy to get. I'm looking for hard drugs." He continued his search of the linen closet but found nothing else. Sasha returned to the bedroom closet. "Find anything?" he asked Darcie.

She was sitting on the floor, going through shoeboxes. "Ashley had more pairs of tennis shoes than I have shoes of all types. There must be a hundred pairs." She was only slightly exaggerating.

"Jealous?"

"No. Maybe. Just an interesting fact."

Sasha smiled. "It may be a fact, but it's not all that interesting."

"Smartass." She opened another shoebox. "And here's another new pair of tennis shoes. In red and gray nonetheless."

"I take it neither you nor Alan has found anything yet?"

From a section of the closet that held a variety of jackets and coats, Alan said, "Mostly, I've found gum, mints, tissues, pens, and stuff like that."

"Mostly?"

"I've found a few pills that need to be analyzed."

"What kind of pills?"

"I've never encountered pills like this, so I can't say." Alan turned and pointed to a shelf above where Sasha was standing. "Each pill is in a separate evidence bag marked with which item of clothing I found it in except for one bag that has two pills. I found them both in one pocket."

Sasha pulled the evidence bags down from the shelf. "So three are different sizes and colors, and two are identical?"

"Yes."

"I'm pretty sure this one is an opioid." Sasha looked over at Darcie. "Do you remember your training on types of drugs, Detective? I'm colorblind."

"It's green and round," she said. "And yes, that looks like an opioid."

"We now have evidence that Ashley had at least one opioid pill in a jacket pocket." Sasha looked at the other pills. "I'm not sure about the others, but I'm going to go out on a limb and say the others are as well. There's no prescription vial for these pills; they're just randomly left in the pockets of coats or jackets."

"I've finished going through all her clothes," Alan said. "Those pills were the only items of interest I found."

"I found nothing of interest in the shoeboxes." Darcie stood up and realized that she was taller than Alan by at least six inches, and she was wearing flats.

"I'm going to go see how Eli is doing," Sasha said. "You two check the basement to see if there's anything of interest down there." Sasha turned to leave the room and look for Eli.

"Will do." Darcie and Alan followed Sasha out of the room and headed down the stairs toward the basement.

Eli was in the front bedroom across the hall from the main bedroom. "How's it going?" Sasha asked.

Eli looked up from the bedside table he was searching. "I've found nothing in these bedrooms other than a few hangers, some extra blankets, and pillows in the closets. There are unopened toiletries in the bathroom drawers and phone chargers in the drawers of the bedside tables, along with books and magazines. These three bedrooms are like hotel rooms."

"I don't know about you, but these rooms are nicer than any hotel room I've ever stayed in," Sasha said.

"Me too." Eli closed the drawer he was searching. "That's it. I didn't find anything."

"Why don't you go downstairs to the basement and see if Darcie and Alan need any help?"

Sasha walked across the hall to the main bedroom door and looked inside the room. He didn't see any reason for them to search Ashley's father's bedroom. Hiding drugs in her father's bedroom seemed counterintuitive.

As Sasha walked into the adjoining bath, Andy turned to him. "I've pretty much gone over everything in here, Sasha. I didn't find anything other than some over-the-counter drugs. I've bagged them so we can confirm that's what they are."

They headed toward the basement and found Darcie standing at the bottom of the stairs. In a hushed tone, she said, "I'm thinking we're not going to find anything else. I don't think Ashley was hiding drugs. I think she thought she was able to conceal her drug use from her father, and he would never have suspected that she was abusing pain meds."

"I agree. That makes sense. I think the pills Alan found were ones she just lost track of; otherwise, she would have taken them."

"When are we supposed to hear from Juanita on Ashley's drug use?" Darcie asked.

"She said Monday. I'm hoping she has it by tomorrow, but with what we've found here, Juanita is going to find opioids in her system. That's what I think anyway."

"The first thing we need to do is to wrap up here so we can let the young lady over there go home." Sasha motioned over at Laura, who was sitting at the kitchen island looking at her phone. "Can you check on the guys in the garage, and I'll find Andy?"

"Will do." Darcie began heading for the garage but stopped and turned back to Sasha. "You should speak with Laura."

Sasha nodded and walked over to the island. "Ma'am?"

Laura pulled off the headphones. "Yes, sir."

"I'd like to ask you a few questions." Laura nodded. "Thank you. I under-stand you told the other detective that you thought Ashley used drugs?"

"Yes. I told the detective I didn't want this to come back to me, though."

"It won't."

"I've got friends who take drugs. Not hardcore or anything. Just recre-ational, you know. At the office, Ashley looked like and sometimes acted like she was on drugs."

"What does that mean?"

"You could look in her eyes, and you'd just know. Or at least I thought she looked like it anyway."

Sasha didn't have any reason not to believe Laura. He was sure she was afraid she was taking a risk by even talking with them about Ashley. "What you tell us will stay with us."

"Ashley was habitually late to work. She would get into arguments with others at work over nothing. Literally nothing."

"Did you get into arguments with her?"

Laura shook her head. "Absolutely not. Never. My job is too important to me."

"Any other symptoms?"

"She seemed to keep losing weight. I know people talk about marijuana and glazed eyes, but I never smelled marijuana on her. Her eyes looked glazed almost all the time." Laura put her phone down on the kitchen island. "You put all those things together, Detective, and she looked like a user to me."

"Okay."

"I've got a cousin who was in a car accident and got hooked on pain meds.

He lost weight, his eyes looked glazed over all the time, and he got into fights over nothing. It almost killed him until he went into rehab."

Sasha nodded. "I understand you've got direct experience with someone who's an addict. I hope that he's recovered and stays that way."

Laura wiped tears from her eyes with a tissue. "I'm sorry. He's doing much better, thanks."

"I think we're ready to roll, Sasha," Darcie said as she returned to the kitchen.

Sasha nodded. "Thank you again, Laura. As I said, we will keep you out of our investigation."

Outside, Darcie looked at her watch and said, "Oh, geez. You forgot about the chief's presser."

"He texted earlier and said he and the mayor would handle it. Glad you remembered to remind me." He smiled at Darcie. "Let's head back and see what the vice unit has for us. I texted R.J. Carlson earlier, hoping he'd have a line on some people we can talk to."

9

It was shortly after 4 p.m. when Darcie and Sasha walked into the conference room back at the station. Sitting at the conference room table was undercover detective R.J. Carlson. He was slumped in his chair, looking like he'd been sleeping on the streets for a week.

Sasha laughed as he approached R.J. "When was the last time you shaved, R.J.? Or showered?"

"Probably yesterday." R.J. stood up and shook his hand.

"Thanks for coming in," Darcie said as she shook hands with him.

"No problem. After looking at your board, it seems you're looking for the names of some perps." R.J. sat back down. "You've got a young lady killed in her expensive car in a neighborhood that doesn't see many BMWs. Anything solid yet?"

"What we have is a dead girl named Ashley Cummins. Likely an opioid addict. By the way, not that it should matter, but her grandfather is a retired judge. They're wealthy and connected. As I said, it shouldn't matter, but—"

"Gotcha. You need to find her killer pronto."

Sasha nodded. "Yes. And the drums are going to start beating if we don't."

R.J. stood up and walked over to the board. "I've got some names of people who sell drugs in the area." The undercover detective started making a list. "The first guy. William Green. He's a player in that area of town." R.J. turned away from the blackboard, "His street name is Sticks." He smiled. "Don't ask."

Darcie recognized the name. "How big a player is Green?"

"Sticks is near the top of the food chain, locally. We think he's got a deal with a Chicago gang that supplies him. Bloomington-Normal is too small-time, so the gang leaves it to local small fry like Sticks to market product for them."

Sasha nodded. "Got it."

R.J. said the next name out loud, then wrote it on the blackboard. "Marvin Milcen. No street name." He turned back around. "Not all of these guys drive Escalades. They make a living selling whatever they can. Guys like Marvin don't cause much trouble. He kinda hides in the shadows of someone like Sticks."

"What kind of living do they make?"

"Somebody like Marvin? Maybe five hundred dollars a week. He spent six years in jail for selling cocaine, but since he got out, he's mostly kept his head down," R.J. answered.

"How about Sticks?" Darcie asked.

"Like I was saying, Sticks supplies dealers in the area, so he makes a lot more money."

"How big is the area?" Sasha wasn't sure why these dealers were on the street if the detective knew who they were, but he decided not to ask why yet.

"Maybe a thirty- to forty-five-mile radius," R.J. said. "Exclude Peoria and Decatur."

Darcie asked, "Why exclude them?"

"There'd be somebody like Sticks in both those cities representing Chicago gangs," R.J. replied. "Next guy is Danny Williams. He's classier than either Sticks or Marvin. Danny's primary customers are college kids. Higher-end users. It sounds like your vic would fit his target customer profile."

"You make it sound like this Danny guy markets like a local retailer."

"He does," R.J. said as he turned back to the table. "Danny goes to clubs. He buys drinks and mingles with the college kids. He's their age. Early twenties. He'd make sure to be available in the best bars in either Bloomington or Normal probably Thursday through Saturday nights."

"How much money does Danny make?" Sasha asked.

"The guy makes money. He often hangs out at Bobcat's. Danny got his start selling marijuana. I doubt he wastes his time with it anymore since it seems like everybody sells on campus. It's easier to buy weed than it is to buy cigarettes."

"So what does he sell?" Sasha asked.

"Pills. His customers are rich kids who normally buy drugs to party over a long weekend."

"We think Ashley was addicted. She had chronic pain from a college sports injury." Darcie thought that if somebody with Ashley's resources couldn't get herself off drugs, how hard it must be for those who couldn't afford to go to a clinic to get help.

"Danny would be happy to supply someone with plenty of ready cash and a drug dependency problem," R.J. said. "He'd be an equal-opportunity supplier." He turned back to the blackboard. "Next name is Charles Johns. His street name is Big G." The undercover detective put the chalk down and turned away from the blackboard. "He's a big dude. Maybe 6' 5" or 6". Weighs maybe 300 pounds. Kinda known as an enforcer working with Sticks. Sticks's a small dude and needs an enforcer to ensure other dealers fear him. I also think he's got the connections to the Chicago gangs. He's from there and moved down here a few years ago."

Darcie asked, "How old are these guys?"

"They're both in their mid- to late twenties. Marvin is the old man at around thirty years old."

Sasha looked up from the notes he had been taking. "So that's everyone?"

R.J. laughed. "Gosh, no. I'm kinda going out, starting at Lee and Oakland. Since that's where the vic was shot, I figured that I'd start there."

"Ashley Cummins." The first time he had called her "the vic," Sasha had let it go.

R.J. had been around long enough to know that Sasha liked to always use a victim's name during an investigation as a sign of respect. "Sorry, Sasha. Ashley."

Darcie broke the awkward moment with a question that had been asked but she didn't think she'd heard R.J. answer. "What do you think somebody like Danny, Sticks, or Big G makes in a year? How much?"

R.J. had been starting to write another name but stopped and turned around. "Oh, yeah. Sorry. Sticks and Big G could bring in ten thousand or more a week. They sell to users and dealers alike."

"Each?" Darcie had an incredulous look on her face.

"No. They're kinda like partners, so they'd split that. Danny might make three thousand to five thousand a week."

"Geez," Darcie said.

"Maybe a little more." R.J. turned back to the blackboard. "Next is a guy who goes by Bones. He sells over in Normal, and we could look at him too." R.J. kept writing and talking. "His name is Carlos Ward-Wallace." He chuckled to himself. "I think he came up with that name Bones himself."

Darcie and Sasha looked at each other and shook their heads. They were both thinking R.J. was having a hard time focusing. "Tell us about him," Sasha said.

"A very low-level guy. Some dealers can't really afford to buy solid street names." He laughed at his own bad joke. "Bones makes less than five hundred on a great week. You've gotta realize some of these guys could probably never get even a minimum wage job. And if they did get one, they'd lose it day one."

"Okay. Anyone else?"

R.J. nodded. "There's Adrian Wolenski. He's kinda like a low-level Danny. I think he may sell for Danny, focusing on junior colleges and technical schools. Different bars than where Danny sells."

"So a low-level guy makes what, then?" Sasha asked.

"Wolenski might make two thousand dollars in a good week." R.J. laughed as he started writing and said derisively, "You gotta love the creativity of these guys."

Sasha leaned back in his chair. "Meaning?"

"Well, we've got a guy named Leon Ross who goes by Jammer." R.J. looked around. "Like I said, don't ask." He turned back to the blackboard. "We've got Darren Redmond, whose street name is Red Red. Jammer and Red Red are on the city's eastside and work together sometimes."

Sasha nodded. "Red Red is a nickname I think I can follow."

Darcie looked up at the board. "I'm assuming all these guys have rap sheets?"

"Good guess." R.J. started passing around the individual sheets detailing their arrests, convictions, and the time they'd each done in jail. "You'll see that all but Danny and Adrian have been in the system since they were teenagers. But none of the others have spent any really serious time in jail or have been convicted of any serious drug offense."

"How's that?" Darcie asked.

"These guys are pretty smart when it comes to making sure they're never caught carrying more than what will get them a minimum sentence." R.J. sat back down. "Judges don't want to put these guys into state prison due to overcrowding."

Darcie looked up from scanning the rap sheets. "What's the worst offense these guys have ever been convicted of, R.J.?"

"Most of them have only spent time in county. Sticks spent two years in Lincoln." R.J. looked at Darcie. "That's minimum security."

Darcie decided she'd let what she thought was the condescending comment go and not reply though she knew what type of prison Lincoln was. "Are these guys smart enough to know not to sell near a school or get caught carrying a gun?"

R.J. nodded. "That's right. They know all the sentencing rules to make sure that judges and prosecutors won't come down harder on them."

"So since there's"—Sasha quickly counted the names on the board—"eight guys you think we should be looking at first, can you help us with some of them?"

"Sure I can help, Sasha."

"Great. How do you want to split them up?"

"I think we should put them in two groups. You and Darcie take one group, and I'll take the other. Sound like a plan?"

"I'd like Darcie and I to take the ones you think more likely to be selling in that neighborhood."

"We can do that." R.J. looked at the blackboard. "Let's divvy them up." R.J. stood up and shook his head while he looked at the names. "All scum, whether they're involved with Ashley's death or not."

Sasha nodded. "Can't argue with that."

"I forgot to ask if you found any prints," R.J. asked.

"Lots and lots of prints in and on the car." Sasha glanced at his watch.

"We would have had a hit by this time if any were in the system." He looked over at Darcie. "You heard anything from Andy?"

"Nothing."

"Okay. So out of this list," R.J. said, "Sticks and Big G probably sell the most in that neighborhood. These two are also the biggest badasses."

The senior detective stood up and stretched. "The witness told us a big guy got into the car just before she heard a gunshot. The big guy could certainly be Big G. So maybe he and Sticks find somebody selling in their backyard, and they confront him. That's got possibilities."

"I agree. How about I take Red Red, Jammer, and Bones?" He placed checks beside their names. "I think you guys should check out Sticks and Big G." R.J. circled both names. "And I think you should do Danny and his protégé, Adrian," he said while circling their names. "I'll also take Milcen."

Sasha looked at Darcie, and she nodded. The senior detective looked back up at R.J. "Sounds good."

R.J. sorted through the rap sheets of those that Sasha and Darcie were taking and slid them over to Darcie.

"We appreciate you taking the time to give us the primer on your world," Sasha said. "We'll start knocking on doors tonight."

"Most of these guys aren't home at night," R.J. said, "as that's when they go out to deal. They're all nocturnal. If you start looking now, you might be able to find one or two of them at home."

"Are the addresses on these rap sheets current?"

"As current as can be. You know these guys aren't the best at keeping their probation officers informed." R.J. stood up.

Darcie stood too. "I know William Green, but he probably won't remember me."

"How so?" R.J. asked.

"We grew up in the same area, but he's obviously much older than me." Darcie smiled at R.J. "But I'm sure you already could see that."

"Obviously," R.J. said with a laugh. "By the way, Danny has a girlfriend and a little daughter. The rest often split their time between different places."

"So you think this could take a couple of days to track down all of them?" Sasha asked.

R.J. walked around the conference table toward the door of the conference room. "Probably. As we look for the guys on our lists, let's reach out to one another if we find anything on the others. Share and share alike."

"Sounds like a plan," Sasha said.

"That way we can compress time like all the business books tell you to do."

Darcie looked at R.J. and laughed. "You're reading business books?"

"I'm not going to be a cop forever."

"If you figure out a way to compress time," Sasha said, "let me know. I could use that concept right now."

"Will do. I'll circle back to you on anything I find," R.J. said.

Sasha nodded. "Deal."

"I'm outta here, Sasha. Nice seeing you, Darcie. Good hunting." R.J. walked out of the room.

Sasha looked at the blackboard. "I think we should start with Danny. What do you think?"

"I agree. He sounds like the kind of dealer Ashley would do business with. Of course, that means we've decided that she is a drug addict."

10

The long day was wearing on Sasha as he sat his desk waiting for Darcie's update from CSI. He made a quick call to let Janet know that he hoped to be home early enough to pick up Chinese.

Darcie walked up to his desk. Sasha looked up at her. "I need to hear good news."

"Andy got a couple of fingerprint hits on the exterior driver's side door handle, door glass, and steering wheel."

Sasha looked at Darcie, waiting to hear whose prints they were. "And?"

"And it's from a guy that did a two-year stint in the Kankakee Minimum Security Unit for robbery."

"Armed robbery?"

Darcie shook her head. "He got caught stealing farm equipment up near Kankakee with a couple of buddies. Class two felony."

Sasha stood up. "The witness didn't see any perps on the driver's side of the car."

"I looked him up. It looks like he got his act together and now works at a local tire store."

"So he worked on her car. How's that good news?"

"He's the only hit that came back on all the prints they pulled. That was the only news that might be considered good." Darcie gestured in air quotes on the final word. "The bad news is that none of the other prints are in the system, and the spent cartridge came back with no match from NIBIN."

"What about prints on the cartridge?"

"Nope. Whoever loaded the bullets in the clip must have done it with gloves on." Darcie shook her head. "Must've watched a crime show on TV and learned that one."

"Nothing else?"

"The drugs found in Ashley's coat pockets all tested positive as opioids."

"No surprise. I talked to Juanita. The bullet came back with no match from NIBIN. What about the prescription vial they found in the car?"

"The vial tested positive for opioids. Andy said they only found Ashley's prints on it."

Sasha nodded. "Juanita also found a partially digested pill in her stomach. It tested positive as an opioid. She thought it might have been the remains of an 80mg tablet. Probably took the pill shortly before she died."

"Are you thinking Ashley met someone to buy drugs on South Lee, then somebody interrupted the sale, and it all went bad?"

"Something like that." Sasha put on his coat. "Let's go find this Danny. I pulled an address from the DMV and googled him too. The address that came up is just a couple of blocks from the scene of the crime. You okay to drive?" He gave her a slip of paper with Danny's address and opened the door for her.

"Sure." They got into her unmarked car. "You want to take the front door, and I'll watch the back?"

"That's what I'm thinking. I don't see the guy as a runner, though. R.J. mentioned a girlfriend and a young daughter. It's dark, so I think we roll up and park around the corner from his house."

"Will do." Darcie pulled out of the parking lot. It was only a few minutes to the address. After driving past Danny's house, she made a turn to park across the street about a hundred feet or so from the back of the house. Lights were on inside.

"Give me a minute to get to the front door. Don't move from watching the back door until I text you, okay?"

"Sounds good."

At the house across the street from where they parked, a dog started barking. Darcie watched Sasha walk down the sidewalk to the corner and cross the street. As soon as he was out of sight, she crossed the street and took a position behind the house. As she waited for Sasha's text, the dog that had been barking walked slowly down the sidewalk toward her. It was some kind of terrier mix whose bark was undoubtedly worse than its bite. Her phone vibrated with Sasha's "OK."

When she reached the front of the house, Sasha was holding the screen door open, talking with Danny Williams.

"Here is the partner I mentioned," Sasha said. "Could she and I step inside and ask you some questions, Mr. Williams?"

"What questions?" Danny turned to his girlfriend, who was holding his daughter. "Everything's okay. Take Kayla to her room."

"What's going on, Danny?" Hallie asked.

"Everything's fine. Please just take her to her room." He turned back to the two detectives. "Please come inside." He stepped back and opened the door wide.

"Thank you, Mr. Williams," Sasha said. "Good evening, ma'am." Hallie didn't move or answer. Darcie closed the door.

"What can I do for you, Detective?"

Danny didn't seem at all flustered that he and Darcie were standing in the front room of his home. "Can we sit down and talk, Mr. Williams?"

"Sure." Danny moved so that the two detectives could sit on the couch. Sasha sat down.

"I'm good, thanks," Darcie said and remained standing.

Danny sat in a recliner and said to Hallie, "Why don't you take Kayla to her room and read her a book?" Hallie studied the senior detective, then nodded and disappeared down the hallway. "Go ahead," Danny said.

"Could I ask where you were at 1 a.m. this morning?"

"Here asleep. Why do you ask?"

Sasha had assumed that would be Danny's answer. "If I asked your wife, would she agree with you, Mr. Williams?"

"Hallie's my girlfriend, and yes, she would." Danny had been questioned by police before and typically wasn't nervous talking with them, but he was struggling to keep calm. He considered himself lucky to have gotten away unscathed, and he just needed to keep cool.

"Do you know a young woman by the name of Ashley Cummins, Mr. Williams?"

Danny had spent the last sixteen hours going over questions he thought the police would ask him if they knocked at his door. Now that the detectives were in his house asking the questions he expected, he couldn't remember the answers he'd formulated. "Ashley who?"

Sasha looked up at Darcie and back at Danny. "Ashley Cummins. Early twenties. You may have heard on the news that she was murdered last night just a few blocks from where we're sitting."

"Sorry, but I haven't had the news on today."

"So you didn't hear the sirens last night? Between 1:20 and 1:30 a.m.?"

Danny took a deep breath. "Yes, I heard the sirens. We hear sirens at all times of the day and night around here. Oakland is just a block away." Oakland was the main traffic corridor and a one-way street that headed west through town. Macarthur was another block over and was one-way, heading east. Both roads saw heavy traffic.

Sasha smiled to himself. "Oakland?"

"Yeah. I didn't see it on the news, but I heard somebody was shot over by Lee and Oakland." Danny wanted only to answer the questions he was asked and was trying not to talk too much. Talking too much could be a problem.

"Who'd you hear that from?" Darcie asked.

Danny turned to her. "Neighborhood grapevine, Detective."

"So I want to ask you again, Mr. Williams. Did you know Ashley Cummins?"

"I already said I didn't."

"You're the first person we've talked with, Mr. Williams. We'll be talking to a lot of people over the next few days." Sasha was sitting on the edge of the cushion and leaned forward. "I think we're going to find somebody who's going to tell us they've seen you with Ms. Cummins. A friend of hers maybe or someone working in one of the college bars you frequent. So why don't you just stop lying to us and tell us the truth?"

Since Danny had told them he didn't know Ashley, he had to commit to that lie. He knew they'd find somebody to confirm that he knew her, but that could take them days. Danny was pretty sure he knew who had put a gun in his face last night, but he wouldn't be talking to the police. "I don't know this Ashley chick." There was no value in helping the detectives find who killed one of the rich girls he sold drugs to.

Sasha stood up. "I'm going to ask Detective Lyman to talk with your wife."

"She's still not my wife; she's my girlfriend."

"Sorry. Detective Lyman is going to ask your girlfriend a few questions." Sasha motioned with his head for Darcie to follow the girlfriend.

When she reached the hallway, Darcie turned back to Danny. "What's your girlfriend's name again?"

"Hallie," Danny said. "She doesn't know nothin' about nothin'."

"Thanks." Darcie smiled to herself and started walking down the hallway.

"Where do you work, Mr. Williams?"

"I'm between jobs right now." Danny didn't have a record, and he'd never had a job, a credit card, or a bank account. He was a street hustler whose grandmother called him a silver-tongued devil.

"What was your last job?"

"I've been outta work for a while."

"I understand. The economy is pretty bad, and the unemployment rate is over nine percent in Illinois." Sasha paused for a bit, but he suspected Danny was too smart and probably couldn't be baited into talking too much. He could probably sit there staring at the detective for hours if he needed to. "If I got the district attorney to pull your tax records, what would we find?"

Danny had never filed a tax return, so he was thinking the joke was on the detective. They rented the house they were living in. He and Hallie both drove nice cars, but not too nice, and he'd bought them from private sellers happy to take cash. He also had plenty of money stashed. "I guess you'll just have to wait until he tells you."

Sasha smiled. Danny had a calmness about him most criminals lacked. He was beginning to see how the drug dealer had been able to get through life without a record. "How about Hallie? Where does she work?"

"You'll need to ask her."

"I'm asking you."

Danny decided he wouldn't reply. He was going with a less-is-more strategy. A minute had gone by with neither of them talking when Darcie returned to the living room.

"What did you find out?" Sasha asked.

"I know you're going to be surprised, but Hallie says they were both here in bed last night." She stood next to Danny. "She says Danny never left the house. They went to bed early after watching some videos with Kayla."

"That's nice." Sasha looked across to Danny. "Which video did you watch?"

"We watched a movie about Tinker Bell. Kayla's favorite." They had watched it several times yesterday and today with their daughter. There was no way the detectives would shake what they had agreed upon as their stories. Just enough truth to be convincing.

Sasha stood up. "Thank you for the time, Mr. Williams. I'm sure Detective Lyman and I will cross paths with you soon."

Danny didn't get up. He gave Sasha a little salute. "You can let yourselves out." He was going to have to lay low for a couple of weeks.

As Sasha was closing the door, he popped his head back inside. "We'll be back, Danny. Meanwhile, you might want to stay out of the bars you've been dealing in. And don't leave town." Sasha closed the door and followed Darcie down the steps and out to the sidewalk.

"His girlfriend didn't give up a thing. My mom used to have a saying: Too cool for school. I'm not sure Hallie has ever sweated a day in her life."

"Danny's the same. He seems to be a natural conman. I can see why he's gotten this far without being arrested. He's smart. He's not going to give anything up unless we find a way to get to him."

"How do we do that?"

"The only thing we can do is to find something to charge him with so we can sweat him."

As they got to the car, Sasha stopped. "I think Danny was there last night. Hopefully, Andy and his team will find something that could tie him to the car. That or he messes up and gets arrested."

"I'm guessing he's going to be spending a lot of time at home over the next few days." Darcie walked around to the driver's side and opened the door. The dog started barking again. "Head back to the station?"

Sasha opened the passenger door. "No. Let's go try to find Green and

Johns. It's early, so we might find them at home." He got into the car and closed the door.

The address Sasha gave Darcie was just a block away from where she grew up. Her mom and William Green's mom were friends. The two ladies both sang in the choir at church. Darcie couldn't remember William attending church much, though. She often thought how lucky she was that she'd gotten out while some of the others had gotten sucked into a life of crime.

A few minutes later, she parked around the corner from the Green home.

"The alley looked a little muddy. You have boots, don't you?"

"In the trunk." Darcie hadn't been a detective long, but she'd picked up a few lessons quickly. Having boots that could slip on over shoes was one of them.

"Let's go." Sasha got out of the car and quietly closed the door.

Darcie got out and opened the trunk. The light was disconnected as were the interior lights of the unmarked police car. She pulled out her flashlight and quickly found the pull-on boots. She watched Sasha turn the corner and walk to the front door. She moved quickly to take up a position in the backyard of Mrs. Green's home.

Sasha knocked and heard a woman's voice asking someone to get the door. The porch light came on and the front door opened, and a man who appeared to be in his mid- to late twenties answered. Sasha had his badge in his left hand and his right hand lightly on the grip of his holstered 9mm semiautomatic. "Good evening. Are you William Green?"

Sticks had assumed the police would come looking for him at either his place or his mother's. He'd had enough run-ins with police officers that he knew how to keep his cool. "Who's askin'?" He pushed the door wide open and crossed his arms.

The floor of the house was maybe four inches above the porch. Sasha thought that Sticks was maybe 5' 8" at the most. He didn't see that Green was wearing boots with two-inch heels. Sasha estimated that soaking wet, the man might weigh 140 pounds. "I'm Senior Detective Sasha Frank. Could I come in and ask you some questions, Mr. Green?"

"Nah." Sticks shook his head. "I don't think so, Detective. Anything you want to ask me, you can do from right there."

Sasha decided Darcie should stay where she was to make sure that no one like Johns left out the back. "That's fine. Can you tell me where you were this morning between 1 a.m. and 1:30 a.m.?"

"In bed."

Sasha expected that answer. At that hour, most people were in bed, but drug dealers tended to be working their customers at that time of night. "Can anyone confirm that, Mr. Green?"

"Wasn't anyone in bed with me, ya know. Momma knows I was here all night. You could ask her."

"That would be great. I would like to confirm that with her. Thanks."

"Momma's not here."

"We can come back later to talk to her. What time did you go to bed?" Sasha asked.

"I dunno. Maybe shortly before midnight."

"What were you doing before you went to bed?"

Sticks smiled to himself, thinking that the detective's softball questions meant they hadn't found any evidence or witnesses who could identify him. "This and that."

"Did you hear that someone was shot and killed over on South Lee near Oakland early this morning?"

"No, I hadn't heard that."

"A young woman, early twenties, was shot and killed in her car last night."

"Okay."

"You hadn't heard that?"

"I already said I hadn't."

Sasha didn't get frustrated talking with potential suspects. At some point during an investigation, the tide would change in his favor. Right now, he wished he could grab Green by his neck and yank him outside. "I would have thought the neighborhood would be talking about the murder."

"Some may be talkin' about it, Detective, but I haven't been outside the house and haven't been talkin' to nobody today." He reached for the door handle. "Is that about it, Detective? Any more questions?"

"No, Mr. Green. I'm sure we'll be talking again soon." Sasha stared for a few seconds, then sternly repeated, "Very soon."

Sticks smiled at Sasha. "Night." He quickly closed the door before Sasha was able to reply.

Sasha texted Darcie to meet at the car, and when he arrived, she was leaning against the back of the car, pulling off her boots. "That was a waste of time."

"Mr. Green not too talkative?" She tossed the boots into the trunk.

"He talked but didn't say anything."

"Did you get the feeling he was involved?"

"Let's get out of here." Sasha moved around to the passenger side of the car and got in.

Darcie got in and started the car. "Did he look like his rap sheet photo?" Darcie put the car into gear and slowly pulled away from the curb.

"Yeah. The guy is maybe five-and-a-half feet tall. And that's a big maybe. Do I think he knows something? Probably. Maybe." Sasha shook his head. "I don't know. He was, of course, home in bed last night."

"Anyone else in the house?" Darcie stopped at the intersection, waiting to hear where they were heading next.

"While I waited for the door to open, I heard a woman's voice. I asked if I could talk to his mother, but he said she wasn't home. I did tell him that we'd be back to ask her some questions. Since you know her, you should do that tomorrow."

"Can do." Darcie was still stopped at the intersection, waiting for Sasha to tell her where to go next.

Sasha got out his cell phone and searched the web for Charles Johns. There were some people with that name in the Chicago area, but none in Bloomington. He pulled out Big G's rap sheet and found the last known address he'd provided to the parole board. Sasha gave the address to Darcie, and she took a right. "I'm guessing we're not going to find Charles at home."

Darcie laughed. "You think Sticks gave him a heads-up?"

Sasha nodded. "The second he closed the door." Sasha wished he'd parked a couple of officers outside Johns's home.

"Assuming he's not there, what's our next move?"

"Head back to the station, get a plan for tomorrow, and call it a day."

"Sounds good, Sasha." Darcie was tired, and she knew that her partner had to be as well. As they drove by the address, they saw there were no lights on in the house. "What do you want to do?"

"Let's head back. I'll call his probation officer to have him set up a meeting at his office. We'll talk to him there."

"What are you thinking?" Darcie asked as she made a turn at the next corner to head back to the station.

"Can you set up meetings with the girls on the friends list so we can hit the ground running tomorrow morning?"

"Sure. What time do you want to start?"

Sasha thought for a second. "Why don't you make the first meet at 10 a.m., then set them up every thirty minutes after? It shouldn't take long to talk to each of them."

"Based on the number, it will take through early afternoon, assuming they're all available tomorrow."

11

As he drove to the Chinese restaurant to pick up the takeout he'd ordered, Sasha massaged his right temple in an attempt to get rid of his headache. He'd spent almost two hours on the phone at the station. After Chief Boyer had listened to Sasha's update on the investigation, the chief said that he'd fielded calls from Ashley's family wanting to know what was being done to catch her killer. Sasha's takeaway from this conversation was that manure ran downhill, and he'd be hearing from the chief several times a day until the case was solved.

When he talked with R.J., he'd already spoken with everyone on his list of potential suspects. Sasha had laughed aloud thinking about the street names these drug dealers were using: Red Red, Jammer. He'd wondered what his would be, but it wasn't worth the time thinking about it. At any rate, R.J. had found no reason to believe that any of the names on his list were involved.

Sasha had had a good call with J'Quon Sweeney, who headed the Adult Probation Supervision Unit for the McLean County Probation Office. He'd always liked working with J'Quon. Although Sasha hadn't graduated from the University of Illinois, he had followed the Big 10 football player's career. Everyone in J'Quon's circle had expected he would play in the NFL, but he decided to stay in college and get his master's degree at U of I. He had dedicated his life to helping keep people out of prison. He also helped ex-convicts stay out of trouble after they were released.

J'Quon told Sasha that Green and Johns had monthly meetings scheduled for the following week, but J'Quon would try moving the meetings up to this week. Getting them to the meetings should be no problem, but getting them to talk would be extremely hard. Since the senior detective hadn't found any evidence to tie them to the murder of Ashley Cummins, J'Quon said it would be hard to flip them. Still, the opportunity to talk to both men in a setting where Sasha had at least some control might get one of them to open up. Although Sasha felt both were involved, if it turned out they weren't, maybe they could shed light on who was.

When Sasha called Andy Simon, the CSI tech confirmed that there was no match in the NIBIN database for the spent cartridge discovered in the car. Other than the set of prints from the employee at the tire dealership where Ashley had work done on her car, there were no other prints found in the FBI database. The pills discovered in the pockets of coats and jackets from Ashley's closet were all confirmed to be opioids. Beyond those pills, the CSI team had uncovered nothing that had provided any evidence pointing to possible suspects in the killing.

Sasha's brief call with Juanita's assistant at the ME's office didn't provide him with any new information. He was just going to have to wait for updates on Monday to find out the results of the evidence collected during the autopsy. The fact that they had found a partly digested opioid pill in Ashley's stomach confirmed the suspicion that she was addicted to the drug. There were too many pieces of evidence that pointed to that fact.

Sasha had decided that he wouldn't tell Charlie Cummins about the drugs they'd found in Ashley's closet. At least not yet. There was no reason to tarnish her memory, especially with her upcoming funeral on Tuesday. Her father had told Sasha of the arrangements he'd made for his only child. It was heartbreaking to hear about the plans for her interment. Mr. Cummins had said his entire family was having a tough time dealing with Ashley's death, especially his parents. Sasha couldn't imagine having to bury a child.

As he was pulling out of the restaurant parking lot, his cell phone rang. Darcie had left him a note while he was on one of the calls, asking him to call her. He'd forgotten. "Sorry I didn't call you. Time got away from me."

"No problemo." Darcie was sitting on her couch in her sweats, eating pizza and drinking a beer. "I just wanted to let you know that I set up meetings with everyone on the list Mr. Cummins provided."

"Great! All of them?"

"Yes. I'm starting with Mindy Sinclair. Everyone was more than willing to meet and talk about Ashley. They were pretty devastated by her murder."

"I'm sure. Did you get anything from any of them? Any of them tell you anything?"

"Just one. Mindy Sinclair went to the concert with Ashley last night. She said Jamie Shunk did too." Darcie took a sip of beer. "Mindy said Ashley was texting someone on her phone on the way back from the concert."

"Did she say who or why she was texting this person?"

"No. Mindy said Ashley was sitting in the back seat of Jamie's SUV and couldn't say."

"Where are you on the warrant for her call history?"

"Ashley's carrier gave us the green light, and we're just waiting for the records to come back. I think we should have it by tomorrow."

"Excellent!" Sasha pulled into the driveway of his home and waited for the garage door to open.

Darcie took another drink. "You know, if she was texting a dealer, it's possible the number she called was a burner phone."

Sasha watched the garage door close behind him. "Yes, that's possible." He turned off the engine and opened his door. In all likelihood, her phone logs wouldn't provide any solid leads, but you never knew. "Listen, try to get a good night's rest, and I'll give you an update on all my calls in the morning."

As Sasha walked through the door leading into the kitchen, Janet was standing just inside, waiting for him. She smiled. "Evening, stranger."

Sasha put the bag of takeout on the counter just inside the door. "It's been a long day, hasn't it?"

"It certainly has been for you." Janet grabbed the takeout and took the food to the kitchen island where there were already plates and silverware out.

He took off the coat he'd been wearing and placed it on the rack by the door. "What do you want to drink?"

"I think I'll have a beer."

"I think I'll have one too." He then removed his gun and holster. Sasha grabbed a couple of beers out of the refrigerator. "Glass or bottle?"

"Bottle is fine, thanks."

Sasha walked over to a kitchen drawer to get a bottle opener. After popping the tops off both beers, he walked around the island, placed the bottles on the counter, and sat down on a stool. He sat at the island and watched Janet remove the containers of food from the bag.

She stuck spoons into each container and pushed the food toward Sasha. "Here you go."

"Thanks, sweetie." Sasha dished out several spoonfuls from each container onto both of their plates. "So what have you been up to today?"

Janet laughed and shook her head. "No way. You first."

Sasha took a drink of beer. "Okay. Can do." He watched as Janet sat down on a stool next to him. Sasha filled her in with all the details of the long, tiring day and ended by telling her about their two best contenders, Sticks and Big G.

"The day hasn't been a bust, then?"

Sasha loved the way Janet put a positive spin on things. "No, today wasn't a total bust. We know a few bits and pieces of information that, with some more digging and a little bit of luck, will lead us to the killer. All is not lost, sweetie. I am hot on the trail." He thought to himself that he was now putting a very positive spin on what little they had discovered.

"Like a dog on a bone. You're tenacious and unrelenting, Sasha."

"Okay. Enough of the pep talk. What about your day?"

She smiled and told him about spending the day with her mother in Champaign.

"That's nice. How is she doing?"

"Great!" Janet took a drink and put down her beer. "I'm more interested in what's going on with you. What's next?"

"Tomorrow I've to spend time going over everything that we've learned so far and work the evidence." Albeit evidence that offers no clear path to finding who killed Ashley, he thought. Sasha just realized that his headache was gone. Talking with Janet was therapeutic.

"It hasn't even been twenty-four hours since her death, Sasha. You'll work the case like you always do." Janet walked over and hugged him. "You're the best at doing what you do. You'll figure it out."

"I'm not throwing in the towel." He opened one of the fortune cookies that had come with the meal.

Janet stood back. "I know. I'm just pointing out that the game has just started. It's like the first batter facing the first pitch in the first inning of the first game of the World Series. The fact is, you're the best at what you do, and I repeat. You're going to figure it out."

Sasha was more interested in relaxing and watching something meaningless on television before heading to bed than in continuing this conversation. He wasn't sure how to end it so that Janet would know that he'd heard what she was saying and would heed her advice. "I hear you. I assure you that we'll figure it out." Sasha looked at the fortune he'd pulled from the fortune cookie, smiled, and read it to Janet. "Hard work pays off in the future; laziness pays off now." He gave his wife a big hug. "I'm going to take a quick shower, and then maybe we can be lazy and watch something light on television before bed. Sound like a plan?"

Janet laughed. "Great fortune. I'll find something for us to watch."

Sasha placed the fortune on the kitchen island, then turned to walk toward the bedroom and the hot shower he had been looking forward to for hours. "Be back in a few." Janet's analogy of a baseball game was a good one. The pressure on him would continue to build until Ashley's killer was arrested, convicted, and finally locked away. In fewer than twelve hours, he would be back at it. He was going to try to avoid giving the case another thought until he walked into the station tomorrow morning.

12

I t was late Sunday afternoon when Darcie walked into the conference room to give Sasha an update on her interviews with Ashley Cummins's friends. Her partner was sitting at the table, staring at the blackboard. She sat down, sipped her coffee, and pulled out her notebook. "It took a while to get Mindy Sinclair to open up. For the first ten minutes, all she talked about how she and Ashley had been friends since they'd first met as eight-year-olds playing youth soccer. She did say that Ashley was her best friend and thought that she would say the same about her. They played soccer together through high school. She said Ashley had been the best soccer player in the area and had been recruited by twenty or more Division I colleges across the country before finally choosing to attend one in California."

Sasha sighed. All he wanted to hear was what Darcie had learned that could help them find Ashley's killer. "Did Mindy have anything of substance, Darcie, or just background info?"

"I'm getting to that." Since this was Darcie's first murder investigation, she wanted to be thorough in relaying what she had learned in the interviews. "Mindy knew that Ashley had been struggling with chronic pain since she'd suffered the injury. She told me she knew that her friend had been buying drugs illegally from a dealer to help with the pain."

Sasha leaned forward. "Okay. Did she know who?"

"No. She didn't have a name." Darcie looked at her notes again, then back to Sasha. "Mindy knew she was buying drugs at a bar in Uptown Normal, but she never actually saw Ashley buy drugs."

"Do you believe her?"

"I think so. Mindy told me she'd been to drug parties with Ashley. Most people who came to the party brought street and prescription drugs and would just drop them in a bowl. They would take turns washing a pill or two down with booze. Bad combination."

Sasha looked at his partner. "Seriously?"

"Yeah, seriously." Darcie shook her head. "I know parties like that take place, but I certainly haven't attended any."

"I'd hope not."

Darcie looked back at her notes. "Mindy said Ashley always brought pills. Mindy insisted that she didn't." The detective looked at Sasha. "Not that that matters."

Sasha leaned back in his chair. "So, yes, she knew that Ashley did opioids and typically bought them in an Uptown Normal bar, but she doesn't know who Ashley bought them from?"

"Correct."

"And you believed her?"

"Like I said. I think so."

Sasha was sure Darcie thought the friend was forthcoming, but he thought she probably knew more. "She didn't know who Ashley texted on the drive back from Peoria?"

"She didn't." Darcie quickly looked at her notes again. "That's it from Mindy."

"That certainly wasn't much. Did you talk to anyone who knows anything that will help?"

"I talked to Jamie Shunk next. She was the other friend who'd gone to Peoria for the concert."

"Did she have anything worthwhile to tell you?"

Darcie knew Sasha was getting irritated, but she decided that she was going to continue to tell him what she'd learned, whether it was important or not. "Ms. Shunk confirmed what Mindy had said about Ashley texting. She wasn't sure who." Darcie looked back at her notes. "She also talked about the drug parties she, Ashley, Mindy, and other friends attended. Ms. Shunk told me she wasn't as close to Ashley as Mindy. Yes, she knew Ashley did drugs, but she didn't know how much. Or if she did, she wouldn't say."

"Others?"

"Most of the girls I interviewed had played soccer with Ashley at some point in her life. Only Mindy and Jamie were on the same high school soccer team with her. They were all aware that Ashley occasionally did drugs." Darcie rechecked her notes. "None of her longtime friends knew of her possible addiction. Rebecca Berens and Danielle Stone became friends with Ashley after she returned to Bloomington from college."

Sasha stood up. "Please tell me one of the two of them knew something?" He was getting very frustrated.

"Yes. These two girls became friends with Ashley because they're also drug users. They say they're not addicted but freely admit they recreationally use drugs. They both met Ashley at Bobcat's. Remember R.J. mentioning that bar?"

Sasha nodded. The bar has been around for ten years or more. He hadn't been there, but he knew young police officers who went there because it was one of the hottest college bars in the area.

Darcie went to the bar occasionally because it was a great place for dancing. "I don't see you and Janet going to Bobcat's for a drink."

The senior detective laughed and sat back down. "Well, we might be a little old to fit in."

"Anyway, both Rebecca and Danielle said Ashley bought drugs from a guy there. They said that he went by D."

Sasha leaned forward. "D as in Danny? Please tell me they positively IDed the photo of Danny?"

"Yes. Rebecca said she introduced Ashley to him at Bobcat's about two years ago."

Sasha shook his head at his partner. "Darcie, you could have told me that at the start."

"Sorry, but I wanted to go through the interview notes with all her friends, and Rebecca and Danielle were the last two I interviewed. What they individually told me all matched up, other than Rebecca telling me that she introduced Ashley to D. Danny Williams."

"We need to go back out and interview Danny again now that we know he was Ashley's dealer." Sasha stood up, looked at his watch, and saw it was 4:40 p.m. "Tell dispatch to send two cruisers to Danny's house to watch it until we get there. I'll call R.J. to let him know what you learned."

"Meet you back at your desk?"

Her partner nodded and watched Darcie leave the conference room then got out his cell phone to call R.J. The vice detective answered on the first ring. "What's up, Sasha?"

Sasha told him what Darcie had learned during her interviews with Ashley's friends. "She knew him by D and made the introduction to Ashley at Bobcat's about two years ago."

"Geez. That's the first time I've heard the guy goes by D. We should've already known that, Sasha. Sorry."

Sasha was thinking the same thing. "It sounds like you need to develop some better confidential informants, though." It was shocking that R.J. wasn't aware that Danny Williams had a street name. How many other dealers were they unaware of in the area? It was astonishing that Danny was able to sell drugs and effectively stay under the radar without being arrested.

"Point taken."

"I'm not being judgmental, R.J."

"I am, Sasha. It's my bad."

"Darcie is over at dispatch to get them to put a couple of cruisers on Danny before we head over to talk with him again."

"Do you want me there, too?"

Sasha considered R.J.'s offer for a few seconds. "Thanks, but no thanks, R.J." Sasha waited to hear the detective's response. There wasn't one. "If you want, I'll give you a call after we talk to him."

"Yeah. That'd be good, Sasha. Thanks. Talk later, man." R.J. ended the call without hearing Sasha's reply.

Sasha wasn't concerned about whether he had ticked off R.J. as he didn't have time to deal with other people's emotions right now.

Darcie was sitting in his desk chair when he entered his office. She stood up. "Ready?"

"Let's roll. I'll drive."

As the two detectives walked to Sasha's unmarked car, he gave her a quick update about his call with R.J.

"So he hung up on you?"

"No, but he was embarrassed."

"Understandable." Darcie got into the passenger side. "When I asked dispatch to send a couple of cruisers to cover Danny's, he decided to send three. He suggested positioning one on both the east and west sides of the house along with one in the alley behind it."

Sasha backed out of his parking place. "Smart call. Since the back is covered, we'll park right out front and go to the door together." Darcie nodded.

The two detectives rode the rest of the short drive in silence. Sasha slowed and saw a cruiser parked in the alley behind a garage, out of view from Danny's house. The officer was out of the cruiser, watching the back door. Sasha wasn't sure who it was, but he appreciated the initiative.

As they made the last turn onto Macarthur and headed east, Sasha stopped at the first cruiser, parked about half a block down from the house, and rolled down his window. The officer in the cruiser rolled down hers, too. Sasha smiled. "Hey, Becky."

Becky Roach had been on the force for about ten years, and for the past three, she'd served as a K9 officer with her German Shepard partner, Lux. "Expecting trouble, Sasha?"

"Just being overly cautious, Becky. How's Lux doing?" The big dog was pacing back and forth in the back seat of the cruiser.

"I think he's hoping for a runner."

Sasha laughed. "Lux may be disappointed. I'm not expecting a runner, but you never know. Keep your eyes peeled, Becky." She gave him a thumbs-up. As Sasha pulled up in front of Danny's house, he spotted the other cruiser parked midway down the next block. "It looks like we're set. You ready?"

Darcie nodded. "Did you notice there aren't any lights on?"

Sasha looked at the house. He'd been looking down the street at the cruiser and hadn't noticed the house was dark. The sun had set about the time they'd left the station, so there should have been lights on if Danny was home. "Crap." The two opened their doors, got out, and walked up to the house. Sasha knocked loudly on the door while shouting, "Police. Danny Williams? Police! Open the door!"

Darcie walked down the steps and looked through the front window. She shined the beam of her flashlight inside. "I don't see anything." She looked over at Sasha. "I don't think anyone's home."

"I sure the hell hope he didn't run."

Darcie walked back and stood at the bottom of the steps. "You want to put an APB out on him?"

Sasha joined her. "No. Call dispatch and tell him to pull the support, but ask him to leave one in place to keep watch on the house."

Darcie made the call and said, "They're pulling the current officers except for Becky. When the unmarked car arrives, they'll have her take off."

Sasha looked over at Darcie. "Let's roll by Johns's house."

"Sounds good." Darcie didn't want to second-guess her partner, but she thought they wouldn't have to try looking for Johns today if Sasha had had his house under surveillance before they knocked on William Green's door yesterday.

As they turned onto Johns's street and rolled up in front of his house, they found that his place was also dark. "I'm sure hoping all three of them haven't left town," Sasha said as he started getting a bad feeling about his key suspects.

"Let's head back to the station and call it a day. I'm going to call J'Quon to confirm the times for the interviews he was setting up."

She shook her head. "I'm going to go back over everything to see if there was something we missed."

"Your call." Sasha turned off the car. "I'm going to head home after I connect with J'Quon, if that helps in your decision."

"I'll work for an hour or two before heading home. I don't have any plans tonight."

———

J'Quon answered on the second ring. "Sweeney."

"J'Quon, it's Sasha Frank. How's your Sunday going?"

"Better than yours, I'm sure. Football season is over, so I'm watching some NCAA basketball."

"Sounds relaxing." Sasha got out his notepad. "What do you have set up for tomorrow?"

"I'm sorry, Sasha, but we haven't gotten either of them to answer our calls. I got ahold of Green's mom, and she told me she thought he'd gone to Saint Louis or Memphis for the weekend."

"You called?"

"Yes. I'm Green's probation officer."

"So you think he ran." Sasha threw his pen at his desk and watched it bounce onto the floor. "What about Johns?"

"I don't know. We finally got through to his mom. She told us she didn't know anything."

"Crap."

"They both have scheduled meetings the week after next. Green is scheduled for Thursday and Johns on Friday. I can guarantee you they won't miss those meetings. But if they're in the wind, all we can do is keep calling them. My guess is they've both turned off the phone we know about and left town."

Sasha was upset at himself for not putting surveillance on Green. He probably would have led them to Johns. "Okay. I'll have officers keep an eye out for them in the meantime."

"We'll keep trying Sasha, and when they do resurface, we'll get them into the office ASAP."

"Thanks, J'Quon. It was my fault for not keeping tabs on Green once we left him at his mom's house."

Sasha started walking to the conference room to give Darcie a quick update. The two detectives were hitting brick walls already and didn't have much to go on.

13

Darcie walked into the conference room, carrying two cups of hot coffee. "Morning, Sasha." She handed him a cup. The senior detective was standing at the table, which was covered with file folders. "I made it just the way you like it."

Sasha smiled. "Thanks." Darcie nodded back at him. "I've been standing here for the past hour looking at what we've got."

"And?"

"And we've got nothing. I talked to R.J. a few minutes ago, and he suggested we send uniforms around to roust the guys on the list that he talked to on Saturday."

"How does he remain undercover if he overtly talks with suspects?" Darcie had wanted to ask Sasha that question since they'd met with the detective on Saturday.

"He just had a casual conversation with each of them to get a feel for what they might know." Sasha sipped the coffee. "You tend to burn your undercover status pretty easily in a city our size."

Darcie nodded. "That what I was thinking." She had been considering applying for the next opportunity to work undercover, but now she wasn't so sure.

"Let's focus on solving this murder." He put his coffee cup down on the conference table and picked up Ashley's autopsy file. "Based on everything Juanita found during the autopsy, we're only waiting for results of blood tests related to alcohol and drug levels, right?"

"Yes, that's right."

"Since she found a partially ingested opioid pill in Ashley's stomach contents, it's a given that she'll test positive for drug use." Sasha turned to look at Darcie. "Whether she abused alcohol or not is meaningless under the circumstances of her death."

"I agree."

Sasha sat back down. "Any additional information we get from the ME and CSI isn't going to move the needle on solving Ashley's murder. We don't have anything."

The two started going through all the files, rechecking evidence and going over information learned from talking with Ashley's family, friends, and coworkers. They reread interviews with every suspect—excluding Charles Johns—and interviews with family and friends, looking for anything that would help. Sasha knew he'd get to talk with Johns soon because J'Quon Sweeney would make it happen. They sat there in silence, looking at the files as they waited for the updates from CSI and the ME's office.

Darcie looked up from the files containing the interviews of Ashley's friends. "Have you talked to the chief this morning?"

"Yes. I saw him at 7:30. Big surprise, he's expecting us to solve the case quickly. I explained to him what little we had to go on."

"She was murdered early Saturday morning, and it's just now Monday morning." Darcie looked at her watch, then back to Sasha. "It's only been fifty-five hours since Ashley was killed."

"He told me again that he's gotten numerous calls from her family. He's also getting calls from the mayor, who's getting calls from the family."

"You've kept the chief abreast of the investigation so far."

"I have. It seems to me that I need to find another way to tell him we have nothing at all." Sasha was trying to stay positive, and it was early, but without any solid leads, they were just spinning their wheels.

Darcie wasn't sure if she should say what she was about to, but she couldn't stop herself. "The young lady put herself in the position to have something go terribly wrong, Sasha. This all falls on her."

He looked at his partner for a few seconds. Darcie was right, but was it fair to blame the victim, he wondered? He decided not to agree or disagree with what she'd said. Being silent was to agree with her. "While we wait for updates, let's talk about Johns and Green."

"Well, they seem to be in the wind. Since we stopped by Green's on Saturday night, neither he nor Johns have been seen on the streets."

"You think Williams is in the wind too?"

Darcie nodded. "I do. Patrol has been keeping a lookout for him with no luck. I talked to R.J., and he wasn't seen in any of the bars Saturday night. He did spot Adrian Wolenski in a bar and casually talked with him. R.J. said Wolenski wasn't forthcoming when he asked about Danny."

"Since Jasmine Warren couldn't ID any of the men outside her home when Ashley was killed, let's put together photo arrays that include Green, Johns, and Williams to see if that will jog her memory. Sound like a plan?"

"Sure. We can do that."

Sasha looked at his partner and said, "Let's do two six-pack photo arrays with pictures of everyone on our list."

"Will do."

"Thanks." Sasha picked up the file on Charles Johns when his cell phone rang. It was the ME's office. "Sasha Frank."

"Hi, Sasha. I wanted to let you know that we got back the preliminary test results on Ashley Cummins."

"Darcie's with me, so I'm putting you on speaker. What'd you find?"

"Hi, Darcie. First, let me stress that these are only preliminary test results. Final results will come in over the next few weeks, up to maybe four more weeks."

"Understood."

"So the prelims are on tissue, blood, and urine. The results show that Ashley abused drugs and that abuse caused damage to her liver and kidneys. These were excessive levels, not toxic, but excessive nonetheless, and far exceeding acceptable levels found in someone who was taking such drugs as a doctor prescribed them."

"No real surprise there," Darcie whispered.

The ME checked her notes before continuing. "In dissecting her bowels, we found distention of the abdomen caused by constipation, which can be a side effect of drug use. You already knew that we found a partially digested pill in her stomach, and as you'd expect, we also found drugs in her urine."

"So no surprises."

"No. None, really. We also found alcohol levels of 0.06. Ashley had been drinking that night, but she wasn't legally drunk. No question she was impaired; a blood-alcohol concentration at that level could have resulted in a DUI if a police officer had stopped her and judged her to be driving under the influence."

Sasha shook his head. "So she had a partially digested narcotic in her stomach and had abused drugs that were causing damage to her internal organs, plus she was drinking at the time she was killed?"

Juanita was tapping her desk with her pen. "Yes."

"What more are you going to learn in the weeks to come?"

"Just more definition to the drug use and toxicity levels."

"Hi, Juanita. This is Darcie. Quick question. The cause of death was the bullet wound, right?"

Sasha looked at Darcie and whispered. "Seriously?"

"Our working theory is that Ashley was there buying drugs, and somehow she ended up shot dead. I'm just pointing out that I'm not sure what more we need from the ME's office to help us solve the case, Sasha."

"Darcie is absolutely correct. Ashley Cummins suffered a single gunshot wound to her right cheek, which severed her brain stem, resulting in instant death."

"Okay, Juanita. Thanks. Let us know if there is anything else that comes up."

"No problem. Good luck." Juanita ended the call.

"Sorry, Sasha."

Sasha pushed his chair back from the table and stood up. "It's not a problem, Darcie. You're correct, and I agree. Let's walk over and talk with Andy."

They took their coats and left the station to walk across the parking lot to the CSI garage. As soon as they walked into the garage, they saw Andy standing at the long counter along the wall.

"Got anything new for me?" Sasha asked.

"I have more info on the pills we found in the Cummins' home," he said.

"As I told Darcie, all of the pills found in the closet tested positive as opioids. If you recall, we found five pills with four different formulations."

"Different formulations?"

"Different chemical formulations. A couple of different brands with different compounds. You know. A certain number of milligrams of x versus y."

"Gotcha."

"But what you're going to want to know about is, drum roll, please." Andy tapped both hands on the countertop. "We found a partial print inside the vial found in the BMW."

"Seriously?" Sasha asked. "Why didn't you call me?"

"Alan just found it forty-five minutes ago."

Sasha was growing impatient. "Has the print been run through IAFIS?"

Andy nodded and looked at his watch. "Alan first checked it against the victim's prints, and it didn't match. He's waiting for the results from IAFIS now, and it shouldn't be much longer."

Alan walked into the garage from the CSI office, saw Andy, and shook his head. "It didn't come back with a match."

Sasha stepped forward. "No match?"

"There's not a match in IAFIS."

Darcie looked at Sasha. "It could be Danny Williams."

"It could be." Sasha thought for a second. "Or it could be anyone who's not in the system. We need to find Williams."

"We'll go back over everything again, but I don't think we'll find anything else."

"The print is in the system now, so as soon as we can get our hands on Williams, we'll check his prints against the vial." Sasha walked up to the CSI technician and patted him on the shoulder. "Great work, Alan."

Alan nodded. "Just doing my job, Detective."

"As soon as we can find Williams and get prints, we'll let you know, Andy." Sasha looked back at Darcie. "Let's head back. We've got work to do."

Darcie waved goodbye and followed Sasha out the door. "What's next?"

"I'm going to talk with the chief to give him the news. Then let's go for lunch."

14

I t was just before midnight when Carlos Ward-Wallace unlocked the front door of the apartment he shared with his girlfriend, Monica. After spending the past four hours delivering drugs to customers, he was happy to be back inside his warm apartment. Since he'd left earlier in the evening, the temperature had dropped fifteen degrees, and it was now just ten degrees outside. With the wind chill, it felt more like zero.

Monica had taken the train to visit her family in Saint Louis on Thursday morning, and Carlos didn't expect her to return until Monday at the earliest. He wished he'd been able to go with her. Being a small-time drug dealer made it difficult for him to leave town for even a few days.

Carlos made money buying small amounts of drugs from his supplier, Sticks, then reselling them. His sales were day-to-day, and it was like being on a rollercoaster, depending on what his customers could afford. It wasn't great money, but it was enough to keep him and Monica in the apartment with food and beer in the refrigerator. Between the money he made selling drugs and Monica's part-time job working at the fast-food restaurant nearby, Carlos had been able to move out of his mom's house.

His mom had been asking too many questions about where he got his money. She thought her son was selling drugs, and Carlos didn't blame her for wanting him out of the house. He'd lived with his mother, younger stepsister, and two stepbrothers in a house on Normal's west side until he and Monica had moved into the one-bedroom apartment last September.

As he stepped inside and flipped the light switch, he looked around the small apartment, wondering where Coco was. A friend had given Monica the tiny mixed-breed dog, and she adored it. Carlos didn't like Coco. The dog was always barking at him, especially when he came in the front door of the apartment, which made him wonder what was up with her tonight. He walked into the kitchen and was fumbling for the light switch when he heard a voice. He flipped the switch and saw a man leaning up against the side of the refrigerator.

"You're Bones?" the man asked.

"Who are you?" Carlos started backing away when he bumped into a second man who had come up from behind him. "What's going on? Who are you?"

"Calm down, Bones." The first man pulled out a gun and started walking toward him. The man laughed. "You scared?"

The man standing behind him was quite a bit bigger than Carlos, and he quickly grabbed his arms, holding him tight. He whispered in Carlos's right ear. "What kinda name is Bones?"

The man with the gun walked up close and pressed the gun against Carlos's cheek. "Yeah. What kinda name *is* Bones?" With his left hand, the man threw a hard punch to Carlos's stomach. Carlos's legs started to buckle, and the man holding him from behind let him drop to the floor.

"What do you want?" Carlos was trying to catch his breath.

Jaime looked down at the man on the floor.

"We need to ask you a couple of questions, Bones." The man who was standing behind Carlos reached down and punched him in the back of his head. "I don't think Teo likes you much, Bones," the man standing in front of him said. He put the gun barrel under Carlos's chin and made him look up at him. "What do you think?"

Teo punched Carlos again in the back of his head.

"What do you want?" Carlos shouted. Fear had overtaken him. The tattoos they had on their necks and hands made him think they were gang members. "You want money? Drugs?"

"No, Bones. We want answers." The man holding the gun knelt and placed the barrel of the revolver to the side of Carlos's head. "You got some answers for us, Bones?"

"Yes, I got answers." He assumed it was what they wanted to hear. Carlos tried to stand up.

"That's good, Bones. That's real good." He raised the gun and swung the butt of the revolver hard against the side of Carlos's head, knocking him to the floor. "Question number one, Bones. Did you sell some little girl some drugs and then shoot her in the head?"

"No, I didn't shoot no girl." Carlos had never touched a gun in his life. Customers liked him, and his supplier knew Carlos wasn't a threat. He wanted nothing to do with guns.

"You sure, Bones?" The man threatened to hit Carlos again with the butt of the gun. "You sure?"

"I don't know anything about a girl getting shot."

"Listen up, Bones. I'll ask you one last time. Did you shoot the girl in her car on the west side last weekend?" As he held the gun on Carlos, he looked at the other man. "What was her name, Teo?"

The big man kicked Carlos in his side. "Ashley."

"That's right, Bones. Little rich girl Ashley."

The kick to his side hurt like hell. "I didn't shoot anyone. I didn't shoot no girl."

"Were you there, Bones? Were you there when she was shot?" The man with the gun stood up and put pressure on Carlos's right knee by pressing his foot down hard. "What you say, Bones? What you say?"

"I tell you, I don't know anything about a girl getting shot."

"That's not what we heard, Bones. We hear you're a suspect." The man with the gun motioned to Teo to kick Carlos again. The big man kicked Carlos hard with his right foot, cracking several ribs.

Writhing in pain on the floor, Carlos shouted, "I don't know anything about some girl getting shot!"

"I heard it was all over the news, Bones." The man with the gun looked around the room. "Where's your TV, Bones? I don't see no TV. How you gonna know what's goin' on if you don't have a TV?" The man motioned again to Teo to kick Carlos.

Carlos let out a groan as several more of his ribs cracked. He could hardly breathe and thought he might have a punctured lung. He gasped for air. "Man, stop. I don't know anything."

The man holding the gun stuck it into his waistband. He slowly bent down on one knee beside Carlos. He pulled up his right pants leg to reveal a large knife in a leather sheath. The man pulled out the knife. "You got any money or drugs here, Bones?"

With his right hand, Carlos reached into his front pocket and pulled out the money that he'd collected earlier selling drugs to his customers. "Here," he gasped, handing the money to the man.

The man counted it. "That all you got, Bones?" He handed the cash to Teo. With the knife in his left hand, he quickly slashed the sharp blade from right to left across Carlos's neck.

Carlos grabbed at his throat, trying to speak as the man wiped the blade clean on Bones's sweatshirt. Blood spewed in all directions. As he lay there, Carlos could hear the man who'd just slashed him with the knife talking to the other man he called Teo. "He's done. Make sure we didn't leave anything, and let's get out of here. And turn off the heater. We want it to get cold in here."

As Carlos lay dying on the floor, he wondered why they thought he shot some girl, why they had beaten and cut him. The last thing that crossed his mind before he drifted off into unconsciousness was Monica's little dog, Coco.

15

I t was almost midnight, and Jammer was walking back from the late-night fast-food restaurant on Veterans Parkway to his apartment on South Prospect Road. He was supposed to have met Red Red, but his friend hadn't shown up. Jammer had a customer who wanted to buy beans from him, and Red Red had agreed to sell him what he needed so he could supply his customer. If Red Red didn't get him the opioid his customer was looking for, he'd lose the sale.

Leon and Darren had been friends since they were kids growing up on Bloomington's west side. They had been selling drugs in an area east of Veterans Parkway for the past few years. They didn't make a lot of money, but they were able to survive. On days like today, the two would often share their stashes instead of having to go to the other side of town to get the drugs they needed from their supplier, Sticks, especially this late at night.

A week ago, Sticks had told them he and Big G were going to lie low for a while since the cops were keeping close tabs on them. That was causing them problems satisfying their customers with the drugs they wanted.

After walking through several dark parking lots, he stopped to cross Stern Drive when a car pulled up next to him. Jammer saw the passenger side window rolling down. He didn't recognize the man sitting in the front seat.

"You Jammer?"

"Who wants to know?" Jammer stepped back from the car.

"Why the attitude, man?"

Jammer didn't know the guy sitting in the passenger seat, and he was wary about talking to someone he didn't know, especially at this hour. "No attitude. I just don't know you, man. I'm just askin'."

"I'm Jaime." He motioned toward the driver. "This is Teo."

Jammer leaned down to look past Jaime and nodded at Teo. "What can I do for you guys?"

Jaime pointed a gun at him. "Get in the car." Jammer froze. Jaime firmly said, "Get in the car now." He stepped out of the car.

Jammer looked around the area to see if there was anyone witnessing what was happening as he slowly moved to the rear passenger side door. He stopped before opening it. "What's going on, man?"

"If you want to live, get in now." Jaime pointed the gun at Jammer's head.

Jammer had never carried a gun, but he knew dealers who had. Right now, he wished he had one. As much as he didn't want to get into the car, he realized he didn't have a choice. "I'm gettin' in, man." He opened the door and squeezed his tall frame into the back seat. The driver was also pointing a gun at him.

Teo smiled at Jammer as he closed the door behind him. "How's it going, Leon?" His name was Leon, but everyone, including his mom and grandmother, had called him Jammer since he was tall enough to dunk a basketball.

Jammer watched Jaime get back into the front seat. "What do you guys want?"

Jaime turned, looked at Jammer, and motioned to him with his gun. "Sit in the middle."

Jammer moved as he was told, then asked again, "What do you want?"

"We just want to talk with you, Leon," Jaime said as Teo started to drive.

"Then put the gun down and talk to me, man."

Jaime handed Jammer an empty fast-food bag. "Get out your phone and turn it off." He watched as Jammer did what he was told. "Put the phone and everything in your pockets into the bag."

Jammer followed Jaime's order, then handed the bag back to Jaime. "Now what?"

"I need to ask you a question. What did you have to do with killing the girl in the car a couple of weeks ago?"

"What?"

"Come on, man. You heard the question."

"Where are we goin', man?"

"Answer the question, Leon."

"I didn't kill nobody, man."

"I'm not talking about nobody. I'm talking about a girl." Jaime waved his gun at Jammer. "Yes or no?"

"I didn't kill no girl, man."

Jaime looked at Teo. "He says he didn't kill nobody." Jaime took his gun and slammed it down just above Jammer's knee.

"What are you, doin', man?"

"Slow down a little, Teo." Jaime said. "We're in no hurry."

"Where are you takin' me?"

"We're going to take you to meet Darren."

"You know Darren?"

"We know everyone, Leon, but let's focus on what's important." Jaime watched as Teo pulled onto the northbound entrance of Interstate 55 on the outskirts of Towanda, which would take them back to Chicago.

"Where's Darren?" Jammer asked.

"Lean closer, and I'll tell you," Jaime said. As Jammer slowly leaned forward, Jaime struck him hard over the head several times with his gun, knocking Jammer unconscious.

Teo looked into the back seat and laughed. "Don't make such a mess."

They had stolen the car they were using earlier in the evening in Joliet, so Jaime wasn't really concerned about bloodstains. Leon's friend Darren was already lying unconscious in the trunk. They'd found Darren Redmond at home in his apartment before they'd forced him into the trunk, after Jaime had asked him a few questions and Teo had hit Darren several times with a crowbar.

"We're going to torch the car when we're done."

Teo looked down at the speedometer to make sure that he was keeping under the speed limit as he drove north on the interstate. "We should be at the lake in about thirty minutes."

Jaime had previously found a deep lake that sat between the interstate and historic Route 66 between Pontiac and Odell.

The plan was, when they got to the lake, they would tie the fifty-pound weights they had put into the trunk earlier to the guys' feet before dumping them in the lake. Lakes like the one they were heading to could be found near the interstates that crisscrossed the United States. They were dug deep to obtain the dirt to build the thousands of overpasses needed for the national roadway system. Most of the lakes were remote, privately owned, and had shorelines with severe drop-offs, which made them perfect for their needs. They had chosen one that was surrounded by trees and overgrown shrubs, which made it appear abandoned and perfect for dumping bodies. With any luck, the bodies would never be found. And even if someday they were, Jaime wasn't worried. Whatever DNA evidence they might have left on the two small-time drug dealers would be long gone after a short time in the water. The gang had used lakes and ponds to dispose of bodies many times before.

Jaime lit a cigarette and looked over at Teo. "Do we need to text Miguel and Antonio to let them know we're on our way?"

Teo nodded. "I told them where we'd meet them in Joliet. They should be waiting for us now." The crew were in two vehicles, and they would give his SUV to Jaime and Teo to drive back to Chicago while they torched the stolen car.

Jammer moved in the back seat. Jaime turned and leaned over the seat and hit him several more times with his gun and waited. "The man is strong," Jaime laughed. "I doubt he'll be able to swim out of the lake, though."

They drove in silence until they reached the lake south of Odell. Finding the area around the lake as deserted as they'd expected, they quickly tied weights to Leon's legs. He was alive but unconscious when Jaime and Teo threw him into the water. There was a thin layer of ice that the weighted body easily broke through. They went back to the car for Darren and found that he had died in the trunk. They attached weights to his body and threw him into the water next to Leon.

Jaime lit another cigarette and stood looking out at the surface of the lake. The two stood at the shoreline for a few more minutes while he finished his cigarette. He wanted to make sure both bodies stayed underwater. Jaime flicked the butt into the lake and said, "Okay. Let's go."

Jaime turned up the music in the car and lit another cigarette as they drove away. As he rode in the passenger seat, he thought that if all went according to plan, within two weeks, the people on the list would be dead. Diego would be pleased.

16

Dustin Benz had been Charles Johns, a.k.a. Big G's, probation offi- cer for the past year and a half since his parole from the McLean County Jail.

Charles Johns had been arrested with almost five pounds of marijuana, but his public defender was able to plead the charge down to possession of over one hundred grams of cannabis with intent to sell, a Class 3 felony. Before being released on probation, Big G had spent a year in county jail. He'd been talking with Dustin Benz in his probation officer's office for about ten minutes when the door opened and in walked J'Quon Sweeney, Sasha Frank, and Darcie Lyman. Dustin looked past Big G, who was sitting with his back to the office door. "Morning, folks."

Big G turned and saw the three come into the office. He only recognized one of them, and he decided he should be friendly. "What's up, Sweeney?"

J'Quon gave the ex-con a hard stare, along with a firm, "It's Mr. Sweeney." It was a longstanding rule that parolees must use the appropriate title when addressing their probation officer. Big G nodded. "Charles, I'd like to intro- duce you to Senior Detective Sasha Frank and Detective Darcie Lyman." J'Quon never used an alias.

Big G remained seated. "Mornin', Detectives."

"They're going to be asking you a few questions."

"Should I have my lawyer present?"

Sasha smiled. "I don't know. Should you, Charles?"

Big G looked back at Sasha with no emotion. "Nope. I was just askin'."

Sasha pulled a chair out from beneath a table at the side of Dustin's desk and sat down. "Detective Lyman and I stopped by your house ten days or so ago, Charles, but you weren't at home." Darcie stood beside the small table, and J'Quon stood next to Dustin.

"Oh, really? I didn't know. Sorry about that, Detective."

The senior detective leaned forward in his chair. "Not a problem. Can you tell me where you were on Saturday morning, February 9th, around 1 a.m.?"

With Sasha leaning forward, Big G leaned back in his chair. "Let me think." Big G looked around the room and furrowed his brow. "I was probably asleep in bed, Detective."

"Really? What were you doing before that?"

"On Friday nights, I normally party." Big G smiled at Sasha. "Yeah. I was partying pretty hard."

Sasha looked over at J'Quon and shook his head before turning back to Johns. "Okay. You were partying hard Friday night, and you were in bed by 1 a.m.? Sounds incongruent to me, Charles."

Big G had no idea what incongruent meant, but he assumed it wasn't a good thing. He sat there looking at the senior detective. "I just told you I was partying, and I was in bed by 1 a.m. Any other questions?"

"Were you with William Green at any time Saturday?"

"Nope. Sticks is on probation, and Mr. Benz says I'm not supposed to consort with other parolees while I'm on probation." Big G looked at Dustin. "Ain't that right?"

Dustin nodded. "That's correct, Charles."

"Do you know Ashley Cummins?"

Big G straightened up. "No."

"Never heard of her?"

"No."

"Did you hear about the young lady who got shot in her car at Lee and Oakland early February 9th?" Sasha leaned back in his chair.

"Nope." The chair he was sitting in wasn't very comfortable, especially for someone as large as Big G, and he tried to reposition himself in it. "Oh, was that the girl you just asked me about?"

"Yes, it was Ashley Cummins. She was killed in her car near the corner of

Lee and Oakland early Saturday morning. Killed by a man that matches your description, Charles."

"Tall and good-lookin', Detective?" Big G smiled. "There can't be too many people tall and good-lookin' like me. But I was in bed when you say she was shot."

"I didn't tell you what time she was shot, Charles."

"You asked me where I was at 1 a.m., then you said she was killed early Saturday morning. I already told you it wasn't me, man. I was in bed and didn't get up until almost noon on Saturday." Big G smiled and leaned back in his chair again. "Partying hard, remember?"

Sasha glanced over at Darcie, and she stepped forward. "Do you know me, Charles?"

Big G studied Darcie for a moment. "Don't know if I do, Detective. Would you like to get to know me?"

Darcie laughed out loud and shook her head. "That's never going to happen, Charles." She moved around to the other side of Sasha and stood next to J'Quon. "I grew up in the neighborhood you live in. I still know a lot of people who live there. When did you move into the area?"

"I got arrested here, Detective, and spent time as a guest in your county jail. When I got released, I decided I liked the area so much I'd call it home. It's a lot less dangerous here than in my hometown, Chicago."

"We know you're William Green's partner selling drugs. Mr. Green matches the description of the other person seen outside Ms. Cummins's car Saturday morning."

"I don't know how you can say that, Detective. Sticks and I know each other, but we don't work together or nothin'." Big G leaned forward in his chair. "And here you're saying that we're partners selling drugs? If that were true, we'd be back in jail as that would be violatin' probation." He smiled and leaned back again.

"You knew before you walked in here today, Mr. Johns, that we've wanted to talk with you about this murder," Sasha said. "We think you and Mr. Green are the two men a witness saw standing outside Ms. Cummins's car early Saturday morning. We believe that you were the man seen getting into

Ms. Cummins's car just before she was shot and killed. Since the day Ashley Cummins was murdered, you've been in our sights, Mr. Johns."

"Well, you can just set your sights on somebody else, Detective. I didn't shoot nobody." Big G smiled, knowing that the detectives obviously had nothing on him, or he'd be back in custody right now.

The senior detective stood up and looked down at Charles Johns. "No, I think we'll keep looking right at you, Mr. Johns. Everything Detective Lyman and I know about Ashley Cummins's murder points to you as the one who pulled the trigger. It was in your neighborhood where she was murdered. You and Mr. Green wouldn't want a rival to be selling drugs on your turf, and you took quick action to deal with someone—someone like Danny Williams—disrespecting you both."

"You're wrong, man. I don't know why you've got it out for Sticks and me, but you need to be lookin' somewhere else."

Darcie stepped up closer to Sasha. "We don't have it wrong, Mr. Johns. We'll be talking with you again soon."

Big G nodded. He looked over at his probation officer. "You got anything more to say to me, Mr. Benz?"

"Not today, Charles. Keep your head down and stay out of trouble."

"That's what I do every day, Mr. Benz. Every day." Big G got ready to stand up. "So we're done?"

"We're done." Dustin stood up from his desk.

Big G stood up and gave a little wave as he walked out of the office. "See ya."

"So I guess that went as you expected?" J'Quon said.

Sasha smiled. "Yes. Exactly as I expected." He turned to Darcie. "What do you think of Big G?"

"I think he shot Ashley. He knows we have no evidence, and he mocked us."

"Yes, he did." Sasha turned to J'Quon. "Ready to talk with Green?"

J'Quon glanced at his watch. "Let's go. He should be waiting in my office. See you later, Dustin. Thanks." He led the way out of the office and turned to head down the hallway to his office, Sasha and Darcie following close behind.

"Good morning, William," J'Quon said when he reached his office.

Sticks didn't turn in his chair to see J'Quon enter. "Mornin', Mr. Sweeney."

"We've got two guests who'd like to talk with you." J'Quon walked around and sat down in his chair while Sasha and Darcie came around and stood at opposite sides of the probation officer's desk.

"Morning, Detective," Sticks said to Sasha. He turned to Darcie. "Morning, ma'am. I'm William Green. It is my pleasure to make your acquaintance." Sticks thought he recognized the woman, but he wasn't sure why.

"William, I understand you've met Senior Detective Frank. This is his partner, Detective Lyman."

Sticks nodded to Sasha. "Detective Frank. A pleasure to see you again." He turned to Darcie and smiled. "Detective." Sticks turned back to his probation officer. "What would you like to talk about today, Mr. Sweeney?"

J'Quon looked across the desk at Green and didn't try to hide the fact that he disliked him. "Today I thought I'd let the detectives meet with you, William. They've been looking for you, and since you've been unavailable, today's meeting seemed like an appropriate time for them to talk with you." He leaned back in his chair and looked at Sasha. "Detective."

"Nice to see you again, Mr. Green."

Sticks smiled.

"I was hoping to talk with you before today. Where have you been?"

Sticks didn't look up. "Here and there, Detective."

Sasha looked across to Darcie and gave a small shake of his head before looking back at Sticks. "Could you be a little more specific, Mr. Green?"

Looking across the desk at J'Quon without answering Sasha's question, Sticks asked, "I don't have to answer his questions without my lawyer present, do I?"

"You have the right to have your attorney present, William, but it seemed like a pretty benign question to me. Why don't you just go ahead and answer the detective's questions?"

Sticks wasn't sure what benign meant. He nodded and looked back at Sasha. "I was visitin' some family."

"Where?"

"I have family in Chicago, so I spent a few days there." Sticks did have family in Chicago, but he hadn't seen any of them since the night Big G had shot the girl in the car.

"Where do you work, Mr. Green?"

"I'm between jobs right now, Detective. Keeping a job isn't too easy for someone like me."

"Someone like you?"

Sticks laughed. "I'm a convicted felon, Detective. I spent a couple of years down at Lincoln as a guest of the state."

"What were you convicted of Mr. Green?"

"I think you probably already know that."

"Humor me."

"I was convicted of possession with intent to distribute." Sticks turned to Sasha. "I wasn't guilty, and the police planted the drugs on me."

"Mr. Sweeney, is Mr. Green correct that he was convicted of possession with the intent to distribute?"

J'Quon knew but fumbled at Sticks's file before answering Sasha's question. "Yes, Detective. He was convicted and sentenced to four years. Mr. Green was released after serving twenty-six months with three years' probation."

"Well, Mr. Green, I can understand then how hard a time you're having finding or keeping a job. I'm not sure how many employers would want to hire someone with that kind of experience."

"That's why I'm between jobs." Sticks was having fun messing with the detective.

"You're partners with Charles Johns selling drugs now, aren't you?"

"No, Detective. That would violate the terms of my probation." Sticks looked back at J'Quon. "Ain't that right, Mr. Sweeney?"

"Last time we spoke, I asked if you knew about the shooting death of a young woman on Saturday, February 9th, and you told me you hadn't heard about it. Have you learned anything about that killing since we last spoke, Mr. Green?"

"Can't say I have, Detective."

"Well, we just spoke with your associate, Mr. Johns, and he told us a similar story. It's really hard to believe you wouldn't know more about what's happening on your home turf."

"I don't have any turf, Detective."

"Mr. Green, did you know that I was raised in the same neighborhood as you?"

Sticks looked at Darcie. "I don't remember you, but Mom does, and she told me that you were a detective now, Darcie. It was nice of you to stop by her house and say hi."

"I always liked your mom, Billy. I still know a lot of people who live in the neighborhood, and most of them know that you control and sell drugs there."

"I go by Sticks now." Sticks sat up in his chair. "I haven't gone by Billy for a long time."

"When I talked to your mom about you, she called you Billy. So did some of the other people I talked to in the neighborhood."

Sticks wasn't used to people disrespecting him like the detective was now, but he also knew that he needed to keep calm. He looked back at J'Quon. "Mr. Sweeney, you said the detectives wanted to ask me questions. They can ask me questions, but I'm not gonna sit here and be disrespected."

"The name of the woman killed in her car on February 9th in your neighborhood is Ashley Cummins," Sasha said. "We have a witness that provided us a description of two men standing outside of Ashley's car at the time she was killed. The description of the two men closely matches you and your partner, Charles Johns."

"You've asked me that question before, Detective. I don't have any idea where Big G was, but I was at home in bed at my mom's house." He turned and looked at Sasha. "Any other questions?"

"So Charles isn't your partner selling drugs?"

"I know who Big G is, but he's not my partner."

"We believe you and Mr. Johns were the two men outside Ms. Cummins's car on Lee Street that night. We also feel strongly that Mr. Johns was the person who shot and killed Ms. Cummins in her car on February 9th."

"Wasn't me, Detective. Like I said, I couldn't tell ya whether Big G was there or not cause I didn't see him."

"There aren't any other questions we have for you today, Mr. Green. We'll be keeping a close watch on you and Mr. Johns."

Sticks smiled to himself. "If you had any evidence, I'd be in jail down the street right now, Detective. You got nothin' on me."

"The detectives are finished asking you questions today, William. Keep yourself out of trouble. On your way out, stop at the front desk. You'll find an envelope with the names of employers willing to hire ex-cons. The next time I see you, I expect that you'll have a job."

Sticks stood up. "I'm happy to talk with them employers, Mr. Sweeney, as I'd love to have a job." He looked around the desk at Sasha and Darcie. "Pleasure talkin' to you, Detectives." Sticks pushed back his chair and left the office.

"How do you think that conversation went, Sasha?" J'Quon asked.

"Darcie certainly rattled his chain a bit, calling him Billy, or maybe he doesn't like women in positions of authority?" Sasha shook his head in disgust. "All we can do is let the two of them know we're keeping a close watch on them and hope they do something stupid."

Darcie smiled. "Well, they're ex-cons, so the likelihood of them doing something stupid is in our favor."

J'Quon stood up. "You could get them to talk if you arrested one of them and charged him with a crime he's committed, something that would possibly send him to prison for some serious time. That's the only way I see that you could you get one of them to flip on the other." He shook his head in disgust. "Both of them are bad guys who need to be locked up. In my opinion, both will ultimately either be killed on the street or become three-time losers sent away for life."

"I can see that."

"Neither of them has any redeeming qualities. I hate to say it because I was pulled out of a bad environment by my brother's probation officer. That man mentored me to become who I am today. Those two will be in and out of the prison system until they're put away for good." J'Quon paused. "Or end up dead."

Sasha nodded. "It's like they're stuck in a hamster wheel. Even if they wanted to get off it, they can't help themselves or listen to someone like you trying to help them." He looked over at Darcie. "There has to be evidence we can find sufficient enough to charge them with Ashley's murder."

"What evidence do you think we're going to find that we haven't already? It's been twelve days since the murder."

Of course, Darcie was right. There wasn't any magical evidence that was going to appear suddenly. "Our job is to find Ashley's killer, and somehow we're going to do just that."

"Well, let me know what I can do to help, Sasha. Whatever you need."

"Thanks, J'Quon. We're going to go back to the station and go over the evidence again. The chief is going to have to decide if he's willing to spend the money for overtime to keep tabs on Green and Johns twenty-four, seven until they do something we can charge them with." Sasha looked back to Darcie. "We also have to consider Danny Williams. He's still in the wind."

"Williams, Green, and Johns have been our primary focus since day one. I agree the three of them were the ones Jasmine Warren saw but couldn't positively ID." Darcie looked at J'Quon. "She's our only witness."

"Since you don't have anything concrete on either Green or Johns, I'm sorry, but there's not much more my office can do for you."

"Today was the opportunity to talk with Johns for the first time and let them both know we're keeping tabs on them," Sasha said. "Thanks for your help."

"No problem." J'Quon followed the two detectives out to the office lobby before saying goodbye. "Good luck."

As Sasha and Darcie waited for the elevator, Sasha said, "That was almost embarrassing. With no evidence, they played us. The only positive out of talking with them might be that they feel more emboldened to do something stupid."

Darcie agreed. "We just need to find the way over, under, or around that wall we keep hitting."

Sasha smiled as the elevator door opened. His partner had used one of his favorite tenets. "Yes, we do." The two watched as the elevator door closed. They didn't talk on the short drive back to the station. Sasha was expecting to be summoned to another meeting with the chief and probably the mayor, too. Sasha knew the Cummins family was calling them to demand justice for Ashley. Yes, it was going to be another long day.

17

As the detectives were in the conference room reviewing what the dealers had said in the interviews, the phone rang, and Darcie picked up the receiver.

Sasha watched his partner as she sat listening to whomever was on the other end of the phone. "What's up?" he whispered after a minute went by.

Darcie held up a finger. "Hold on a second, Detective. I'm with my partner, and I'd like to put you on speaker." She put the call on hold and hung up the receiver. "You're going to find this interesting." Darcie hit the speaker button. "You there, Detective Murphy?"

"Yes."

"I want to introduce you to my partner, Senior Detective Sasha Frank." Darcie paused. "Sasha, this is Chicago Police Department Detective Damien Murphy."

"Morning, Detective Frank."

"Good morning, Detective." Sasha looked at Darcie, wondering why they were talking to the Chicago detective, and she smiled. "To what do we owe the honor of your call?"

"Well, as I was beginning to tell your partner, it looks like we've got a shooting that's connected to a murder you're investigating."

"Can you start from the beginning please, Detective?" Darcie said.

"Sure. Yesterday morning, we had a shooting on the South Side." Damien paused. "Well, actually, we had several, but the one I'm calling you about happened around 11 a.m. in the Chatham neighborhood. Are you familiar with the area?"

Sasha first glanced at Darcie, then answered, "No, we're not."

"It's one of the most dangerous parts of Chicago. We have a lot of gang activity in that neighborhood related to drugs. Yesterday morning, 911 got calls reporting gunfire." Detective Murphy paused. "When police arrived on scene, they found two men dead and one badly wounded."

"Okay."

"All three were members of a gang that operates in that area. What we know at this time is that a van pulled up at the corner, the sliding side door opened, and an unknown number of people opened fire."

Sasha whispered, "What else has he told you?"

On a notepad, she wrote, "Nothing."

"The three men on the corner didn't return fire. Two of the three were dead at the scene. The third man is not expected to live."

"What does this have to do with our murder investigation?" Sasha asked.

"Does the name Jordan Orman mean anything to either of you? He's the one on life support."

Sasha looked at Darcie, and she shook her head. "No."

"How about Edgar Johnson or Daniel Matheson? They're the two dead at the scene."

Again Darcie shook her head. "We've never heard of them, either," Sasha replied.

"Okay. I just wondered." They could hear the Chicago detective paging through his notes. "Doctors were able to remove three slugs from Orman. All three bullets were matches to the gun used in a murder that took place in Bloomington on February 9th."

Sasha was stunned. "Well, that's an interesting development. Were the others shot with the same gun?"

"No. Just Orman. He's a twenty-one-year-old male who's been in the system since his early teens. As an adult, he has arrests for multiple assaults and was currently out on bail for a drug charge. Not your model citizen."

"You have any idea who shot them, Detective?"

"No. The only good thing about yesterday's shooting is that no bystanders were involved."

Darcie sat back down in her chair. "I'm guessing that the gun that shot Orman wasn't found at the scene?"

"Correct. Three guns were found at the scene, and they belonged to the three victims because their prints were on them. Interestingly, none of the spent cartridges found at the scene are a match to the cartridge in your case. All we have are witness statements saying a white panel van was involved. We don't know for sure how many shooters were inside. As you can imagine, getting witnesses to cooperate on gang shootings is impossible."

"So what are you thinking, Detective?"

"I'm not. I'm just passing along information and seeing if you have anything helpful on your end."

Sasha leaned back in his chair and started rubbing his temples.

Murphy continued, "We solve under twenty percent of the murders committed in Chicago. Unless we find the gun in someone's hand, this shooting will probably remain unsolved. Even if we did, we would need an eyewitness positively IDing them as the shooter."

Darcie stood up again. "We're not going to be any help, Detective."

"That was what I was expecting, but I needed to give you a call."

"Keep us informed if you find out anything new. We'll do the same."

"Certainly. I just wanted you to know that the gun in your murder was used here yesterday. I'm not sure if that information helps or hurts you."

"Thanks," Sasha said. "If you could send us all the forensics you've got related to the bullets that would be great. We'd also take all you can send us on Orman and the others."

Once the call ended, Darcie asked, "Do you think our killer is from Chicago?"

Sasha shook his head. "I don't know what to think. I find it hard to believe someone from Chicago was down here and shot Ashley. Why would Chicago gangbangers be at Lee and Oakland early on a Saturday?" He stood up and pushed his chair back. "It doesn't make sense."

"No, it doesn't."

The senior detective started walking around the room but stopped when his mobile phone rang. "It's Janet. I'm going to take the call."

"I'm going to go out and get some good coffee. Want some?"

"Yes, thanks." Sasha watched Darcie walk out of the conference room, then answered Janet's call. "Hi, sweetie."

"I wanted to see if you were willing to have some family over this weekend?"

Sasha had three children with his first wife, Julie. His daughter, Emily, her husband, and their young son lived nearby, while his other two children lived outside the area. Sasha's mom and dad lived in nearby Springfield. "That would be great. Was that it?"

"Yes. Sorry to bother you."

"You didn't bother me. I just got off the phone with Chicago PD." Sasha told Janet about the call.

"What are you going to do?"

"I don't know. Darcie and I will have to give it some thought. It's not like we were about to solve the case." He shook his head. "It's just so frustrating." He sat down in his chair and ended the call. Sasha started rubbing his temples again.

Sasha leaned back in his chair. How could Johns and Green be his prime suspects for Ashley's killing and be involved in a shooting in Chicago? They couldn't be involved in both shootings; they were here in Bloomington yesterday morning. It made no sense. As he sat there awaiting Darcie's return, he could only think that somehow they were being played. Could Johns have used the gun to kill Ashley and then gotten somebody in Chicago to use it to deflect suspicion?

Darcie walked back into the conference room and set Sasha's coffee down in front of him on the table. "What are you thinking?"

"I'm thinking somebody is messing with us. We were with Johns and Green yesterday when the shooting took place in Chicago. I don't believe in coincidences. That had to have been planned."

"You think they're that smart?" Darcie sat down across from him.

"No, I don't. I think *they* think they are, but no way are they smart enough to have done this on their own." Sasha sipped his coffee. "We need to start looking at known associates to see if anything pops."

"Okay. I'll talk with R.J. to see if he can help us with that."

"I still believe that Johns killed Ashley, and that means they have to be working with somebody in Chicago to deflect our focus."

"I'm on it." Darcie got up and walked out of the conference room to talk to R.J.

Sasha stood up and headed for the chief's office for a conversation he didn't want to have.

18

It was almost two weeks ago when Adrian got a call from Danny letting him know he was driving to Florida with Hallie and Kayla for a little getaway. Danny didn't say how long he'd be out of town. With the winter weather in Illinois, Adrian was jealous of his boss's beach vacation.

Danny asked him to take care of his customers at the local college bars where he could make big money. Adrian had spent the past two weekends making sure he was available for Danny's clients. His boss also texted customers to keep a lookout for Adrian, who could take care of them while he was out of town.

Adrian was just leaving a bar on Bloomington's east side, where his customers knew he would be around this time every Saturday night. It was just after eleven when he pulled out of the parking lot of the bar and headed back to his apartment to pick up more product.

After making the five-minute drive to his apartment, Adrian pulled into a parking space across from his townhouse. He got out of his SUV, locked the doors with his remote, and put his hands in his coat pockets to shield them from the cold night. As he walked past the back of his SUV to cross the parking lot to his apartment, a vehicle suddenly accelerated toward him. Adrian turned quickly, trying to move away from the car, but he was knocked to the asphalt. Then the car drove over him.

On his back and severely injured, Adrian looked up and saw the stars in the night sky. He tried moving his arms and legs but couldn't. He was sure his left leg was broken. The backup lights of the car came on as he slowly turned his head to look toward it. The car started moving back toward him. He couldn't move, and he couldn't scream. Just before he fell into unconsciousness, the vehicle backed over him, killing him instantly.

Teo got out of the car they'd stolen earlier that evening in Kankakee and took a picture with his phone. He showed it to Jaime. "He's dead."

Jaime smiled. He knew the police would never be able to determine who had run over the man. "I'll send it to Diego."

"When do you think they'll find him?"

"It's hard to say at this time of night. The parking lot looked full, so maybe not until morning if we're lucky."

In the airport parking lot, Teo parked beside the SUV that Jaime had driven behind him as they drove down from Kankakee. The two had been wearing gloves while riding in the stolen car, and it would be unlikely that the police would ever be able to connect the vehicle to the killing of Adrian Wolenski. Regardless, they quickly used wipes to remove any possibility that their DNA was left inside the car.

Jaime got behind the wheel of their SUV and started driving east on Route 9 to Towanda Barnes Road, then out to the interstate. "We should be back in Chicago in a couple of hours."

"So far, the job that Diego gave us to finish for him has gone well, no?"

Jaime was about to reply when he received a return text from Diego. "VERY GOOD!"

As he steered onto the highway, Teo said, "When do we strike again?"

"Earlier today, Diego told me that our friends in Miami would deal with one of the names on the list." Jaime lit a cigarette and offered one to Teo. "That means our job is almost done."

Teo nodded as he drove cautiously through Towanda and onto the northbound entrance of the interstate.

19

Hallie, Kayla, and Danny had enjoyed the past two weeks on the beach at the five-star hotel on Key Biscayne, just south of Miami Beach. Miami's downtown was only twenty minutes away from the hotel, which gave Danny and Hallie the chance to enjoy the city's outstanding night-life. The Florida getaway was a welcome break from the past four months of winter in Illinois and Ashley Cummins's ongoing murder investigation.

The three of them had spent a lot of time on the beach, which Kayla had enjoyed. The two-year-old had never seen the ocean before, and she could spend hours looking for shells on the beach with her mother and father. Hallie was enjoying the time she spent in the spa while Danny enjoyed early morn-ing runs and swimming in the warm ocean waters before having breakfast with his family.

Danny hadn't noticed they were being watched round-the-clock. Since they'd been there, eyes had been on them wherever they'd gone at the resort. They were being followed even while Danny and Hallie hit the clubs.

It was early when Danny left their corner suite on the resort's twelfth floor for his daily run. Sunrise wasn't for another fifty minutes or so. He would miss these runs along the deserted shoreline when they returned to Bloomington next week.

As he walked out of the elevator, a man in the lobby radioed to others and watched. Danny walked by the restaurant, then followed the path to the hard-packed sand on the ocean's edge. He watched the gentle waves coming into shore and thought how great it would be to have daily runs on the beach for the rest of his life. He took a deep breath and began running south along the shoreline.

At this hour of the morning, there were only a few people out walking on the sand. No one was running. As soon as he reached the northern boundary of the state park, he had the beach entirely to himself. Danny wasn't aware that there were several men with binoculars watching him from the tree line of the park. When he reached the south end of the island, he ran in place for a minute. As he looked east and south, he could only see water and a few lights from boats bobbing far offshore. They were probably fishermen.

Danny started heading back to the resort, where he would go for a swim in the ocean, something he looked forward to every morning. After running a few hundred yards, he could see two men walking on the beach a short distance in front of him. As he got closer, he realized they were pointing guns at him, and he quickly slowed.

"*Buenos días,* Señor Danny."

"What's going on?" This was the second time in less than two weeks a gun had been pointed at him.

Enrico waved his weapon at him. "*¿Hablas español?*"

"Not so much." Danny could order a beer or maybe a couple of kinds of rum drinks, but that was it. His clientele in college bars all spoke English, so the need to learn Spanish was low on his list of priorities.

"I see." Enrico looked at Javier and laughed. "*Estás en Miami y no hablas español.*" Javier shrugged. Enrico pointed his gun at Danny's head. "You're in Miami, and you don't speak Spanish, Danny? I need you to take off your running shoes."

Danny didn't understand. "What?"

"It's very easy. Take off your running shoes." Enrico lowered his gun and pointed at Danny's feet. "Quickly, please."

He took off his running shoes, then looked up at the man pointing the gun at him. "Now what?"

"I need you to place them on the sand over by that coconut." Danny did so. "Now, I need you to walk into the water."

"Okay." Danny looked out at the water and saw the other man hand his gun to Enrico. "What's going on here, man?"

Enrico pointed both guns at Danny. "Javier will be joining you on your swim, Danny." He motioned for Danny to get into the ocean. "Please."

Danny didn't move, and Javier moved toward him. "I need you to get into deeper water."

"Why?"

"I'm tired of all the questions, Danny. This is your morning to die." Enrico fired a single shot a few inches from Danny. A silencer muffled the sound of the gunshot, but Danny clearly understood that he needed to move into deeper water.

"Why are you doing this?"

"As I said, I'm tired of your questions, Danny." Enrico had killed more times than he could remember. Few of those he had murdered were allowed to ask questions. "This is your fate."

"What? Why are you doing this?"

Enrico relented. "Someone asked my boss to do him a favor. I know nothing more than that."

"Who asked your boss?"

"A friend."

"A friend?"

"So many questions." Enrico followed Danny and Javier into the water. "Keep walking." When the water reached his knees, Enrico stopped. "A man by the name of Diego."

"Diego? Who's that?"

"I don't know. You asked, I answered. Diego asked a favor, and we are in the business of—what do they say, Javier? '*Me rascas la espalda y te rascaré la tuya?*'"

Javier smiled. "Sí. You scratch my back, I scratch yours."

"Yes, that's it, Danny. A favor given is a favor owed."

The sun peeked over the eastern horizon far out in the Atlantic, and Enrico signaled to Javier. Javier quickly dropped under the surface and grabbed Danny by his feet, lifting the smaller man upside down in the chest-deep water. Javier held on tight to Danny as he struggled to keep his head above water. Before too long, he was able to force Danny's head underwater until the smaller man's body finally went limp.

Enrico watched as Javier let go of Danny. The body surfaced and bobbed in the water face-down. Javier then pulled Danny's body back into shallower water to where Enrico was standing. "*Nuestro trabajo se hace aquí, mi amigo.*"

"Si." Their work was done. They walked out of the ocean and about fifty yards up the beach on the hard-packed sand before heading to the parking lot where their car was parked. Enrico got on his radio to let the men know to head back to Miami. "Santos will be pleased," Enrico said.

20

Sasha was sitting at the conference table late Sunday morning when his cell phone rang. "Morning, R.J. I'm looking for some good news. I hope that's why you're calling."

"I've got news, but I don't know if it's good or bad. Somebody on our list got run over by a hit-and-run in his apartment parking lot last night."

Sasha stood up. "Who?"

"Adrian Wolenski." R.J. paused. "911 got a call around 5 a.m. reporting a male lying in an apartment parking lot on the east side of town. He was run over several times."

"Is he in the hospital?"

"He was found dead. ME's best guess was sometime around midnight last night. It got down to freezing overnight, so she can't be more accurate on the time."

"Is that where he lived?"

"Yes. Wolenski rented a townhouse at that address."

"You live in his world. What do you think happened?"

"It's hard to say, Sasha. It wasn't accidental."

"If it was murder—"

"I don't think there's any question about that."

"Who would kill him?"

"It could be a disgruntled customer. A rival drug dealer. Right now, it's tough to say. He could have been caught messing with someone's wife or girlfriend."

"We're talking about Bloomington, Illinois, R.J. People here don't kill other people over things like this."

"Times have been tough the last few years. Anything's possible. It wouldn't surprise me."

"Yeah, I'm just not seeing it, R.J."

"I just wanted to give you a heads-up. I've got another case I'm working. Why don't you give the ME a call to find out more?"

"Thanks for the heads-up." Sasha ended the call with the vice unit detective. He sat back down at the conference room table just as Darcie walked in. "R.J. just called to tell me Adrian Wolenski is dead. He was run over multiple times in the parking lot where he lives."

Darcie sat down at the conference table. "Any idea who did it?"

"No idea." Sasha called the ME's office to speak with Juanita. As he was on hold, he gave Darcie more details from his call with R.J.

"Hi, Sasha."

"Darcie's with me. I'm going to put you on speaker."

"I assume you're calling about Wolenski?" They could hear Juanita shuffling papers.

"Yes. Wolenski is an associate of Danny Williams, who we consider a person of interest in Ashley Cummins's murder."

"Okay. What do you want to know?"

"I understand that he was run over by a car multiple times."

"Absolutely. The injuries he suffered are consistent with being struck by a car but to an extent I've never seen."

"So you believe it was intentional and not accidental?"

Juanita looked at the pictures in the file. "Wolenski suffered broken bones in the left leg, fractures in his right leg, and his pelvis was shattered. Both arms suffered broken and fractured bones, along with multiple broken and fractured ribs. His right lung was punctured, and he had lacerations on both kidneys and his liver. If all that wasn't enough, the coup de grâce was his skull getting crushed."

"Geez. Somebody must've really wanted to send a message."

"I don't have an opinion on that, Sasha. The one thing I can tell you is that whoever killed Wolenski wanted him dead in that parking lot. I would estimate that after he was initially hit and knocked to the ground, someone then drove backward and forward multiple times. I estimate that he died around midnight. He wasn't discovered until 5 a.m." Juanita paused. "It is my opinion that in the absence of the head injury, considering the totality of injuries sustained, the other injuries alone would have caused him to bleed out."

Sasha scribbled on a file folder, "Sending a message." Darcie nodded.

"It would seem so."

"Thanks for telling us what you found, Juanita."

"Certainly. Can I ask you a question?"

"Sure."

"How's the investigation going into finding Ashley Cummins's killer?"

Sasha sighed and rolled his eyes, then looked at Darcie. "It's been over two weeks, and we have suspects but no evidence."

"I'm sorry to hear that. My daughter has told me that family and friends aren't dealing very well with Ashley's death."

"Who could?"

Juanita closed the Wolenski file on her desk. "No one. Sorry. Busy morning here, and I've got things to do."

Sasha ended the call. "Somebody is sending a message. I've never seen the sheer brutality of something like this around here. Maybe Chicago or Saint Louis, but not in Central Illinois."

"Then you think whoever did this is from out of town?"

"I think they have to be." Sasha took a sip of coffee. It wasn't hot anymore. "Let's go through the files again."

21

A fter the call came in from Diego Reyna, Sticks immediately wondered who had given the Chicago gang leader his number. Few people had it. The number was under his older sister's name, and she paid the bill with money he gave her each month.

Everyone like Sticks had a private number where certain people could always reach them. Only family members called him on that number. He couldn't think of anyone else. How had Diego gotten ahold of it?

Regardless of who had passed it on, the call was an interesting one. Diego told Sticks he wanted to set up a meet to discuss selling drugs for him in Central Illinois. Diego knew that Sticks sold drugs for a rival gang, but he hinted that he was looking to expand his gang's reach and influence in Illinois. Diego wanted to find someone who could take over his drug distribution downstate. Sticks told the gang leader he'd be willing to meet. Diego told him that he'd send a text by early afternoon with a time and place to meet that night in Chicago.

When the call ended, Sticks's first thought was maybe this would be an opportunity to go out on his own. Currently, he and Big G bought drugs via Big G's Chicago connections. Diego was asking him to distribute all their product south of Interstate 80, and the deal could be worth many times over the half a million dollars he and Big G currently raked in.

Could he handle that kind of volume on his own? If he tried to do it without his partner, Sticks would need new muscle to replace Big G to ensure that he'd be able to control the vast territory Diego was offering to him. There'd be no easy way to walk away from their current supplier without Diego's help in providing protection, and Sticks would probably have to deal with Big G if he decided to go it alone. After taking the time to think about what his options were, he believed that the risks of going alone were worth the rewards.

He turned on the television in the living room. He needed to chill out and decided to watch some sports or something that would calm his nerves. Going it alone was a big decision. He'd been unnerved ever since the two detectives had surprised him by walking in on his meeting with his probation officer Thursday morning. It was evident that the cops hadn't found anything to connect them to shooting the girl over on Lee Street a couple of weeks ago, but still, something was bothering him, which was out of character. Based on the questions they'd asked, there may have been a witness who'd seen them that night. But the detectives could be lying about the witness. Still, if there really was a witness, they couldn't have positively IDed anyone, or the meeting with the detectives would have ended differently.

Killing the girl in the car was the first time either of them had ever shot anyone. Sure, he and Big G had waved a gun in someone's face once or twice. Sticks had even taken wild shots at a couple of bangers just to scare them. But killings brought cops, so they'd done their best to keep their hands clean.

He chuckled out loud, thinking about Rattler arranging the shooting of a rival gang member on Chicago's South Side with the gun used to shoot the girl at the same time he and Big G had their probation meetings. Who could have predicted those two detectives would walk into their meeting? How lucky was that? Sticks knew that when the bullets removed from the gangbanger were checked out on the FBI database, they'd find a match to the bullet found in the little girl. And Big G always loaded bullets right outta the box and into his 9mm while wearing latex gloves. There'd be no prints on anything connected to that bullet or cartridge casing. Surely the detectives had found out about the gun by now. He wished he could have seen the look on the old detective's face when he'd heard the news. It would be priceless.

Thirty minutes later, while he was watching a sports talk show on television, Sticks received several texts from the number Diego had called him from earlier. "Meet in bar parking lot. South Indiana Ave. Just south of East

144th Street. Across from railyard. 10 p.m." Sticks didn't know the Chicago area well, but he thought that sounded like the Riverdale area on the South Side, which he knew was part of Diego's turf. That would be a great place to meet. There was little chance he'd be seen by one of Rattler's gang. Rival gang members rarely ventured into another gang's territory unless they went in heavy with men and weapons. Sticks texted back, "See you then." Sticks had never met Diego, but by all accounts, he was a ruthless SOB.

Sticks gave his partner a call to tell him he was going to lie low. "I'm gonna have some fun tonight, so don't be lookin' for me."

Big G laughed. "I think I'll be lookin' for the same."

Sticks ended the call happy that he was going it alone in Chicago. He needed to be careful and would be carrying a 9mm in case the meeting didn't go well.

22

The bar was in a part of the far South Side of Chicago that Sticks knew was the turf of Diego's gang, so he was being cautious. As he pulled up, the first thing he noticed was that there were only two cars in the lot. Ten o'clock on a Monday night was probably early for the patrons of this bar. Sticks parked the Impala away from the other two cars. He texted Diego. "Here." A text message came back immediately. "Come on in."

Sticks was eager to hear what the man had to say. As he got out of the car, he looked around the parking lot. He knew he should be ready for anything. For the first time, he began feeling a bit nervous meeting the head of a gang that was a big rival of Rattler's. If Sticks decided to work with Diego, it would inevitably lead to escalating violence between the two Chicago gangs. Sticks reached back and touched the 9mm semiautomatic he had tucked into his belt at the small of his back.

Sticks opened the door and entered the bar. Once inside, he quickly looked around. At the end of the long room to his left, he saw a lone man standing behind a bar counter, drinking a beer.

"Welcome, my friend. I'm Diego Reyna." Diego set his beer down on the counter. "Please come sit and have a drink with me."

Sticks walked over to the bar. "I'm Sticks." He shook hands with Diego.

Diego motioned for him to sit down. "Please make yourself comfortable." As his guest sat down on one of the stools in front of the bar, Diego slid open a case filled with cold beer and took out two bottles. He popped off the caps on the side of the case and put one of the bottles in front of Sticks.

Sticks clinked bottles with Diego and took a drink. "How do we start?"

Diego was a big man at 6' 8", and he smiled at the small man across from him. "So are you eager to talk about the future?"

"I'm interested in hearing what you've got to say, Diego."

"Good. Word is you do a good job in the area Rattler allows you to operate in on his behalf." Diego knew Rattler's gang had fifteen or more people like Sticks and his partner selling drugs for them downstate. Rattler didn't want the people who sold for him to have too large of territories or make too much money, so he limited their ability to sell outside their designated areas. Diego assumed the man sitting in front of him wouldn't appreciate hearing him say that Rattler had total control over them. No man in their line of work could appear weak, and he wasn't sure whether he would appreciate his take on their situation.

"I do a lot more for Rattler than sellin' his drugs. I provide him muscle and keep those who sell his drugs in line." If Diego wasn't aware that he and Big G were key players for Rattler's gang, then Sticks would make sure that he was. "I just met Rattler tonight, and he wants us to take on more for him downstate." That wasn't true, but Sticks thought it would make him sound more important than he was.

Diego smiled. "Oh, I have no doubt." He'd struck a nerve. "I see the value that you bring." Diego took a drink of his beer. "That is why I reached out to you, to talk with you about distributing product for me."

Sticks sat up on his barstool, trying to seem bigger. "I'm listening, Diego."

"I want to pay you seventy-five thousand per month to handle product for me south of Interstate 80 in Illinois." Diego took another drink of beer. "I will add Saint Louis and Indianapolis to the area I want you to cover for me." Diego wondered what Rattler saw in Sticks. "You will also receive ten percent of all sales that you handle for me. Of course, you may split the ten percent between you and your partner if you'd like." He smiled. "This is a good proposal, no?"

"It's a good proposal, but not a great one." Sticks didn't know what to expect from his first meeting with Diego, but what he did know was that the proposal was worth millions each year. Millions to both him and Big G if Sticks decided he'd bring his partner into the deal. "I think what I offer is worth more."

To Diego, it really didn't matter what the little man thought he offered. "I'm sure that's true. How about I make it fifteen percent instead of ten?

After all, we are friends here, and we should expect to make a lot of money together."

"I agree with that, Diego." Sticks smiled and reached out his bottle to Diego.

"Excellent!" Diego reached out with his beer, and they clinked bottles. "Cheers, my friend." Two men entered from the door at the end of the bar and took up positions next to Diego. "Ah, Jaime and Teo. I'd like you to meet our new partner who will be working with us downstate."

Jaime and Teo nodded at Sticks. Jaime could tell that the man sitting at the bar seemed at ease with Diego.

Sticks raised his beer to the two men. He was relieved that he'd quickly cut a deal with Rattler's competitor that would change his life. "Nice to meet ya." He turned to Diego. "When do we start?"

"First, would you like another beer?" Diego asked. Sticks nodded yes. "Excellent." He opened the case holding the beer, reached inside, and pulled out a sawed-off shotgun. At the same time, Jaime and Teo each pulled guns and pointed them at Sticks. Teo moved slowly, repositioning himself behind the man sitting at the bar.

"What's going on?" Sticks asked.

"Put your hands down on the bar. Slowly. Very slowly." He did as he was instructed. "Teo, would you please check to see if he's carrying any weapons?" Teo quickly found and took the 9mm, then returned to his place beside Jaime.

"What's going on, Diego?"

"Well, Sticks, I hate to tell you that I've changed my mind. You're not someone I would enjoy working with."

"What do you mean?"

"I understand you recently found yourself a suspect in the killing of an innocent young girl." Diego looked at the man sitting across the bar from him and smiled. "Someone asked us to do him a favor, and we feel obliged to do so. We are indebted to him."

"I don't understand. What favor?"

"Your name appeared on a list, my friend. We are taking care of those on the list." Diego looked at Jaime and Teo. "These two have already dealt with many men on this list."

"It's not true. I haven't killed anyone, Diego."

"It may be that you did not kill this young girl, my friend, but your name is on the list of people the police believe may have killed the girl, so I'm sorry that you must pay with your life." Sticks started to stand. Diego motioned with his shotgun. "Not a good idea. Sit." Sticks sat back down.

"Listen, Diego," Sticks said. "I don't need fifteen percent of the sales. Ten is more than enough."

Diego laughed out loud. "You are very funny, my friend. There was never a deal for you here. Only death was your fate." He motioned toward Teo to use the zip ties he was carrying to tie up Sticks. "Teo and Jaime will be taking you away now. We don't want to make a mess here in my bar now, do we?"

Teo lifted Sticks up, then searched his pockets and found the car keys. He jingled them before he pushed Sticks toward the door that led to the back of the bar where they'd entered a few minutes earlier.

Diego watched as Jaime and Teo led him out. Then he followed them through the door leading to the back parking lot. Jaimie took Sticks's billfold, cash, and phone. Teo drove up to the bar's back door with the car they had stolen earlier in the day. To send a strong message of disrespect, they'd torch the car with Sticks's body in the trunk in the parking lot of Rattler's apartment building. One of Jaime's crew would be taking the car that Sticks drove to Chicago to a chop shop where it would be dismantled, and within an hour, it would be as though the car had never existed.

Diego walked back into the bar, placed the sawed-off shotgun back into the case, and pulled out another beer. As he took a drink, he thought to himself that everything was going as planned.

23

After a late night of drinking and dancing at a country and western bar, Kelly Moran accepted her friend Jenna's invitation to crash on the couch at her Downtown Bloomington apartment instead of driving back to her own apartment near the airport. Jenna's one-bedroom apartment was in the attic of an old home that had been converted into apartments a few years earlier.

Kelly quickly fell asleep but was soon awakened by a series of loud bangs. She sat up just as Jenna came out through her bedroom door. Jenna was pointing a flashlight at Kelly. "Did you hear that?"

"Gunshots?"

Jenna pointed the flashlight toward the only door in the apartment. "They sounded close." She quickly walked over and looked out the small window above the kitchen sink.

Kelly rose from the couch and joined Jenna to look out the window. "Do you see anything?"

"No." Jenna looked down at the alley that ran past the back of the old house. There was a black or dark blue sedan parked in the alley behind Kelly's car.

They heard more noise, and Kelly and Jenna looked at each other, wondering what it was.

There was yet another loud noise out back of the apartment. They then heard someone hurrying down the stairs that led from the third story to the ground floor deck. Two men appeared in the driveway and ran past Kelly's car in the alley, then quickly sped off.

Jenna leaned over the sink, looking out the window. "What's that?"

"What's what?" Kelly was taller than Jenna, and she leaned forward, looking out the window. She could see what looked like flames and smoke coming up from the back of the house. "Something's on fire."

"On *fire?*"

"Yes, at the back of the house."

Jenna looked at her friend. "*That stairway is our only way out.*"

Kelly was standing in the kitchen, barefooted. She knelt and touched the floor. "The floor feels warm."

Jenna crouched down and did the same. "Very warm." She looked up at Kelly. "The downstairs apartment must be on fire. I'm calling 911."

Kelly walked over to the door that led to the landing at the top of the stairs. She touched the doorknob and quickly recoiled. "*It's hot!*" She ran back to the kitchen counter, grabbed a towel, ran it under the faucet, and tried turning the doorknob again. The stairway below was fully engulfed in flames.

As soon as the 911 operator answered, Jenna started shouting. "I need to report a fire! My apartment is on fire!"

Calmly, the 911 operator asked, "What's your name and address?"

Jenna gave the operator her information.

"I've alerted the fire department and the police. Both are on their way. Are you outside and safe from the fire?"

"*No!* My friend and I are inside my third-floor apartment! The stairs outside are on fire, *and that's our only way out!*"

"Please try to stay calm, Jenna. You and your friend should go to the bathroom, fill the bathtub with water and soak towels so that you can breathe through them."

"*What we need is for someone to get us out of here now!*" Jenna yelled at the operator. The two friends heard what sounded like firecrackers going off coming from the apartment below and looked at each other.

The door of the apartment that Kelley had left open was now fully engulfed in flames. Kelly looked at Jenna and shouted. "*We have to get out of here!*"

Sirens wailed in the distance. Jenna glanced toward the kitchen window and the two windows in the apartment's living room, but all she could see was smoke and flames outside. She looked around the apartment and saw smoke coming up from the corners where the floor met the walls. The friends had no options. "*Come on!*" Jenna yelled.

Kelly followed her to the small bathroom and watched as Jenna filled the bathtub with water. "What are you doing?"

Jenna grabbed several towels and threw them in the tub. "The 911 operator told me we needed to do this."

Smoke was filling the apartment. They began to cough, and the ceramic tiles on the bathroom floor had almost become too hot to stand on. Kelly sat down in the tub and took the soaked towel and draped it over her head. She started yelling, trying to get the attention of whomever was outside the house. Jenna got into the tub with her and did the same.

———

The fire department started hosing water into the house as soon as they arrived on scene, but the fire was raging. Clark Parsons, a fire department battalion chief and arson specialist, was coordinating the fire company's actions. The stairs at the back of the house were badly burned and had been heavily damaged by the time the fire crew had arrived and didn't offer firefighters access to the upper floors. All three stories of the house were ablaze.

Clark got on his radio. "There's no way we're going to get ladders up to the windows in the attic. The flames are making that impossible." He looked around, trying to decide what to do. He made another call on his radio. "Get more water on the back of the house." He shook his head. They'd received the call less than ten minutes ago, and the fire was already out of control.

Clark was walking around the house, checking on the efforts of the crews. As he was walking around the southeast corner, several first-floor windows blew. The force of the blast knocked him off his feet. He slowly got back up and momentarily felt groggy. He said out loud to no one, "911 got the call just a few minutes ago!"

———

After he pulled himself together, Clark got out his phone and called the 911 center. "Was there more than one caller from inside the house?" he asked.

"No. The only call from inside got disconnected. Perhaps she was overcome, or maybe she got out."

"Thanks, I just wanted to know if you could give me any more information on what happened here." Clark ended the call.

One of the crew chiefs walked up to him. "I'm sorry, Chief, but there was nothing we could do to access the apartments."

Clark nodded. "There's nothing any of us can do until we get those flames under control." He knew it was too late to save anyone inside.

24

I n less than thirty minutes, the roof and most of the walls of the house had collapsed into the basement. Clark walked to the back of his SUV, opened up the hatch, and started removing his firefighting gear so he could begin his arson investigation. He had just settled onto the back of his SUV's bumper when he heard a familiar voice.

"Morning, Clark. Any chance you could provide me an update on what we've got here?"

The battalion chief smiled and stood. "Kinda early for you to be here, isn't it, Sasha?"

"You of all people know that when duty calls, you step up." The senior detective shook hands with his friend, then turned and looked at the smoldering remains of what had once been a home. "Fill me in?"

Clark sat back down. "Sure." He took several minutes to provide Sasha with what he'd found since arriving on scene. "This was a three-story apartment house when I got here, and now all you see is the smoldering remains in the basement." Clark explained he would shortly start his arson investigation next.

Sasha looked up and down the street. "Was this house a similar size to the others on the street?"

"Pretty much. I'd guess the homes on this street were probably built around the 1920s. All-wood construction. Probable accelerants didn't help." It was Clark's job to determine how the fire had started, and he'd be able to find out soon enough whether there were accelerants present.

Sasha nodded. "Based on 911 calls, you expect there'll be multiple bodies found in the debris?"

Clark took a moment to look over at the scene. There were still fire hoses streaming water on the area at the southeast corner of the basement where there still appeared to be one hot spot. Firefighters had set up floodlights, which cast an eerie scene of shadows and smoke across what remained of the house. "We think we're going to find at least one body. Maybe more."

Given the fire and the amount of water used to extinguish it, Sasha knew that if there were bodies found in the debris that it would be highly unlikely any physical evidence would be found other than the residue of accelerants. "Okay. What're your next steps?" Sasha asked.

"First thing, I'm going to be taking some samples. Based on the burn rate and what the neighbor reported seeing, I'm sure we're going to find that some liquid or chemical accelerant present. Then I'm going to have the water pumped out of the basement."

"I'm going to talk with neighbors and wait around to see what you find out."

"Sounds good. As soon as the water is gone, we'll be able to at least do a quick look around." Clark eyed the debris piled high in the basement. "Have you called in a cadaver dog?"

"It's already been requested. I'm not going to alert the ME until we get confirmation of DBs."

"Sounds good." Clark stood up. "You'll hear from me when I find something interesting."

Sasha stood watching Clark as he shouted instructions to fire crews on the scene. The water that had been pouring on the smoldering debris since he'd arrived had stopped, and several water pumps were beginning to drain water out of the basement. He knew that those pumps could move about three hundred gallons per minute, so it wouldn't take long for Clark to gain access to the basement as he looked for evidence.

While the senior detective awaited Darcie's arrival, he walked over to the smoldering remains of the house to get a closer look. A few minutes later, Sasha spotted the K9 officer and her dog walking toward him, and he met her at the front of the lot. "Morning, Becky."

"Hi, Sasha." Becky had a strong hold on her dog, Lux. "Where do you want us to start?"

"You'll need to wait until we get clearance from Clark." Sasha bent down and patted Lux. Although his first pet was a German Shepherd, he now preferred English Bulldogs.

Lux was pulling hard at his leash and started barking loudly. There was a strong smell in the air of burnt wood, plastic, and other terrible, indistinguishable odors. Perhaps that was causing him to act the way he was.

Becky shouted "Fuss!" and the dog stopped barking and stood quietly at her side. "Sorry about that." The officer reached down and gave the dog a pat. "Sitz."

"That was impressive. I figure 'sitz' must mean sit, but what does the other word mean?"

The German Shepherd focused on Becky. "It means heel. Not that many perps we encounter can speak German, and we only give commands in German or Dutch." Becky smiled. "We don't want a perp shouting out commands they understand to try and confuse them."

"I'll keep still and try not to look like a perp."

"Lux would do whatever I commanded him to do." Becky smiled. "So you should always be nice to me, Sasha."

Sasha smiled. "No problem." He turned and looked over his left shoulder at the smoldering remains. Clark gave them a thumbs-up for the dog to start the search.

"I'm going to start at the northwest corner and continue around the perimeter of the house," Becky said. "If I don't get an initial response from Lux, I'll ask that the lights be directed to the debris field and walk Lux over it. When I get a reaction, I'll alert Clark, and he will take it from there."

Sasha nodded. "Let's get started." He watched as Becky and her dog methodically worked the perimeter.

After about ten minutes, Lux started to bark loudly, focusing his attention on the west side of the basement foundation. "He's got something. Can we get some more light over here?" While the lights were being repositioned, Becky took a set of boots for the dog's paws from a coat pocket. She put them on and loosened the leash, allowing the big shepherd to move onto the pile of debris. Several minutes passed, and Becky whistled to get Sasha's attention. "Got something!" she shouted.

"What'd you find?"

"Looks like a DB."

Sasha called dispatch to report that the dogs had found a DB and to alert the ME, then he alerted Clark.

Clark motioned to several of the firefighters to come to the area Lux had found. "This shouldn't take long, Sasha."

Clark and Sasha watched the fire crew begin their search. "I'm afraid we're going to find multiple bodies in there." Clark looked at his friend. "While the dog was searching, I was taking samples from debris to determine whether accelerants were present. I also called the state police headquarters in Springfield and asked them to send up a dog trained in detecting accelerants. I was just informed they're here."

"They've got dogs for everything."

"The dog should be able to quickly find the location of accelerants in the debris pile."

The two stood watching the fire crew start moving through the debris as Becky and the dog continued their search.

Clark turned his attention to Lux. "Will the dog have a problem with the state police dog?"

"She's almost finished, so I'll tell her to put her dog in her cruiser when she's done." Lux started barking again, and the fire crew began digging through the charred rubble in the area the dog had flagged.

As Becky was walking Lux back to her vehicle, Sasha saw an Irish Setter coming down the alley beside his handler. Clark was standing at the back of the house to meet them, and the senior detective joined them. The dog quickly began its search, and it only took about ten minutes for the state police's Setter to start barking.

The dog's trainer turned to Clark. "Dóiteán found something." The trainer kept the Irish Setter moving through the area, searching for additional signs of accelerants.

"Dóiteán translates to fire in Gaelic," Clark said to Sasha. "I'm not sure if we're going to be able to find out where the fire initially started, but with the accelerant traces being found near the top of the debris pile, that would lead me to believe that the fire started on the second or third floor."

Jesse, the handler, came over with the dog at his side and talked with Clark, pointing out the three areas where Dóiteán had found traces of an accelerant. The arson investigator quickly bagged debris evidence from the specific spots the dog had discovered.

"Thanks again, Jesse." Connor reached down and petted the Irish Setter. "And thank you, too, Dóiteán."

"We're always ready to help out. If you don't need us anymore, we'll head back."

"My gut tells me one of the bodies in the debris will have gunshot wounds," Clark said. "Accelerants are often used by arsonists to try to hide evidence of a crime."

One of the fire crew in the basement looked up and shouted. "Clark!"

"Yeah, Freddie."

"We've found another two bodies!"

"Okay!" Clark looked at Sasha. "The 911 call originated from inside the third-floor apartment and indicated that we could find at least two bodies." Clark and Sasha turned to look where the team were searching in the northeast corner of the basement where Lux had alerted them earlier.

"I don't see the ME," Sasha said. "I'm going to let dispatch know you've now discovered three DBs."

"Sounds good." Clark looked back to where the team had found the third body and shouted, "Let's make sure that we mark the location of all three bodies for the ME and her team." The ME was going to be busy today.

25

Darcie arrived on the scene and parked her unmarked car in the lot of a hair salon on Washington Street directly behind the house that had burned down. As soon as she stepped out of her car, the acrid smell of smoke made her gag and her eyes begin to water. She reached back into her car for her water bottle, took a swig, and swished it around in her mouth. She spat it on the ground and got on her radio to let dispatch know that she had arrived. Darcie ended the call and opened the trunk to retrieve a pair of boots. The detective expected the ground around the house to be a mess. The city had been blanketed with several inches of snow, and with the fire department dumping water on the house to put out the fire, she expected the ground to be covered with mud or ice.

As she walked past one of the fire trucks parked in the alley behind the house, she saw her partner. She walked over to where he was standing. "Morning, Sasha."

Her partner turned. "Morning, Detective."

"So what's going on?"

"Evidence points to the fire being intentionally set. Do you know Clark Parsons?" Sasha motioned to Clark, standing beside him. "He's a battalion chief and the lead arson specialist with the fire department."

Clark shook hands with Darcie. "Pleasure to meet you, Detective."

"Same here. Dispatch told me you found DBs?"

"Fire crews searching through the debris in the basement found three." Sasha pointed over to the ME team that had arrived ten minutes earlier standing next to what was left of the house. They were all dressed in overalls, boots, gloves, masks, and head coverings. "They're going to take photos of the debris around the bodies before they remove them."

"Okay. Have you talked with the ME yet?"

"No. Clark has."

"I updated the ME on where we found the three bodies. All appear badly burned and unrecognizable as to gender. Based on a 911 call from the third-floor apartment, we should find that two of the three are women."

"Dispatch told me. A woman and a friend on the top floor?"

"Yes." Clark looked over at one of the fire crews packing up equipment. "If you two need anything further, let me know." He walked away.

Sasha took the opportunity to give Darcie a brief update. He looked around the scene. "I also had the adjacent homes on the block canvassed by several officers earlier. We need to find out what they've learned." He and Darcie went to find the officers.

———

Sasha and Darcie learned that the owners of the property were a couple named Baughman who were in Florida this time of the year. A neighbor who lived across the street provided contact information for them, and the detectives decided they'd wait to reach out to them until after they had left the scene and were back at the station. Officers had only been successful learning the name of a man who lived with his girlfriend in the first-floor apartment. Luckily, the two were out of town on a ski vacation. The neighbor that had given them his name said they would give him a call to let him know what had happened. None of the neighbors knew both the first and last names of the tenants who had rented either the second- or third-floor apartments in the house.

After learning what the officers had been told by the people they'd interviewed, the two detectives decided that they only needed to speak with the owners of the two houses on either side of the house that had burned to the ground.

Sasha thanked the officers, then looked at Darcie and said, "Let's first talk with the neighbor to the east who called in first hearing gunshots, then called back to report the fire."

"Sounds good." Darcie followed close behind Sasha as he walked toward the neighbor's house. They walked up the front steps of the house and knocked on the front door and waited.

Doug Archer opened the front door. "Good morning."

"Good morning, sir," Sasha said. "Sorry to knock on your door so early. Are you Mr. Archer?"

"Yes, I am. I was already awake, so it's no problem. And my friends call me Doc."

"Can we step inside and talk?"

"Sure. Come on in." Doc stepped aside as the detectives walked into the foyer of the old home, and he closed the door behind them. "Would you like to come into the kitchen and have some coffee?"

"Yes, thanks. I'm Senior Detective Sasha Frank, and this is Detective Darcie Lyman." They shook hands and followed Doc into the kitchen, which was toward the back of the house. The man motioned for them to sit down at the kitchen table. They watched him get out two mugs.

"Can I ask if you are alone in the house?"

Doc handed them their coffees and sat down in a chair across from them. "Right now I am. My wife and I have children who have all graduated from college. My wife is visiting friends in Texas."

Darcie pulled out a pen and notepad from her jacket pocket. "We understand that you called 911 at 2:03 a.m."

"Yes, Detective. It was around then." Doc paused. "I'm a light sleeper. I heard several gunshots and looked out my bedroom window."

"Where is your bedroom located?"

"Directly above the kitchen. The window looks out on this side of the Baughman's house, the backyard, and the alley."

Sasha nodded. "We understand the owners turned the house into apartments."

"Yes. Chuck and Betty Baughman lived next door from us for years until the house got too big for them after the kids all went off to college and got married. Maybe five years or so ago. They moved into a small duplex on Hershey and spend their winters in Florida. I'm sure they're down there now."

"Okay. Thank you," Darcie said. "Could you go on with what you saw and heard?"

"Like I told the police officers, I heard several gunshots."

"Do you know how many exactly, sir?"

"I can't be positive. I would guess two or three gunshots."

Darcie wrote down the information. "Please go on, sir."

"Please call me Doc. I got out of bed and looked out the window. There's no longer a garage behind the Baughman house, but there is a garage on the other side of the alley that has an outdoor light. With what little light there was, I could see two men running down the back stairway. When Chuck and Betty decided to turn the house into apartments, they added the back stairway to gain access to the second floor and attic apartment."

"Where did you first see them on the stairway?"

"I first saw them on the steps just below the second-floor landing. They were running down the stairs when the second man stopped on the lower landing. I saw a small flame from a match or lighter, lighting what must have been a Molotov cocktail. He threw it up to the second-floor landing. As soon as it landed, it exploded and started burning."

"Would you be able to identify either of the two men?"

"I don't think so. They were both light-skinned. I can't be positive, but that's what I think."

"Okay." Darcie continued to write notes. "Go on."

"Well, the smaller of the two was driving, and the bigger man who threw the Molotov cocktail got in on the passenger side. The car they were driving was a dark blue sedan."

"Do you know the year, make, or model, sir?"

"It would be a guess if I did. So many cars look the same nowadays."

"Yes, sir. I know what you mean. What would you guess?"

"Well, if I were to guess, I'd say it was some kind of GM mid-size sedan." Doc shook his head. "That's a guess, though."

"That's fine. But you said it was dark blue?"

"Yes, Detective. I could tell that for sure." Doc got up and poured more coffee for the three of them.

"What else can you tell us?"

"Well, I called 911 again shortly after the first time to tell them there was a fire. By the time I hung up, the fire had really taken off, especially inside the second-floor apartment. I don't know what was in there, but the fire moved fast through the second floor."

"Did you know anyone who lived in the house, Mr. Archer?"

"There was a guy who lived on the second floor. I never saw any women around him much. Men, either, for that matter. He wasn't all that friendly and kept to himself. I don't know his name." Doc sat back down at the kitchen table. "There was a girl who lived in the attic apartment. She was friendly and parked her car next to the side of my garage. Her name was Jenna. I don't know her last name."

"I understand there was also a first-floor apartment."

"That's right. There's a couple that lives together there. The man's name is Collin Jaron, and his girlfriend is Tabatha Wardman or Warman. You know, I'm not sure, but it's something like that anyway. I'm pretty sure they're out west on a ski trip. Colorado, I think. They're both nice people."

"Do you know how to reach any of the people who lived in the house, sir?"

"I might have Collin's mobile number, but I don't have any way to contact any of the others." Doc looked at his phone and showed the detective contact information for Collin Jaron. "Did the guy and girl in the upper apartments get out okay?"

Sasha thanked John for the contact information, then looked at his partner. "Darcie, have you heard anything yet on the people living in the apartments?"

Darcie looked back at Sasha. Knowing that three bodies had been found in the debris, she followed his lead. "We're waiting for an update from the fire investigator, so I don't know."

"Is there anything else you can tell us, Mr. Archer?"

"I don't think so. I'd like to thank the fire crew for the job they did to protect my house. That house was burning down so fast, I was afraid my house would catch fire, too. They kept spraying water on the roof and walls that faced the Baughman house. I appreciated that very much."

"I'll be sure to let them know that." Sasha stood up. "If there's nothing more you can add, I'd like to leave you my card. If you think of anything more, give me a call. We want to thank you for the hospitality and coffee, too."

Darcie stood up. "Yes. Thank you."

"No problem." Doc took Sasha's card and followed the two back to the front door of his house. "If I can be of any further help, please let me know."

"We will, sir. Thank you again." Sasha shook hands with Doc, and the detective followed Darcie out the door and down the stairs.

"So you're thinking that maybe those two guys shot somebody and then lit the house on fire to cover it up?"

They stopped at the sidewalk in front of the house. "It does sound that way. If the fire took off the way he described it, they must have doused the inside of the apartment with gasoline or something. Clark can let us know his theory on that."

The two detectives walked toward the house on the west side of the Baughman's. There was a man with a dog standing on the sidewalk.

"Good morning, sir." Sasha reached out to shake hands with the man. "Can I ask your name, sir?"

"I'm James MacKenzie."

"Mr. MacKenzie, Detective Lyman and I understand that you were one of the people who called 911 to report gunshots."

James picked up the small dog, which had started barking. "Quiet, Jack. Yes, I did, Detective. I heard gunshots shortly after 2 a.m."

"Did you see anyone outside after the shots were fired?"

"No." James turned and pointed to the back of the house. "My young sons share a room on the east corner of the house back by the alley. Our bedroom is across the hall on the west corner. When I heard the gunshots, I looked out our windows. Then I heard the sound of a— I don't know. I hate to say explosion, but I guess a small explosion."

"Did you see anything when you heard the noise?"

"I can't say I did. I went to the boys' bedroom and looked out their window that faces the alley. I could see flames at the back of the Baughman house. I started to go to the other window to see if I could get a better look when I heard a car in the alley. At first I couldn't see it because it must've been parked behind our garage. But then I saw it drive by, heading west."

"What kind of car was it?"

"I sell cars for a living, Detective, and the light coming from the back of my garage gave me a pretty good view of a Chevrolet Cruze, a dark-blue sedan. Maybe 2011?"

Darcie looked at Sasha, then back at the man. "You're sure?"

"Yes."

"Okay. Is there anything else you can tell us about the vehicle? Anything specific?"

"It had one of those Illinois license plates from a college. I can't be sure, but if I were guessing, I'd say it was the University of Illinois Chicago. I'd guess UIC."

"Did you see the license plate number?"

"I know the last two numbers were a 1 and a 4, but I can't tell you the rest of the plate number. Sorry."

"This will be most helpful, sir." Sasha turned to Darcie. "Could you call dispatch with the description of the vehicle Mr. MacKenzie just provided?" Darcie nodded and walked a few feet away to call in the license plate to dispatch.

"Could you, by chance, identify anyone in the car?"

"There was someone in the passenger seat who was wearing something dark. Maybe black. I couldn't see a face."

"You've got pretty good eyes, sir."

"I had laser surgery on my eyes in November. After years of wearing glasses, I've got 20/15 vision now."

"Detective?"

Sasha turned to Darcie, and she motioned for him to join her.

"Excuse me, sir." Sasha walked over to where Darcie was standing. "What did you find out?"

"Nothing specific. With that much detail, dispatch thought it wouldn't take very long to run the search. We should find out pretty quickly."

"Okay." Sasha walked back to Mr. MacKenzie. "Is there anything else you can tell me, sir?"

"I think that's it, Detective."

"How about your wife?"

"She didn't see anything. She talked with your officers earlier when I took the boys across the street to our neighbors after the fire started. She told me she mentioned to them that I saw a car leave."

"We may want to follow up with you later as part of our investigation."

"Any time, Detective."

"Thank you very much for telling us what you saw, Mr. MacKenzie. Your information was very helpful." They shook hands, and Sasha walked back to check on what was happening at the burned house.

"That went well."

"Yeah. We should've talked with that guy first."

The two stopped and watched the ME team gently place a victim into a body bag. Sasha reached for his ringing phone. "Frank. Yes. Yes. Okay. Thanks."

"What did you find out?"

"That was dispatch. The car MacKenzie saw is registered to a Qiang Zheng who lives in a condominium on South Prairie Avenue in Chicago. He said he would reach out to Chicago PD to ask them to go to the address to speak with Mr. Zheng."

They watched the ME and her team raise the body bag up to the waiting arms of several firefighters at the west side of the basement. The sun was up, and it was lightly snowing. There were already two body bags lying on the ground. "Let's talk with Juanita," Sasha said.

The detectives walked over near the body bags. Juanita was climbing up a ladder the fire crew had earlier used to access the basement.

She stepped off the ladder and onto the ground. "Morning, Detectives."

"Are you all wrapped up here, Juanita?"

The ME took off her latex gloves and put them in her pocket. "We are." Juanita looked down at the body bags. "Based on the condition of the bodies, we will have no chance of finding fingerprints, so dental records, DNA, or maybe other medical records will be required to provide positive IDs."

"That bad?"

"Yes."

"Okay. I don't see any reason to attend the autopsies. What do you think?"

"That's your call. I can tell you that each will be painstakingly long."

"I think our time would be better spent working with Clark to find who-ever set the house on fire."

"Understandable. We're going to head back to the office and start as soon as we can. If I find anything interesting, I'll give you a call. Sound good?"

"Yes, thanks. Talk to you later, Juanita." Sasha and Darcie watched as the ME spoke with her team. The team quickly placed each of the body bags on stretchers and began moving the bodies to the ME transport vehicles.

Sasha turned to Darcie. "I'm going to talk to Clark before heading back to the station. Why don't you head back now and call the owners and find out the possible identity of the victims? Clark will be here for hours. The two of us can circle back to him later."

"Deal. I'll head back now."

As Darcie walked back to her car, she started thinking about what they'd learned from the interviews with neighbors. The fire must have been started to obfuscate what the two men had done. Taking on this investigation with the ongoing Ashley Cummins investigation was going to make for more long days for the two detectives.

26

Darcie was sitting at her desk at the station when Sasha returned from the scene of the fire. "Anything new from Clark?"

"Not really. He's waiting for the results from the lab."

"I waited for you to reach out to the Baughmans. Let's go to the conference room and make the call." Darcie stood up and walked toward the conference room they'd been using for the Cummins investigation, and Sasha followed. Darcie sat down, put the telephone on speaker, and began dialing the Baughmans' number. The call went through, and they heard the phone ringing.

Chuck Baughman was standing in front of his condo in Port Charlotte, Florida, talking with a couple of friends after returning from breakfast, when his cell phone started ringing. He didn't recognize the number, but it was an area code from home, so he answered. "Hello?"

"Is this Mr. Baughman? Chuck Baughman?"

"Who's calling?"

"I'm Detective Darcie Lyman. I'm with the Bloomington Police Department, sir. Also on the call is Senior Detective Sasha Frank. Is this Mr. Baughman we're speaking with?"

Chuck immediately started worrying that something had happened to one of his family members back home. "Yes, that's me. What's going on, Detective?"

"I'm sorry to tell you that your former home off Clinton Street in Bloomington was burned to the ground early this morning."

"Are you serious?" Chuck was relieved that the detectives were just calling about the rental house. "Oh my gosh. I was afraid something happened to a family member."

"No, sir. Sorry to worry you. Could you answer a few questions for me?"

"Certainly. Go ahead."

"Could you please provide us the names and contact information for the tenants renting apartments from you, Mr. Baughman?"

"Was anyone hurt?"

"I'm sorry to say there were several fatalities, sir."

Chuck started shaking his head. "Oh, my gosh! I'm so sorry to hear that. What happened?"

"Right now, we believe this to be a case of arson."

"That's terrible."

"Yes, it is." Sasha motioned to Darcie to keep the conversation going. "We need to know who was living in the apartments. Any information you have would be helpful, sir."

"Well, certainly, Detective. I can get you their names and telephone numbers now, if you'd like. My son takes care of everything at the house for us. You can contact Charles, Jr. to see if he has additional information at his office that would be helpful."

"That is very kind of you, Mr. Baughman. I'll take whatever information you have now, and if you could provide us with your son's contact information, we'll also reach out to him." Darcie gave Sasha a thumbs-up.

"I should probably go up to my condo and call you back, Detective. The names and numbers for the tenants are on my phone, and I'll need to write them down before I call you."

"You could text them to me."

"Sorry, but I don't text."

"That's fine. Will it be only a few minutes?"

"Yes, I'll go up right now. Call me back in a couple of minutes. Would that be okay?"

"Yes, sir. I'll call you back shortly. Thank you." Darcie disconnected the call and the two detectives talked for several minutes until she called Mr. Baughman back.

"I've got the names and telephone numbers of the renters," Chuck said. "Marvin Milcen, Collin Jaron, and Jenna Jameson."

The two detectives looked at each other. Darcie asked, "Was the first name you mentioned Marvin Milcen?"

"Yes, Detective. Marvin was on the second floor. Collin and his girlfriend on the first floor. Jenna in the attic apartment."

Another one of the original suspects in the Ashley Cummins murder could be dead. "What do you know about Marvin?"

"Well, Marvin changed jobs a lot, so I'm not sure. This last time, I heard he was working as a janitor over at the tire plant. My son may know. Marvin was a nice guy. He had been on probation, but I think that's over now."

"Can you tell us anything you know about the others?"

"Collin works at a sporting goods store, I think. Jenna works as a bartender."

"Do you have the name and number for Collin's girlfriend?"

"No, I don't. I think she's a new one."

Sasha motioned for Darcie to end the call. "Thank you, sir. Do you have any other information that would be helpful?"

"No, but my son has all the paperwork they filled out. You can call him."

"Thank you very much for your help, Mr. Baughman. If you could let your son know we'll be wanting to talk with him, that would be great."

"Certainly. I'm going to call Charles now to let him know what happened. I was happy to help."

Darcie disconnected the call and turned to Sasha, who was beside her, leaning back in his chair. "What the heck?"

"So that's two on our list killed under suspicious circumstances," Sasha said. "That can't be a coincidence."

"Want to talk to R.J.?"

"Yes. Let's go." Sasha stood, and Darcie followed her partner to R.J.'s office. The door was open, and the vice unit detective was sitting with his feet up on his desk, dressed in blue jeans and an old sweatshirt.

"I see that your dress code hasn't changed much," Sasha said, entering the office.

R.J. smiled. "I've got to dress like my friends out there. Why are you slumming it in my office?"

"One Marvin Milcen."

"What's Marvin done now?" R.J. took his feet off the desk.

"We think he's gotten himself dead."

"No way!" R.J. sat up. "How?"

"Death by arson to start. Maybe gunshot too. Provided that the ME identifies one of three bodies found in the debris as Milcen."

"When?"

"Early this morning. Milcen had a second-floor apartment in an old house near Clinton and East Washington." Sasha handed R.J. a sheet showing the address reported to 911 and told him what they had learned. "A neighbor says he saw somebody throw a Molotov cocktail."

"That's the address where Marvin lives, alright. I guess somebody didn't like him?"

"Guess not. You said he was lying low."

"I told you Milcen was a convicted drug dealer. He's not on probation anymore, and I view him as a fairly low-level dealer. I didn't think anyone saw him as a threat." R.J. stood up. "He basically stays under the radar."

"Well, we now have two on the list dead." Darcie looked at the file she was carrying. "So why would somebody want him dead, R.J.?"

"I can't imagine."

Sasha started pacing around the small office.

"I've got to believe that somebody is sending a message."

Darcie looked at her partner. "What's the message?"

"I don't know, exactly, but two of the guys on our list are dead, and both could be related to Ashley Cummins's murder. All this doesn't pass the proverbial smell test."

27

Sasha and Darcie were driving back to the station from lunch, and as Sasha pulled his car into the parking lot, Darcie asked, "The original theory was that Wolenski was killed by someone who had a beef with him, right?"

"Yes, that was our original thinking. With what happened last night, that view is evolving." The senior detective pulled into his parking space, and the two got out of the car, walked into the station, and headed straight to the conference room. They'd been working together there every day for the past two weeks or more.

They'd only been in the conference room for a few minutes when the phone rang. Darcie answered and put the call on speaker.

"What have you got for us, Juanita?"

"Once we were provided with the names of the tenants, we were able to access dental records that positively identified two of the bodies discovered in the debris." Juanita paused. "We've got one male by the name of Melvin Milcen and a female identified as a Jenna Jameson. We're waiting on dental records to confirm the identity of the third body, which is also female."

"Can you give us the identity of the second female?"

"We tentatively believe it is a Kelly Moran. A single mother of two. As you probably already know, a car registered to Moran was parked at the back of the home, and her mother has confirmed that she was out last night with Jameson. Jameson told 911 a friend was with her in the apartment. We're assuming dental records will confirm that it is Moran."

Both Sasha and Darcie were writing down the information the ME was providing. Sasha asked, "You're aware of the reports of gunshots shortly before the fire. Did you find anything related to that report?"

They could hear Juanita typing on her keyboard. "Alright. I'm just going to start talking. You can stop me if you have any specific questions." Juanita paused for a few seconds. "Like I said, we've completed the preliminary autopsies on the bodies recovered from the debris." She paused again. "Jenna Allison Jameson was a twenty-nine-year-old female. Her body was very severely burned. So much so that she could only be identified using her dental records. Jenna's airways, her nasal cavity, and entire respiratory system, the throat and lungs, contained soot from the fire. There were clear signs of inhaling hot smoke, which would have caused her to suffer from hypoxia. It is my medical opinion that Jenna drifted into unconsciousness before she died from a combination of smoke inhalation and burns."

Sasha said, "Quick question. Was there any physical trauma to the body before death?"

"The body was subjected to significant and extensive trauma. The intense fire caused extreme trauma to tissue, internal organs, and bones. I understand Jenna lived in the attic apartment, but with her body being found in the debris in the basement, she had broken and cracked bones. We're waiting for the results of blood tests, but her blood will undoubtedly show extremely high levels of carbon monoxide. I don't believe that there was trauma prior to unconsciousness. I could go into great detail, Sasha, but there is no question that her death was caused by the fire."

"I understand, Juanita. You've made your point. I'm assuming that you found the same with the second female?"

"Yes. The injuries on the second female are consistent with Jenna's."

"What about the male?"

Juanita reached for the manila folder containing the autopsy of Marvin Milcen. "The male victim is Marvin Andrew Milcen. A thirty-one-year-old male. Identification was made with dental records from the Illinois Department of Prison due to the condition of the body. The key difference between Milcen and the two females is that his respiratory system showed no indication of soot or smoke, so—"

"So he was already dead?" Sasha said.

"*Sasha.*" Juanita was annoyed by the interruption. "I was obviously about to say that. The damage to Milcen's skull and body was extensive due to the fire. I'm not going to go into great detail on this call discussing the wound profiles, but I believe that Milcen was shot multiple times in the head and at least once in the upper torso." She picked up a small evidence bag holding a bullet. "The damage to a human skull from the extreme heat of a fire can make it difficult to determine the occurrence of entry wounds, but I believe that I've identified at least one, and perhaps two, entry wounds in the skull. More importantly, I'm holding a 9mm bullet that was found lodged at the C3 cervical vertebral bone near the top of the spine. Mr. Milcen's death was from a bullet or bullets. He did not succumb to the fire."

"So the gunfire resulted in Milcen's murder at the hands of the two men seen leaving the scene by our witness, Mr. Archer," Darcie said. "Obviously, they also were responsible for setting the fire."

"Is there anything else you need from me, Detectives?"

"No, Juanita. We can circle back later this afternoon. Can you let us know when you've got a positive ID on the second female?"

"Certainly. Talk to you later. Good luck." Juanita ended the call.

R.J. walked into the room just as the call with the ME ended. "You're not going to believe this."

"Believe what?"

"On the morning of Thursday, February 21st, a woman in Normal called 911 to report finding her boyfriend dead in their apartment. The boyfriend's throat had been slashed, and Normal police thought he was the victim of a robbery."

Sasha shook his head. "So?"

"So the ME said he'd been dead for several days."

"Who's the boyfriend?"

R.J. walked over to the board and pointed. "Carlos Ward-Wallace."

Sasha stood up. "Why are we just hearing about this?"

"There was an article about it in the paper last Friday or Saturday, and a guy in dispatch asked me about it after lunch. He said a guy was found by his girlfriend, who'd been out of town visiting family. She comes home and finds her boyfriend and dog dead." R.J. picked up a piece of chalk. "I assume the newspaper got his legal name reported correctly. What I wrote here is wrong.

It's not Carlos Ward-Wallace. I just called and talked with a Normal Police Department detective." He tapped the board with the piece of chalk. "This guy's legal name is Carleton Ward." He crossed out Wallace with the chalk.

Darcie looked at Sasha. "You wrote his name down wrong?"

"I asked the detective about that. Carlos Ward-Wallace was not his legal name. Ward's mom got remarried when he was something like two years old to a guy with the last name of Wallace. His mom and stepdad had three kids together, and those kids' legal last names were Ward-Wallace. They just started calling Carleton by the other kids' last name of Ward-Wallace without legally changing it."

Sasha looked incredulous. "What about his first name?"

"The detective said his mother told him he always hated Carleton, and when he was five years old, he announced to everyone that he wanted to go by Carlos. And it stuck."

R.J. crossed out the *o* and *s* in Carlos and added "eton." "Voilà. Carleton Ward."

Sasha shook his head. "You said his throat was slashed?"

"Yes. Normal PD has no suspects, but believe he was killed by either a rival dealer or maybe a drug addict wanting whatever drugs and cash he was holding."

Darcie stood up. "You said they killed a dog, too?"

"Both Ward and the dog had their throats slashed. Normal PD will send everything they have over to us."

"So these three have been murdered." Sasha walked over to the blackboard and picked up a piece of chalk. He marked through the names of Ward, Wolenski, and Milcen. He looked back at Darcie. "We have to go out and find the remaining guys."

"Why don't we immediately put out APBs on each of them? Then we can talk with them when they're brought in."

"Good idea, Darcie. Talk to dispatch now." Darcie got up and left the conference room. Sasha looked at R.J. The senior detective was angry about the mix-up with Carleton Ward's name, but he'd talk with him about that later. "Thanks, R.J."

"No problem, Sasha."

The senior detective sat down and thought to himself that R.J. had set the investigation into Ashley Cummins's murder back by getting the name of one of their suspects wrong. "Why don't you circle back to your list and check to see where they are?"

"Okay. I can do that." The two continued to talk about re-canvassing the remaining names on the blackboard before R.J. went back to his office.

———

"Dispatch is putting out APBs," Darcie said as she walked into the conference room and sat back down. She saw that Sasha was deep in thought. "That was an unexpected twist."

Sasha looked up, nodded, then stared at the list on the blackboard. "I knew there was a murder in Normal, but what I heard just mentioned that the guy was found dead by his girlfriend. That's on me for not digging deeper with Normal PD."

"Don't beat yourself up." Darcie pointed at the blackboard. "With R.J. messing up the guy's name, how could you have ever suspected?"

Darcie was right, of course. Sasha recalled that the young man's rap sheet showed he'd been in and out of juvie since his early teens before being sentenced at age seventeen to four years for a Class 3 felony. Ward participated in a criminal conspiracy related to selling cannabis.

Sasha looked back at Darcie. "You know Ward was sentenced to Taylorville Correctional Center because the judge cut him a break in hopes that he'd change his ways. Guess he didn't."

Darcie repeated what she said when she walked into the conference room. She didn't think Sasha had heard her. "Dispatch is putting out APBs."

"Right. We need officers finding each one of these guys ASAP." Sasha stood and began to pace, wondering if someone was really targeting guys on their list or if these deaths were coincidences. He didn't believe in coincidences.

The senior detective sat back down. "So we've got Milcen on the receiving end of gunshots, then whoever shot him started the fire to cover it up. That's our theory, right?"

His partner leaned forward. "Based on our eyewitnesses and what Juanita told us, yes."

"Let's switch gears. Dispatch told us that when officers started asking around at a few bars about Wolenski, they were able to piece together a partial timeline of his movements the night he was killed. He was last seen leaving a neighborhood bar off East Empire."

"Yes."

Sasha opened the file they had on Wolenski. "One of the bartenders told them he'd seen Wolenski go outside and meet with multiple patrons numerous times that night. He knew the man sold drugs and had even pointed it out to the bar's owner previously. The owner had told the bartender to stick to the bar's policy of don't ask, don't tell."

Darcie smiled. "It's universal. I worked as a bartender in college. I don't know of any bar that would say anything."

Sasha shook his head. "I know. I'm just saying that Wolenski sold drugs for a living, and nobody turned him in or bothered him. Based on what officers heard, everybody loved him. R.J. couldn't"—the senior detective shook his head—"or *wouldn't* get the goods on him and arrest the guy."

"Somebody didn't like him."

"True."

The phone rang, and Darcie answered it. "Yeah? Okay." She put her hand over the mouthpiece. "Danny Williams was found dead in the ocean off Miami Beach."

28

Harvey said goodbye to his wife in the kitchen before opening the door to the attached garage and getting into his car. Today was going to be the fourth time he'd met with John, his friend of over twenty years, to discuss the plan they had hatched two weeks ago. Harvey sighed as he started the car, backed out of the garage, and left for the short drive to his favorite downtown restaurant for breakfast.

The goal of their plan was simple: rid the Twin Cities area of the vermin selling illegal drugs. Law enforcement wasn't doing enough to stop the flow into the area, and since they weren't doing what was needed to protect its citizens, John and Harvey had decided they would.

As he pulled into the parking lot of the downtown breakfast spot, Harvey watched his friend John enter the restaurant. He parked his car, got out, and zipped up his leather coat to shield himself from the cold morning wind and quickly walked into the restaurant. He moved through the restaurant to where John was sitting in a back booth.

The waitress came over with two pots of coffee. "Good morning, gentlemen. Pour you a cup?"

"Yes, thanks." Harvey smiled up at the waitress who had been serving coffee to patrons of the restaurant for many years. "I think I'll have a full cup this morning, Blanche." He looked down to see the familiar faded logo on the bottom of the old, green, and heavy porcelain mug that waitstaff had been pouring coffee into for almost fifty years.

Blanche Collins knew her longtime customer had been coming to the restaurant four or five times a week for breakfast long before she'd started working as a waitress over thirty years ago. She knew Harvey had a heart condition that restricted him from having regular coffee, so she filled his mug from the pot of decaf. "Here you go." She looked at John. "Coffee for you this morning?" John nodded, and she poured him a mug of regular. "I'll be back in a few minutes to take your order, gentlemen."

Harvey waited to talk to John until Blanche had gotten out of earshot. The restaurant was busy this morning, but there wasn't anyone sitting in the booth directly behind John. Harvey leaned over to talk in a hushed but firm tone to his friend. "Can you explain to me what went so wrong?"

John shifted uncomfortably on his side of the booth. "The simple answer is that they weren't aware someone was living above Marvin Milcen."

"Weren't aware?" Harvey looked with disbelief at John. "Only dealers were supposed to be killed. Not two innocent women."

"I know, Harvey. It's a tragic accident."

Harvey shook his head and let out a heavy sigh. "A tragic accident? One of them had two small children—a daughter and a son, for God's sake!"

Blanche came back, took their orders, and returned to the front of the restaurant. Harvey looked back at John. "This wasn't supposed to happen."

John turned to make sure no one was close to the two men. "I understand, and I'm sorry. But things happen."

Harvey raised his voice. "Things happen? *Seriously?*"

Other customers in the restaurant turned and looked toward them. John said in a firm whisper, "Calm down. When we started down this path to get rid of these vermin, I told you there could be unintended consequences." John took a sip of coffee. "I understand that two young women were tragically killed, and I feel bad about that, but we embarked on this together, and we're not going to stop until we accomplish what we agreed on."

Harvey shook his head. "Killing innocents makes us no different from those we are having killed."

John turned around again to see if Blanche was coming with their breakfast orders. When he saw that she had stopped at another table, he looked back at his friend. John started to raise his voice uncontrollably. "It was my daughter who died seven years ago, Harvey." He caught himself and returned to a whisper. "Killed by a man who I had successfully defended a year earlier after he was arrested and charged with a murder he said he didn't commit. How did he repay me for me getting him off?"

"I know how he repaid you, John."

In a calmer tone, John replied, "You know that the day that scum killed my daughter was the last day I defended any more like him."

Blanche returned to their booth with their orders. "Here you go, gentlemen." She looked at them. "Anything else I can get you two?" The friends shook their heads, and she smiled and turned to head back to the kitchen.

"Since Bonnie's death, you've become one of the finest prosecutors I've ever known." Harvey knew he needed to tread carefully in what he would say next. "Your conviction record is second to none, and the passion you have fighting for justice for not only the victims of senseless crimes but for victims' families as well has earned you a great amount of respect." He paused and looked at his friend. "The reason we agreed to do this now was to make sure people didn't get away with killing or hurting innocents."

John nodded. "We've been talking about doing this for years. Having arranged the deaths that have taken place so far is something we both signed up for, and I'm sorry that the girls died."

"That fact alone changes everything."

"We're almost done, Harvey."

"Yes, I know." Harvey took a sip of his coffee and shook his head again. "Innocents were killed."

"You haven't been listening to me, have you? You know no one else is willing to take the steps we have taken."

Harvey lowered his head. "I have been listening, but can't you see what we've done?"

"Okay. So you want to take some time and reassess."

Harvey looked up from his coffee cup. "I think we have to. Their deaths are all I've been thinking about." He saw Blanche heading toward them with two pots of coffee. He hadn't touched the English muffin she'd brought him earlier.

"Something wrong with the food?"

"We've just been talking. I'll take more decaf, though." Harvey wasn't hungry. He watched her fill his cup. "Thanks, Blanche."

"My pleasure." Blanche raised her eyebrows at John, but he covered his coffee cup with his hand. She nodded. "I'll be back in a few minutes to check on you."

"I want to take a few days to determine the best way to move forward," Harvey said.

"Our plan is nearing its end, and if we pause, it would require a reengagement with our friends in Chicago."

"They're not my friends."

"Friends. Associates." John shrugged. "Whatever." He was responsible for recruiting those required to execute the plan. He'd first encountered them while he was a public defender, defending a man arrested for attempted murder. While preparing for trial, John had learned his client was a known member of a Chicago narcotics ring. The gang's leader had provided him with the names of rivals who could also be possible suspects for the murder. John had also discovered that crucial crime scene evidence might have been mishandled by investigators just before the trial. As an idealistic and energetic public defender, he'd been able to convince the jury that there was reasonable doubt his client was guilty of attempted murder. The gang and its leader were forever in John's debt. Even after he'd become a downstate prosecutor, John had maintained a relationship with the gang's leader and that gave him an opening to ask for their assistance. In the back of his mind, John knew he would be indebted to the gang, but he didn't give that any consideration as they formulated their plan.

John and Harvey had convinced each other that to remove existing dealers from the area would allow law enforcement the time, with help from the two of them and other leaders in the community, to put into place programs to eradicate drug use and dependency. Their rationale was that they could stop residents from buying the drugs they craved from new dealers willing to fill a market need.

John sat back in the booth, recalling their initial discussions and the time when they'd set the plan in motion, and he realized only now how delusional their idea, driven by revenge, really was. Regardless, they'd come this far. They needed to see it through to the end. He took another sip of his coffee and found that it was cold. He motioned for Blanche that he needed a refill. "I need to know you're still on board."

Harvey looked at his friend and shook his head. "I just feel so bad about the two girls."

Blanche came to the table, then returned to the coffee station to get John a fresh mug. The two friends sat in silence as they waited for her to return. John thought back to when they'd hatched their plan and he'd purchased prepaid burner phones at a store in a small town miles away on the Indiana border. John knew the calls and texts made on those phones would never be traced.

Blanche returned with the coffee and dropped off their check. "Thank you, Blanche," John said. She smiled and walked away with plates.

John looked across the table at his friend. "So what do you want to do, then, Harvey?"

"I don't know if I want us to stay on plan, John."

"Let's get together in a couple of days to talk again. Is that okay?"

"That sounds like a good idea." Harvey looked down at the table. "This is just eating me up."

"I understand. Ready to go, my friend?" John reached into his pocket, pulled out a fifty, and left it on the table for Blanche. He followed Harvey out to the parking lot, where the two stood at the back of John's car and shook hands. John watched as his friend got into his vehicle and pulled out of the restaurant parking lot. After listening to what Harvey had to say, John decided he'd have to deflect responsibility for the murders onto someone else quickly. He got into his car and made a call on his burner before heading home.

29

Sasha and Darcie finished their late-afternoon meeting with the chief in his office and returned to the conference room. The chief wanted an update on all that had transpired in the Ashley Cummins investigation over the past day or so. He was not happy about what had been discovered just that afternoon.

The meeting was prompted initially by the house fire and what the chief had learned about Carleton Ward. Even though Ward had been murdered in Normal almost two weeks ago, the two detectives tried explaining to the chief that Ward's true identity had been unknown to them. Sasha also told the chief that blame couldn't be placed on R.J. for providing a wrong name for Ward because the man had been convicted and sentenced to prison under the surname Ward-Wallace.

During the meeting, the two detectives also let the chief know that they'd learned earlier that Danny Williams had died in an apparent accidental drowning last Sunday morning while on vacation in Florida with his girlfriend and daughter. The coroner's inquest had determined that Danny was inexperienced and unaware of the riptides that occur just off the island's shore, which often take tourists unfamiliar with them out to deeper waters where they can become exhausted and drown.

They also told the chief that they were informed a short while ago that William Green, who they believed to be one of the suspects outside Ashley's car, was also found murdered. Green's mother had called in an hour ago to say that a detective from the Chicago PD had called her this morning with news that he'd been found dead in a stolen car. The vehicle had been torched on Chicago's South Side early last Tuesday morning. It had taken the ME in Chicago several days to identify the remains.

Sasha let the chief know he'd spoken with police investigators in Chicago as soon as he had learned of Green's death, and that they had no suspects for the killing of Green. The bullets recovered from the body didn't match any in the NIBIN database. Green had been shot multiple times. Investigators believed that he was the victim of ongoing gang violence related to drugs, and they held out little hope of finding those responsible.

Danny Williams's alleged associate, Adrian Wolenski, had been killed the night before Williams was found dead in Florida.

The chief knew that Milcen had been murdered and was aware of the tragic deaths of the two women. Sasha and Darcie told the chief that there was one solid lead being pursued with the help of Chicago PD related to the car and partial plate number a witness had seen driving away from the fire. With the partial plate number, they'd been able to identify the registered owner of the car who lived in Chicago's South Loop neighborhood.

After speaking with the car's owner, a college student by the name of Qiang Zheng, Chicago police officers had discovered that the vehicle was not in its designated parking space at the owner's downtown condo parking garage. The owner hadn't driven during the past several weeks and gave police officers the only two sets of keys to the car. He told police that after his father had purchased the car for him, he'd never driven it outside the city limits. Chicago Police told the two detectives that they had no reason to disbelieve what the owner had told them. The vehicle was assumed stolen from the parking garage, and there was little hope it would be recovered. Police believed the car had already found its way into a gang chop shop—yet another dead end in Ashley Cummins's murder investigation.

In summary, they told the chief that in the few weeks since Ashley Cummins was killed, five men on their list of potential suspects had been confirmed dead. APBs were out on the remaining three men on the list—Charles Johns, Darren Redmond, and Leon Ross. Sasha was sure Johns had gone into hiding after William Green was found dead in Chicago. He told the chief that if and when any of the three men surfaced, they would immediately place them under twenty-four-hour surveillance.

Sasha and his partner had interviewed family and friends of the missing men, none of whom had been seen for days. All those interviewed said it wasn't unusual for the men to go underground from time to time. With police asking questions about the whereabouts of these men, family members were concerned for their safety.

It was now evident to the chief, Sasha, and Darcie that the men on their initial list had been explicitly targeted. The chief and his detectives agreed that identifying the person or persons responsible for those already dead and those currently missing would be difficult. Police in Normal, Chicago, and Bloomington hadn't arrested any potential suspects in the deaths because there was little or no evidence pointing to those responsible.

When the meeting was over, the chief ordered Sasha to find out who in the department was aware of the list of possible suspects in Ashley's murder.

Darcie looked across the conference table at Sasha. "There weren't many even aware there was a list."

Sasha nodded. "I always intended to keep the names close to the vest. The only ones who knew about the list were R.J., the chief, maybe the mayor, the dispatchers, and you and me. Right?"

"Yes, but if the door was open, anyone walking by the conference room could have seen it."

"True." Sasha leaned back in his chair. "I'll start. Darcie, did you talk with anyone other than R.J., the chief, dispatch, or me about the names?"

Darcie smiled. "No. How about you, Sasha?"

"The only person I mentioned a couple of the names to was Janet, but I never told her all the names."

"Janet wouldn't have passed along anyone's name. I'll mark you down as a no."

"I really can't imagine anyone passing along the names. It doesn't make sense."

"It may not make sense, but it's the only explanation." Darcie turned around to look at the list of suspects. "I'm assuming you'll agree that the chief is a no?"

Sasha nodded.

"I'll check with the chief, then, on what the mayor may know, but I think that's another negative."

"I'll have to talk to the mayor."

"You're kidding, right?"

"No, I'm not. I'll personally ask the mayor. Together we will talk with the others. We might as well get started now." Sasha stood to leave the room, as did his partner. They walked down the hallway to R.J.'s office. He wasn't in. "We can talk to him later. Let's go talk to dispatch."

"Deal." Darcie walked with Sasha to the dispatcher's desk, where he was on the phone.

The dispatcher looked up at the two detectives standing in front of his desk and nodded. He ended the call and hung up the phone. "What's up, guys?"

Sasha looked around the area to make sure that no one was close enough to hear what he was about to say. "I need to ask you a serious question."

Sasha's tone made him sit up straight in his chair. "Okay. Shoot."

"Did you talk with anyone other than R.J., the chief, other dispatchers, or the two of us about the list of suspects we compiled in the Cummins murder investigation?"

He leaned back in his chair. "Not that I'm aware of."

"Not that you're aware of?"

"Correct. I don't think I talked with anyone but the two of you about the list, Sasha."

"You're certain you didn't talk about the list with any of the others I just mentioned?"

"I might have spoken with the other dispatchers about the list in passing when we'd start or finish each other's shift. But I'm sure I didn't talk to anyone else about it." He paused. "You know, there *were* a few patrol officers used for backup when you and Darcie were out looking for potential suspects. They were only given addresses, though."

Four other dispatchers could have been on duty since the night Ashley was murdered, and they would need to talk with them as well. Sasha changed his tone. "Okay. Thanks. Please understand we're not making any accusations. We're just interested in understanding who was aware of all of the names on the list."

"No problem, Sasha. What's going on?"

"We're just tying up loose ends."

Darcie tapped her partner on the shoulder and turned to walk back to the conference room. "Come on, Sasha."

Back in the room, Sasha said, "I probably need to ratchet down my delivery, don't I?"

"I think so. I don't believe any of the people we're going to be asking gave somebody that list on purpose. Think about who we're talking about."

"I can't believe it, either, but somehow somebody got ahold of those names." Sasha rubbed his temples. Headaches seemed to be developing into a routine. "We need to call R.J. and get him in here to talk with us."

"I'll call him." Darcie pulled out her cell phone and called the vice unit detective. R.J. didn't answer, and she left him a message.

"I'm going to get some coffee," Sasha said. "Want some?" Darcie nodded. The senior detective decided to give Janet another call as he walked down the hall to the kitchen. Talking with her always had a calming effect on him.

She answered on the first ring. "Hi, Sasha."

"Hi. How's it going today?"

"Probably better than your day."

"We just finished a meeting with the chief."

"How'd that go?"

"With all we've learned in the past twenty-four hours, he was a bit grumpy, but that's understandable. I'm a bit grumpy too." That wasn't quite the right word, but it would do. Since yesterday morning, they'd gone from one person dead under suspicious circumstances to five, with three missing. "The body count in the wake of Ashley Cummins's murder is crazy."

"Based on what you last told me, somebody has been very busy settling a score."

"The number one question is who and how they learned about the list."

"You'll figure it out."

Sasha smiled to himself. At times like these, Janet often reminded him of his mother. If he was feeling down because something wasn't going well,

Alyona would be ready with an old Russian folk saying that would give him some positive reinforcement and make him feel better. Regardless of the situation, his mother and now Janet were there to make sure he was on an even keel. "Thanks, sweetie. I gotta go. Talk to you later." Sasha ended the call, poured two cups of coffee, and headed back.

Sasha handed Darcie a coffee and sat down. He pointed over to the blackboard. "Who could be passing along the list? Either innocently or purposely." He leaned back in his chair. "Regardless of the reason, someone outside this building learned about the list, and they're taking retribution."

"Who do you think would want to do that?"

"I obviously don't know. We should consider Ashley's father. The chief doesn't believe he's involved." Sasha leaned forward. "I'm not sure what I'd be capable of if someone had killed one of my children."

Darcie looked at her partner and thought about what it would take for her to seek retribution. "What's next?"

"We need to go back out and talk with Charlie Cummins." The senior detective looked at the blackboard and shook his head. "Anyone walking by this room could have seen that blackboard."

"Who's on your shortlist of likely suspects?" Darcie asked. "Besides her father, who would do this?"

Sasha stood up. "I don't know."

Darcie stood up and walked to the blackboard and pointed at the list of names. "Our goal was always to find out who she was there to meet, hoping that would lead us to who killed her."

"True. But all of these murders have to be tied to her murder. Without her, I don't believe that any of them would have taken place. These aren't coincidences."

"Okay. You convinced me."

"We've talked to everyone but R.J. about who could have passed along the list and to whom. That one detail alone could help us solve her murder."

"I agree. But where do you want to start?"

"First, we need to make sure that Johns remains alive. Next, we need to talk with Charlie Cummins."

30

The two detectives drove up and parked in front of Charlie Cummins's home on Stonebrook Court a few minutes ahead of the time they were scheduled to meet with him. "I'll take the lead on questioning Mr. Cummins," Sasha said. "The chief wants us to be very respectful."

"Is that fair?"

"Fair?"

"The Cummins family has clout."

"There doesn't need to be any space between being respectful and doing our job." Sasha and Darcie got out of the SUV, walked to the front door, and rang the doorbell.

Charlie Cummins opened the front door and let the two detectives inside. "Morning, Detectives." He led them to his library, where he'd first met with them and motioned for them to sit down. "What can I do for you?" he asked, sitting across from them.

"Thank you for agreeing to meet with us, Mr. Cummins. I need to ask your whereabouts on some dates."

"I'm happy to answer your questions if I can, Detective."

"Thank you, sir. Where were you on the evening of February 15th?"

Charlie stood up and walked over to the chair behind his desk. "I need to check my calendar." He picked up his mobile phone off his desk and touched the calendar icon. "On the evening of February 15th, I was at my sister Tina's house. She had a get-together for the family."

"How long were you there?"

"I picked up my parents around 5. Then we drove to her place. Before you ask, we stayed there until 10 or so. I drove my parents home, and I stayed to have a drink with my dad. I left around 11:30. I would have been home ten or fifteen minutes later."

Sasha knew the ME had placed the death of Carleton Ward between the hours of 6 p.m. and midnight on February 15th. If Charlie did what he said he'd done that night, it would have been possible—but a stretch—for him to kill Ward. "I assume you have no problem with us checking with your sister and parents on what you recall?"

Charlie looked at the detective taking his measure. "None whatsoever. You're looking at me as a suspect for something. What exactly?"

"There have been several murders following Ashley's death that appear to be related." Sasha saw the bewilderment in Charlie's eyes. "Can I ask you about some additional dates?"

"I have nothing to hide, Detective." Charlie leaned back, looking Sasha in the eyes. "Ask away."

He immediately knew asking Charlie Cummins questions about the men on the list of suspects would be a waste of time. Regardless, he continued asking Charlie his whereabouts on the other dates. Charlie checked his calendar and offered alibis for each night. The senior detective learned that Charlie Cummins had been spending a great deal of time with his parents and siblings since Ashley's murder. He'd even spent time in Chicago with his brother David.

After about twenty-five minutes with Mr. Cummins, the detectives excused themselves. As they drove back to the station, Sasha shook his head. "That is a part of the job I don't like."

"We had to ask him."

"Yes, but suggesting to a grieving father that he was involved with the killing of the men on our list was a stretch. His answers to our questions were honest and forthright. He had no idea what we were talking about."

"Regardless, we had no choice." Darcie slowed as she approached a red light. "Now we can move on."

31

With his mom and two sisters in Chicago for the weekend, Charlie had made plans with his father to go out for breakfast on Saturday morning. He knew his father had a favorite diner in Downtown Bloomington, but Charlie was going to take him to a spot on Veterans known for its pancakes.

About six inches of fresh snow had fallen over the city overnight, but the streets had already been plowed and cleared before he'd driven over to his parents. It was still lightly snowing as Charlie pulled into the driveway. He had texted his father before heading over, telling him to come on out if he was ready, but he still hadn't heard back from him. After waiting a few minutes, he got out of his car to walk up to the front door.

He rang the doorbell, and when there was no answer, he knocked. He went back to his car and got his set of house keys out of his console. Once inside the large home, he shouted for his father, but there was no response.

Charlie wandered through the two living rooms and into the kitchen. His father's nightly ritual was to get the coffee maker ready for the next morning by putting in a fresh filter, their favorite ground coffee, and filling the tank with water. The coffee maker was prepared to make coffee but hadn't been used. Maybe his father had forgotten their plans and had gone out for coffee. He walked through the mudroom and opened the door to the garage and saw both his parents' cars. He turned and started walking through the kitchen to the sunroom at the back of the house. The sunroom was empty. He was getting worried.

He looked down the hallway that extended from the sunroom to the foyer at the front of the house. He started walking down the hall and stopped at the double doors of his father's library. The room was dark as the wooden shutters at the far end of the library were closed, which was odd. His father always left them open. He stepped into the library and flipped the switch that turned on four lamps in the room. His father was slumped over at his desk. Charlie rushed over and found his father dead.

His father was sitting in his desk chair, leaning to his left. There was a gunshot wound in his father's right temple. There was a trickle of dried blood on his father's right cheek, and blood splatter covered parts of the desk and floor, including the shelves ten feet away.

Charlie reached to turn on the light switch on the wall behind him. The two ceiling lights lit up the desktop. A blood-splattered handwritten note was lying on the desk in front of his father. There was a .357 revolver lying in his father's lap. Being careful not to touch anything, he leaned over and began reading what his father had written.

With the police unable to find the person or persons responsible for Ashley's death, I took it upon myself to find justice for my granddaughter. I planned and hired those who could carry out the killing of men I learned could have been responsible for her murder. After the death of the two innocent women in the fire earlier this week, I can no longer live with what I've done. I have no choice but to take my own life. I did this alone. I ask that my wife and family forgive me.

After he finished reading the note, Charlie cried softly and said, "Dad. What have you done?"

He took one more look around the desk before he walked through the library and headed to the foyer. Charlie stopped and sat at one of the chairs sitting on both sides of a large mirror in the entry foyer. He dialed 911 and described the scene to the operator.

"I'm dispatching police officers and an ambulance to the address, sir. Is there anyone else with you?"

"No. I'm by myself." He lowered his head, thinking about the calls he would have to make to his mother and siblings.

"Police should be arriving momentarily."

He heard sirens and watched a single police car pull into the driveway. "A police officer just arrived," he told the operator.

"Thank you, sir. I'll stay on the line with you until the police officer identifies himself as Timothy Darby."

"Thank you." Charlie watched as the officer got out of his cruiser and jogged to the front door.

"Good morning, Officer."

The officer stopped at the front door. "I'm Officer Darby. Are you Mr. Cummins, sir?"

"Yes, I am."

"You can end your call with 911, sir."

Charlie thanked the operator for her help and said goodbye. He asked the police officer to step inside.

Darby closed the door behind him. "There will be additional officers arriving shortly. Can you please tell me exactly what happened here?"

Charlie explained that he had found his father dead in the library and led the officer to the scene.

Darby stopped beside Charlie and looked at the slumped body sitting behind the desk. "How long ago did you find him?"

"Ten minutes or so."

"Did you touch anything in the room?"

Charlie sighed heavily. "I flipped on the light switch just inside the door on the wall here. Then I flipped on the switch on the far wall that lights up my father's desk."

"Nothing else?"

"No. Nothing else."

Darby nodded. "You didn't touch the body or the desk or anything else in the room?"

"No. Just what I told you." Charlie shook his head as he looked at the body of his father. "I don't know how this could have happened."

Darby looked around the room. "I'm going to walk over to the body. Please stay here. As other officers arrive, could you please let them in?"

"Certainly." Charlie watched the officer walk toward his father. Darby turned on his flashlight and scanned the floor with the beam. He stopped at the front of the desk when he saw blood spatter on the wood floor to the right of it. Darby shined the beam at the man and found the entrance wound. The left side of his head had a large exit wound. There was blood spatter on one side of the top of the desk and a revolver lying in the man's lap. Darby shined the flashlight's beam on the sheet of paper and read the note.

"Did you read this note, sir?"

"Yes, officer." There was a loud knock, and Charlie said, "I'll let them in."

Darby nodded and stepped away from the desk. He got out his cell phone and called dispatch to give them an update on what he'd found. He didn't want to use his radio for everyone to hear. Dispatch told him that detectives would be alerted and would be on their way to the scene. Darby ended the call and turned to see Charlie Cummins standing at the double doors of the library with K9 Officer Becky Roach.

Becky met Darby's eyes, then addressed Charlie. "Could you please go sit in the foyer, sir?"

Charlie nodded.

Darby looked at Charlie. "Mr. Cummins?"

"Yes, Officer."

"Please accept my sincere condolences. I'm deeply sorry for your loss."

"Thank you. I appreciate that very much." Charlie turned and walked to the foyer.

Becky watched him walk away, then turned back to look at the judge slumped over in the chair. In a low voice, she asked, "What happened?"

"It looks like a self-inflicted gunshot wound." Darby didn't tell her about the note.

"Oh, no!" Becky shook her head. "Well, he did lose his granddaughter last month." She turned and walked to the front of the house to join Mr. Cummins. As she stopped and stood beside him, she could hear him talking to what sounded like maybe a sister telling her that their father had taken his own life. How sad, she thought, for the family.

32

Whe Sasha Frank arrived at the Cummins' home, there were already four police cruisers, an ambulance, and a Mercedes sedan parked in the driveway. Darcie was standing beside her unmarked car as Sasha pulled in.

"Good morning," Darcie said to her partner as he walked over to her. "You know I've driven by all the big houses on this street countless times over the years." She had heard that doctors, lawyers, and insurance business executives who worked in the area owned most of these homes. "This is a really nice part of town."

Sasha looked around. "Yes, it is." It was still snowing lightly, and the outside temperature was in the mid-twenties. The senior detective could see that the front door of the house was partially open. "Let's get inside."

As soon as they walked in, they saw Charlie Cummins sitting in the foyer. The two detectives offered him their condolences.

Charlie stood up and shook hands with them. "Thank you, Detectives."

"We'd like to talk with you, but I would first like to talk with the officers on scene."

"I'll be here when you need me." He sat back down.

Sasha and Darcie walked down the hall to where Officer Tim Darby was standing.

"Morning, Detectives."

The two detectives stopped at the double doors of the library and saw Judge Cummins at his desk. Sasha turned to Darcie. "Quite a mess we caught this morning."

Darcie nodded and pulled on a pair of latex gloves. "How do you want to start?"

"Slowly." Sasha put on his latex gloves and moved to the front of the desk. Darcie was close behind. He pulled out his flashlight and began looking around the library.

Making sure she didn't step on any blood, Darcie carefully walked around the desk and read the note out loud. She looked up at Sasha. "Geez." He nodded. She noticed the pen the judge had used lying next to the note. She shined her flashlight on the revolver in the judge's lap. "Looks like a .357 five-shot." She moved the beam to the entry wound in the judge's right temple.

Sasha had followed his partner's movements from the note to the revolver to the gunshot wound to the shelves covered in blood, brain matter, and bone fragments. He shook his head. "He must have been pretty upset with the deaths of the two girls."

"I was in the judge's courtroom a few times. He was tough on criminals." Darcie shined the beam into the judge's face. "I guess he was pretty frustrated with our not finding his granddaughter's killer."

"Dispatch told me that one of the officers was checking the outside of the house. How'd that go?"

"When I got here, Becky Roach told me she had cleared the house. She didn't see anything. She's doing a walk-around now."

Sasha nodded. "No one else home?"

"Charlie told officers that his mother was in Chicago with his two sisters. They went up yesterday morning to see a play or something. A brother lives up there, too."

"So the judge was home alone last night?"

"Yes. Charlie evidently made plans with his father to have breakfast this morning. He'd texted the judge before he'd left his house. Didn't get a reply."

Sasha had heard Darcie read the note the judge left, but he moved around the desk to read it himself.

Darcie pointed her flashlight at one of the windows on the back wall. "Darby said Charlie told him he's never seen these shutters closed before. Not sure that means anything."

"Let's have CSI check them for prints," Sasha said. He'd been on the witness stand at least fifty times in Judge Cummins's courtroom. The judge regularly doled out maximum sentences to guilty defendants. It didn't surprise him that he would hold himself up to the same standard by which he judged others.

Darcie looked at her partner. "Sasha." She waited several seconds. "Sasha!"

"Yes." He turned. "Sorry."

"No problem. What are you thinking?"

"Unless CSI finds other evidence, the judge died by his own hand. Knowing the judge only from the time I spent in his courtroom, I can see how he wouldn't be able to live with what he'd done. He held himself up to the same standard of justice he wielded as a judge."

Darcie nodded. "It appears that way."

"Detective." Officer Becky Roach was standing at the library's open door.

"Find anything?"

Becky stepped inside the library. "It snowed more than six inches overnight. There are plenty of animal tracks in the fresh snow, but I didn't see anything else."

Sasha walked around to the front of the desk. "Did you check all the doors and windows?"

"I tried all the doors," Becky said, "and all were secure. I did a visual of all the windows, and I didn't see anything out of the ordinary."

"Did you see anything outside these two windows?"

"Nothing suspicious."

"Okay." Sasha nodded. "Thanks."

Sasha looked at Darcie. "I'm going to give dispatch a quick call and ask them if they've called the ME and CSI. Then let's go talk with Mr. Cummins."

"Sounds good."

As soon as Sasha finished his call, he turned to Darcie. "ME was waiting for us to give her the green light. CSI will follow her in."

"Could you stay posted at the door and only let the ME in when she arrives?" Darcie asked Becky. She turned to Sasha. "Is Juanita coming?"

"Yes."

Sasha started for the foyer. "Let's go talk with Mr. Cummins." His partner followed him out of the library.

Charlie Cummins was still sitting in the foyer and talking softly on his cell phone. When he saw the two detectives standing near him, he ended his call. "I was talking to my brother."

"Can we step into another room to ask you some questions?"

"Yes, Detective." Charlie led them into one of the front living rooms. They sat on a couch while Charlie sat on one of several wingback chairs.

"I know this is difficult," Sasha said, "but we have some gaps we need to fill, Mr. Cummins."

"I understand. I'll help you as much as I can."

Sasha nodded. "Thank you, sir. Could you walk me through what your father did over the last twenty-four hours or so?"

"Certainly." Charlie leaned forward in the chair. "My mother and sisters went to Chicago for the weekend. My sisters thought taking her to the city for a couple of dinners, some shopping, and to see the symphony would be good for her." He dropped his head and looked at the floor. "Ashley's murder has been hard on all of us, especially her grandmother. Ashley was her only granddaughter, and she meant a lot to both my parents."

"That's understandable."

"They were staying at a hotel downtown. My brother and his wife live in the same tower. They were planning on spending a lot of time together."

"Your father decided not to go along?"

"No." Charlie chuckled. "He called it a girls trip. My father didn't like going to Chicago, and he wasn't a big fan of the symphony like my mother is." Charlie leaned back in his chair and sighed.

Sasha nodded. "Please go on, sir."

"Oh, yes. I'm sorry. My mother and sisters and brother will be on their way back home soon."

"Were you aware your father was capable of doing something like this?"

Charlie leaned forward again. "Well, I would have sworn to you before this morning that it wouldn't be possible, but after reading the note, I don't know what I believe anymore."

"Just to be clear, do you believe that he could have orchestrated what he took responsibility for in his note?"

"I reread the note several times, Detective. There's no question it was written by his hand, so it's difficult to sit here now and say he couldn't have."

Darcie asked, "So there's no question that he wrote the note?"

"It's his handwriting."

"Do you have any idea who your father could have found to commit the murders he referred to in the note?"

Charlie shook his head. "When he was a judge, I sat in his courtroom just two times—on the tenth and twentieth anniversaries of him becoming a judge. All the family was in the courtroom to celebrate with him. Other than those two times, I didn't interact with his legal world. When he was a prosecutor, I never watched him in court. As I sit here telling you this, I wonder, what kind of a son does that make me?"

Sasha had spent hours listening and learning about what his dad did at the FBI, which had led him to law enforcement. Quite different from Charlie and his dad. "I understand what you're saying. So you have no idea how your father might go about finding someone to kill the men he mentions in his note?"

"Obviously, no."

"I'm sorry if I was indelicate, sir." In the back of his mind, Sasha was questioning whether Charlie might have had some knowledge of his father's actions. "Have you talked with your father since the house fire that killed the two young women on Wednesday morning?"

"I called him yesterday to see if he'd go to breakfast with me this morning. Dad said he'd look forward to it." Charlie dropped his head again and teared up.

"I'm sorry to ask you these questions, Mr. Cummins." Sasha looked at his partner and motioned for her to take over.

"Mr. Cummins." Darcie paused. "I understand that the past three weeks has brought a great deal of heartache to you and your family." Charlie nodded. She asked, "I have a few questions, sir. Did your father own the revolver in his lap?"

"Yes. That's the Ruger .357 he kept in his desk drawer."

Darcie wrote his answer down in her notepad. "Are there other guns in the house?"

"Yes. There's a gun safe with rifles, shotguns, and several handguns in an upstairs bedroom closet."

"I'd like to understand your father's state of mind in the past three weeks. Could you tell us about some of the conversations you and your father have had during that time?" Darcie asked.

"I had to tell my mother and father about Ashley's murder shortly after you told me. It was one of the hardest things I've ever had to do. Since then, we've probably talked more than we have in years. We talked every day. He was very unhappy with the lack of progress in finding Ashley's killer. I'm sure you know he called or met with the mayor and chief almost daily, wanting updates on the investigation."

Sasha nodded. "We are aware."

Charlie thought back to his father, talking with the mayor and chief. "Some days, he called them several times asking for updates. Dad was unhappy, and he let them know it."

"In his note, he takes responsibility for killing a number of men." Darcie paused to let that sink in. "Are you surprised by that admission?"

"Very much so, Detective. It crosses a line I wouldn't have thought he'd cross. Dad ruled his courtroom with an iron fist, enforcing laws and doling out sentences for the past twenty-five years. It's difficult for me to see him so blatantly violating the law he revered by killing men not given a chance to defend themselves." Charlie leaned back again in his chair. "I also have difficulty believing that he could have committed suicide, but the evidence and the facts clearly show that he did."

"You don't believe he could have shot himself?" Darcie asked.

"I'm saying I'm shocked that he could have, that he would. He believes— he *believed* in God." Charlie paused to try to get control of his emotions. "I can see how he could get drawn in, get blinded by anger, and seek revenge on anyone who might have murdered Ashley. He often talked about the important role of the courts, the importance of his role in keeping the public safe from criminals." Charlie looked at Darcie. "If he did what he said, then the deaths of the two women would have haunted him forever."

Sasha glanced at Darcie, then looked at Charlie and asked, "So he was capable of shooting himself?"

Charlie shrugged. "It would appear so." He then dropped his head into his hands.

Sasha gave Charlie a minute to compose himself before continuing. "How do you think he could have accomplished the killing of all these people?"

"I already told you I have no idea, Detective." Charlie paused. "As a judge, he came into contact with all kinds of bad people."

Sasha's cell phone buzzed. "Excuse me for a moment." He stood up and walked into the foyer. A moment later, he returned. "Sorry about that. The ME will be arriving shortly." Charlie nodded. "I just have one more question. After finding your father this morning and reading the note he left, do you believe that he is responsible for arranging the killings before committing suicide?"

Charlie looked up at Sasha and let out a heavy sigh. "Based on what I've seen, yes."

"Thank you, Mr. Cummins. If we have further questions, can we give you a call?"

"Certainly."

Sasha nodded. "As I mentioned, the ME will be arriving shortly as well as the Crime Scene Investigation team."

"Okay."

Darcie moved closer to Charlie. "I'm sorry, but we're going to have to ask you to leave the scene until we've finished our investigation, Mr. Cummins."

"Yes. Of course. I understand, Detective." Charlie walked out into the foyer, picked up his coat from a chair, and walked out the door.

33

Medical Examiner Juanita Gordon was waiting in the room across from the foyer where Sasha and Darcie were talking to Charlie Cummins. She wanted to talk with them before she and her team started their work.

After ending their meeting with Charlie Cummins, the two followed him into the foyer and waved to Juanita as they watched him walk out the front door.

"Morning." Juanita looked around the house. "Looks like you've got a lot going on today."

"Yeah." Sasha looked at his watch. "How's Beff doing?"

"She's doing well. Bonding with the new baby."

"You want to follow me to the library? I can tell you what we know so far."

"Sounds good." Juanita motioned for her team, who were standing behind her, to follow. "This is a very nice house."

Sasha stopped just short of the library and turned around. "This is the biggest house I've ever seen. Two living rooms at the front of the house. You won't believe the library." He turned, and Juanita and Darcie followed him.

Juanita looked at the body slumped in the desk chair. "So that's Judge Cummins?"

"Indeed, it is." Sasha walked in and stopped short of the desk. "The judge shot himself in the right temple with a .357. You can see the damage all over this side of the room." The detective waved his arm toward the bookshelves.

Juanita followed him. She looked at the floor in front of the desk to make sure there was no blood spatter, then at the body. "He sure made a mess of himself."

"Yes, he did." Sasha turned to Juanita. "He left a note, too."

"What's it say?"

"Take a look." Sasha pointed at the note lying on the desk in front of the judge's body.

The ME walked past the two detectives and around the back of the desk. She scanned the area to make sure that she wasn't disturbing the crime scene, then leaned over and read the note. She looked up at the two detectives after reading it. "Oh, my."

Darcie nodded. "Yep."

Before they entered the house, Juanita and her team had put on the protective gear they wore at crime scenes. She pulled on a pair of latex gloves, pulled down her mask, then took the flashlight out of her pocket. She first focused on the entry wound on the judge's right temple. "Based on the stippling pattern on his skin, the gun barrel was held no more than an inch away."

"So after he shot himself, the gun just dropped into his lap?"

Juanita looked at the gun and nodded. "He would have died instantly. Muscle control, muscle response with an instantaneous death could have resulted in either immediate relaxation or constriction of muscles controlling his right hand. The evidence would suggest immediate relaxation with the gun falling from his hand onto his lap."

"You don't see anything that would suggest something other than what we're seeing?" Sasha asked.

"Well, I've only been observing the scene for a couple of minutes, but it appears to be a self-inflicted gunshot wound to me." She shined the beam from her flashlight onto the judge's chest. "We'll test clothing for GSR as the gun fell from his hand, and it could have come in contact with his sweater, leaving evidence." The ME moved slowly around the back of the chair, focusing her flashlight on the floor, checking for spatter. She shined the light on the massive wound on the left side of the judge's head. "Isn't it amazing the brutal force a bullet inflicts on the human body?"

It occurred to Sasha that the ME might be looking forward to this investigation. "You seemed pumped."

She looked over at Sasha. "Sorry. A suicide like this isn't something I see very often in Bloomington." Juanita smiled sheepishly. "I feel like I hit the lottery."

Darcie knew how the ME felt and what she meant. "I get it."

"Me too. It wasn't a criticism, Juanita. It was just an observation."

The ME nodded. "We're going to get started, so I need to ask you both to leave the room, please."

"No problem. We're going to look around the house. If you find anything interesting, you'll let us know?"

"Yes, I will."

The detectives turned and walked out into the hallway. "I think you and I should nose around the entire house."

"Sounds good. What do you want me to focus on?"

Sasha looked down the hallway to the back of the house. "You start at the back, and I'll start at the front." He looked at Juanita, talking to her team in the library. "Check out the entire house. Top to bottom. If we get two pairs of eyes on everything, we'll be sure not to miss anything. This suicide is going to be a high-profile investigation, so we'll need to make sure we do everything right and don't miss anything."

"Understood." Darcie looked toward the front of the house. "Chief's arrived."

Sasha turned and looked toward the foyer. The chief was talking with a couple of the uniformed officers keeping watch. "Not unexpected." He gave the chief a casual salute, then looked at his partner. "You start back here. I'll talk with the chief."

The chief saw Sasha walking toward him in the hallway. "Morning, Detective."

"Chief." They shook hands. "Glad you came over."

The chief smiled to himself as he doubted his detective meant that. "Walk me through what you've found so far."

"Let's talk in the living room." Sasha led the way into the living room where he'd met with Charlie Cummins earlier. "You want the short or long version?"

"Short now. Long later."

Sasha nodded and proceeded to tell the chief what they had learned. When he finished, the chief asked him, "Did you take the picture of the note that was texted to me?"

"No. That was Tim Darby."

The chief looked over to the foyer where Darby was standing and called him over.

"You took a picture of the note the judge left?"

"Yes."

"Delete it. Now."

"Sure." Darby pulled out his cell phone and deleted it from his phone.

"Delete the text as well." The chief watched as Darby opened the texts on his cell phone. "Thanks, Darby. I just want to keep control over the note. I'm not suggesting anything by asking you to delete it."

"I understand. Dispatch asked me to take a picture and send it, so I did."

"Not a problem."

"Before you ask, neither Darcie nor I have a copy of that picture." Sasha understood why the chief wanted to keep the exact contents of the suicide note private.

The chief nodded. After Darby walked away, he asked Sasha, "So what are you thinking?"

"I'm very shocked and surprised that the judge was involved." Sasha looked down the hallway toward the library. "But the evidence paints a different picture."

"The judge was one of the first people I met when I took the job. When I talked with him, there was no mistaking that he was a strong law-and-order advocate."

Sasha looked around the room they were standing. "No question about that."

The chief lowered his voice. "Just keep following the evidence in each of your investigations. The judge's involvement will certainly be a distraction, but keep your head down, stay on task, and wrap them up as soon as you can." Sasha nodded. "It seems that the judge wrapped it all up in a bow for you."

"Well, we still don't know positively who killed his granddaughter."

The chief looked at his senior detective and nodded. "True."

"Juanita and her team are in the library now, but do you want to see the scene, Chief?"

"Yes. If I could have a quick look, that would be great, but I don't want to get in the ME's way."

"That won't be a problem. You can see everything from the hallway."

The chief nodded. "Okay. Let's take a quick look, and then I'll get out of here. I have to meet with the mayor."

Sasha led the chief down the hallway to the library. They stood in the doorway and watched the team from the ME's office go about collecting evidence.

The chief quickly scanned the room, and Sasha looked it over again as well. The library appeared to be at least eighteen to maybe twenty feet wide and well over twenty-four feet from the doors to the far wall. Bookshelves lined the walls except for an area behind the desk. On that wall was a large painting of the judge sitting in a chair wearing his black robe. Like the ceilings in the rest of the house, these had to be at least twelve feet high. The shelves were full of books, pictures, and mementos accumulated over a lifetime.

"Where did he leave the note?" the chief asked.

"On the desk in front of him. His son confirmed his father wrote it."

"What about the gun?"

"Identified as one the judge kept in a desk drawer. Ruger .357 short barrel."

The chief looked around the room. "This is a big house." Sasha nodded his agreement. "Okay. I'm going to head out. Keep me informed, okay?"

"Will do, Chief." Sasha watched the chief walk down the hallway before stepping a few feet into the room in hopes of getting Juanita's attention.

She was standing beside the desk when she noticed movement in the room. "Need something, Sasha?"

He took a couple of steps into the room. "How's it going?"

Juanita watched two members of her team photographing the desk, floor, and bookshelves. "We're close to being done taking pictures. Next, we'll start gathering the physical evidence."

"Have you done anything more with the body yet?"

"No. We have to collect blood, bone, and brain matter before we tackle the body." She looked around the room. "Best guess would be a couple more hours."

Sasha watched as the ME techs finished taking pictures of the scene. "Find anything interesting so far?"

"Nothing specific, but everything about this investigation is intriguing."

"Intriguing how?"

"This all started with the killing of a young woman. Now you have a lot of men that were considered suspects either dead or missing. Then a couple of days ago, two innocent young women were killed. Now the judge here leaves a note stating that he was responsible for all those deaths and commits suicide."

"If what you mean is that after three weeks it's curious that so many cases seem to have been solved with a single gunshot, I'll agree with you. The judge secured help from someone to carry out what he's taken responsibility for initiating. We still need to find Ashley's killer and find out who did the killing for the judge."

"It just amazes me how all the cases are so intertwined."

"Yes, they are," Sasha said. "I'm going to be around the house for a while if you need me." He left the library and started his search of the big house.

———

Darcie had finished her search of the house and was sitting on a couch in the living room where they'd talked with Charlie Cummins when Sasha walked in and sat down across from her. "Find anything?"

"Not really. There are a lot of pictures in this house." Sasha glanced around the living room. "Don't forget we need to get the combination to the gun safe just to check it out."

Darcie added that to her notebook. "What are you thinking, Sasha?"

"Two days ago, we learned our list of suspects got out. Today, we get confirmation Judge Cummins was responsible for the deaths of most of the men on our list. First thing is we've got to find who killed for him." Sasha leaned back into the couch and looked at his partner. "Everything changed today."

34

When Juanita and her team had finished with their work at the Cummins' home, she told Sasha that she would give him a call after she'd completed her autopsy. There wasn't anything Sasha and Darcie needed to do at the house, so they went to lunch before heading back to the conference room to sift through the interviews and evidence they'd collected.

After the two detectives had been working in the conference room for an hour, Sasha's phone rang. He could see it was the ME. "Sasha Frank."

"Hi, Sasha. I just finished the judge's autopsy." Juanita paused as she finished pulling up the details on her computer. Sasha put his phone on speaker. "Sorry if I'm restating things you may know, but I'm just going to briefly download information. The judge had an entry wound located at his right temple. The size and shape of the entry wound is consistent with a .357 bullet. The immediate damage to the skull from the bullet is comparable to the cracking exhibited in an egg's shell when it's dropped onto a hard surface. After traveling through the brain, the bullet exited the left side of the judge's skull. The skull shattered, exploding brain, blood, and bone fragments. Death was instantaneous. Any questions or comments?"

Sasha looked at Darcie, and she shook her head. "None here."

"The judge was a seventy-two-year-old male. He was 5' 10" and weighed 141 pounds. During the autopsy, I discovered that he had cancer."

Darcie mouthed, "Cancer?"

"He had Stage IV stomach and pancreatic cancer. Those cancers spread to other vital organs."

"Any idea how long he had to live?"

Juanita thought about Sasha's question for a moment. "The short answer is that I'm unable to say with specificity as I haven't spoken to a family member to ask about his doctor's diagnosis or prognosis. I would estimate that the judge had no more than a month to live. Two, tops."

"We have to assume that he knew he had cancer. Knowing that he only had a short time to live may have led him to believe he had nothing to lose in seeking revenge for his granddaughter's murder." Sasha looked at Darcie. "What do you think, Darcie?"

"If a family member of mine was shot and killed, and if I knew that I was going to die in a few months, I might do what he did."

Sasha didn't think he could do what the judge did, but you never know what you'd do when confronted with that reality. "Anything else that was interesting?"

"If you recall, one of the first things we did when we arrived at the scene was to test for gunshot residue, and we did find GSR on the judge's right hand. I learned from CSI at the scene that his fingerprints were already in the system. Regardless, I also took a complete set of prints during the autopsy."

Darcie leaned forward in her chair to get closer to the phone. "Did you find any drugs in his system?"

"We took blood samples. The tests won't be back until Monday at the earliest, so I can't answer that question, Darcie. His stomach contents contained partially digested food, but nothing relevant to his death, in my opinion. We did not find any bullet or bullet fragments during the autopsy. I assume that CSI did after we left, but you might know something about that. That's about it, folks. I didn't find anything inconsistent with suicide."

"Okay, Juanita. Thanks for the information." Sasha ended the call and turned to his partner. "Would you agree that if the judge hadn't written the note before committing suicide, we wouldn't be any closer to solving all the other cases?"

Darcie gave her partner a puzzled look. The answer to Sasha's question seemed obvious. "If he hadn't left a note, none of our investigations were close to being solved. Solved only means that the judge admitted his involvement."

"Okay. So the note the judge left points to the deaths of the two innocent women as the trigger for his committing suicide. Charlie Cummins said that his father's mental state hadn't changed." Sasha stood up. "We need to go see Charlie Cummins yet again."

"About what?"

"We need to find out if he knew his father had cancer."

"I think we need to give him a couple of days, Sasha. He's going to be pretty busy with family obligations right now."

Sasha sat back down and thought for a minute. Darcie was right. "It can wait until the first part of the week."

Darcie nodded. "I don't think there's anything else we can do here today. How about heading home for what's left of the weekend?"

"Good idea." Sasha needed to take a couple of days just to think. He looked at his watch. It was 4:35 p.m. "Let's step back until Monday morning. Then we'll get back to it."

Darcie stood up. "I'm all for that."

35

R.J. Carlson walked into the conference room shortly after 9 a.m. on Monday morning. "How's it going, guys?"

Sasha looked up. "It's going. How was your weekend?"

"My girlfriend and I spent it in Chicago. It was great. We stayed downtown in River North, went to some great restaurants, and hit a couple of clubs."

"Sounds nice." Sasha looked at Darcie.

Darcie looked up at R.J. "You want to take a seat?"

"Sure." The detective sat down. "What's up?"

"I'm not sure what you know about what's happened in our investigation since you were away." Darcie looked at Sasha before looking back at R.J.

"Nothing really."

Sasha looked up from his notepad. "Five on our list are dead. Two are missing, and we're still looking for Big G. The families of the missing have no idea where they are. It's like they've dropped off the face of the earth."

R.J. sat across from them and said nothing.

Sasha leaned forward in his chair. "So we've got several questions, R.J." He pointed at the whiteboard. "Question number one is who did you talk to about the list you wrote on the board?"

"What do you mean who did I talk to?" R.J. shifted in his chair.

"I mean other than Darcie and me, who'd you talk with about the list?" Sasha paused. "You know, any other detectives or dispatchers, uniformed police officers? Who other than us?"

"I don't think I talked to anyone around the station about the list."

"Just so we're clear, we've asked the same question of dispatchers, detectives, even the chief and the mayor." Sasha looked at Darcie. "Am I missing anyone?"

"Nope. That's it."

"Like I just said, Sasha, I don't think I talked to anyone in the station about the list."

"Okay. We'll mark you down as telling no one outside of our group about the list."

"Right." R.J. stood up visibly upset. "Is that all you needed?"

Sasha leaned back in his chair. "It was. Thanks." R.J. turned and walked out of the conference room.

"What do you think?"

Sasha looked at Darcie. "If none of us told anyone about the list, then somebody walked by the room and saw the names."

"If that's what happened, we'll never know who gave them to the judge."

"We know that the judge got his hands on it, so maybe his son could shed some light on the how." Sasha got out his cell phone. "I don't want to wait any longer to talk with Charlie Cummins. We need to find out what he may know."

Darcie watched as Sasha called the judge's son. She had already voiced her view that they should wait to talk with him.

Sasha ended the call and said, "He's at home now and has an appointment at a funeral home at 10 a.m. before he heads over to his parents' house to be with his mother and family." The senior detective stood up and looked at his watch. "He said we could come over now and talk with him." Sasha grabbed his jacket and headed for his car in the parking lot.

Darcie watched as her partner left the room. She shook her head and followed him to his car for the ride over to Stonebrook Court.

———

Although it was just above freezing outside, Charlie Cummins was standing outside smoking a cigarette. He walked over to greet them as they got out of the car. "Good morning, Detectives. What questions do you have for me?"

Sasha reached out to shake hands. "We're very sorry to bother you at this time, Mr. Cummins. Thank you for agreeing to meet with us."

"It's not a problem." Charlie shook hands with Darcie. "I'm happy to help in any way I can."

"We just have a few questions, sir."

Charlie nodded his head and threw his cigarette into the front yard. "Go ahead."

"I'm sure you must have given some thought to who your father may have been working with to kill the men we considered suspects in your daughter's death."

"I have, but I haven't been able to come up with anyone." Charlie shook his head. "Quite frankly, I'm still having a hard time believing that Dad committed suicide."

"Your father left a note taking responsibility."

"I understand that, Detective. Last Saturday, I said that suicide wasn't acceptable to my dad, so I'm struggling with that. You also have to know that taking part in killing those men—" Charlie paused. "It just wasn't who my dad was. He firmly believed in the rule of law and the police's and court's roles in doling out justice."

Sasha was beginning to agree with Darcie. He understood Mr. Cummins couldn't help them get into his father's head to comprehend how the judge rationalized the killing of five men and two innocent women before committing suicide. "I understand, but is there no one your father might have turned to for help?"

"For the entirety of his career, my dad's world intersected with police, prosecutors, attorneys, judges, and the criminals that they revolved around." Charlie lit another cigarette. The stress of the past month had caused him to go back to a habit he'd kicked almost twenty-two years ago. "I would guess that Dad would have had to have sought help from one of those on the good-guy side, because I'm finding it hard to believe that Dad knew a single bad guy well enough to ask them to carry out the killings."

Darcie looked at Sasha. She didn't understand pressing Charlie Cummins when it was apparent he didn't know anything that could directly help in their investigations. "There's no one you can point us to right now that you think could have helped your father?"

"No. I'm sorry, but I can't help you, Detective."

She nodded. "Do you know of anyone your father has spent a lot of time with lately? Perhaps you could ask your mother?"

"Until Ashley's death, I spoke or saw my dad maybe once or twice a week. Over the past three weeks or so, I've either seen or touched base with both him and mom several times a day." Charlie thought for a few seconds. "Other than at Ashley's visitation and funeral, I don't recall seeing or hearing my dad talk with anyone specific."

Charlie lit another cigarette from the one he was finishing. "I wished I could be more help."

"We appreciate it. If you have the chance to ask your mother about your father meeting or talking with anyone more than usual lately, we would be interested in hearing what she might know."

"I will, but I'd rather not say anything to her that could upset her as she prepares to bury her husband." Charlie voice was trembling. "Surely, you understand that while my daughter's killer remains free, it's difficult to ask my family to help you find anyone that might be involved with killing men you believe could be responsible for her death."

The senior detective was under no illusion that they'd provided the Cummins family with the closure they desperately needed. He realized that he may have crossed a line with Charlie. "I'm deeply sorry, Mr. Cummins. Please accept my apology for my insensitivity."

"Thank you, Detective."

Sasha handed Charlie a manila envelope he had brought with him. "I wanted to give you several photos taken in your father's library during our investigation. The photos are of the note he left, as well as the top of the desk." He paused. "There is blood splatter in the photos, but I wanted you to have them as we won't be able to return the note and some of the evidence to you or your family."

Charlie nodded but did not speak. The two men shook hands, then Darcie reached out and shook hands with Charlie. She told him her thoughts were with him and his family.

The two detectives got into their car. "You were right, and I was wrong, Darcie." Sasha pulled back onto Stonebrook Court for the quick drive back to the station.

"The man is hurting, Sasha. Losing his daughter and his father in three weeks can't be easy." Darcie looked over at Sasha. "I'm not giving up, but I don't know how we're ever going to solve the case of who killed Ashley."

"In my gut, I believe those responsible are already dead." Sasha turned left onto Veterans Parkway to return to the station.

36

After the two returned to the station, Darcie began poring over each piece of information they had gathered during their investigation into Ashley Cummins's death, looking for any clue they might have missed that would lead them to her killer.

At the same time, Sasha began looking at evidence and other information they had pieced together on the deaths of the men on their list. They were at a standstill with both the hit-and-run and the fire investigations. There were no witnesses who could ID anyone, and they had zero leads on the year, make, or model of the vehicle that had run Wolenski down. Officers working with them had been searching for video camera footage in the immediate area in the hope of finding the vehicle involved in the hit-and-run, but nothing had been found. The Chicago PD informed Sasha that images were found showing the two men speeding away from the fire that killed Milcen and the two young women, but they'd lost track of the vehicle when it had headed south from the city. Both occupants were wearing balaclavas, so they'd hit another dead end.

The Bloomington and Normal Police Departments had also searched the area for camera footage of the car while it had been in Bloomington. Although they'd found footage, they'd lost track of the vehicle once it had headed east on Route 9 and out of the city.

"Did anything come back from NIBIN on the bullets recovered from Milcen?" Sasha asked his partner.

"I told you, there were no hits." Darcie went back to searching her files.

Sasha shook his head, remembering that Darcie had told him there was no match for the bullet that had killed Milcen. He was beginning to think he was losing his mind. His cell phone rang. "Frank. Yes. Yes. Okay, Mr. Cummins. We'll be right over." He looked over at Darcie. "The Cummins family wants to talk with us. They're all at the house on East Washington."

"What do they want to talk about?"

"Charlie said they have new information they thought we needed to hear." He got up. "He didn't offer any specifics. Let's go."

———

When Sasha and Darcie arrived at the Cummins' home on East Washington, the judge's widow and her four children were waiting for them in a living room. Once introductions were made and everyone was seated, Charlie Cummins spoke for the family. "First, we'd like to say we appreciate you giving us time to grieve our loss." He looked at his mother. "I'll get right to it. None of us were aware that our father had cancer. We were told that the ME discovered that during the autopsy, and Mom had a call with his doctor this morning. The doctor discovered he had cancer while running routine tests in mid-January for his annual physical."

"The family didn't know?" Sasha asked.

Charlie shook his head. "He hadn't told Mom or any of us anything about the diagnosis. His doctor said he might have had only a few weeks or a month to live."

Marjorie Cummins, the judge's wife, added, "The doctor said the cancer was causing him a great deal of pain. I knew that something was wrong, but he wouldn't tell me what was going on. He wasn't a complainer."

"We believe this explains the actions he took," Charlie said. "Please know that we're not suggesting in any way that a cancer diagnosis gave him the right to do what he did." All of the Cummins family nodded in agreement.

Sasha nodded. "Obviously."

Charlie continued, "We have all looked at the photos you gave me this morning." He looked over at his sister Deborah. "Deborah pointed out that both the note and pen looked oddly placed on the desk."

"Oddly placed?" Sasha asked.

Charlie motioned for his sister to explain. "Dad was left-handed, and the paper was positioned on the desktop as though he were right-handed." She reached down and picked up the manila envelope holding the pictures, pulled out one of them, and handed it to Sasha. "The paper was lying opposite the angle Dad would have written it as a left-hander. If you look closely, the pen is also lying at the wrong angle."

Darcie mentally imagined positioning a piece of paper and pen as Deborah had described. Sasha looked at the picture, then at Darcie, who nodded. He then he turned back to Deborah. "We understand what you're saying, but what do you think that means?"

"We're not suggesting that the note wasn't written and signed by Dad's hand. His handwriting style was unique. Regardless of the circumstances of why he wrote the note, we believe he purposely positioned it and the pen that way."

"With Deborah questioning the note and the pen, I started thinking about the gun," Charlie said.

"Thinking what about the gun? You're questioning whether he shot the gun?" Sasha didn't want to be insensitive, but GSR tests performed at the scene and during the autopsy by the ME's office confirmed that the judge had recently fired a gun. His fingerprints were on the gun, and the striations on the bullet removed from a book on the library shelves matched. "What are you saying?"

"I'm not sure if you are aware, but my dad had a concealed carry permit. He was around guns his whole life and was proficient in their use." Charlie paused. "As Deborah noted, Dad was left-handed, and he would have never used his right hand to shoot."

"Okay. What are you thinking happened here?"

Marjorie leaned forward in the couch. "We believe the judge was leaving us a message."

The two detectives glanced at each other. "A message?" Sasha asked. "What kind of a message?"

"My husband was a man with a lot of habits. We're convinced he would never have positioned the note and paper the way he did, and he would have never used his right hand to shoot a gun. If you don't believe us, then talk with his friends, former law partners, clerks, and staff, and ask them what they think about these inconsistencies."

"We will certainly look into what you're suggesting," Sasha said, "but—"

"There's more, Detective," Charlie said. "When Mom was reading the note this morning, she"—he looked at his mother—"she immediately saw that 'granddaughter' was misspelled in the note."

"Misspelled?" Sasha asked. Ten to fifteen people must have read that note, and no one had picked up the spelling error.

"Dad's penmanship wasn't the easiest to read, and Mom is the one who knew his writing the best. When she read the note, she told us with Ashley being his only granddaughter, he would most certainly know how to spell what was dearest to him. We believe that this is another message left by Dad."

Sasha stood up. "Detective Lyman and I are going to step into the foyer for a minute." Darcie got up, and the two walked into the foyer.

"What are you thinking?" Darcie asked.

"My mind is whirling. The family has certainly convinced themselves that he sent them unmistakable messages that something was amiss."

Darcie nodded. "You can't get around that he took responsibility for killing all these people, which seems pretty amiss to me."

"Yes, the family sees inconsistencies in the pictures and believes the judge was under duress that evening."

"Think about what they're saying, Sasha. It seems like they're reaching a bit."

"Maybe, but I see what they mean. We're both right-handed. Whenever we write something down on paper, we tilt the paper a little to the left. When you or I finish writing, we naturally put the pen down on the right side of the paper. We'd never finish writing and reach across the paper and place the pen on the other side." Sasha looked at his partner. "Right?"

Darcie wasn't convinced. "So he was telling his family he didn't want to do this?"

"Maybe. I'm just saying it's possible."

Darcie was struggling with the thought that the judge was sending a message. "How? How could somebody make the judge do that? He was going to die in a few weeks anyway. There needs to be a quid pro quo. What's the judge get for offing himself?"

Sasha sat, looking at his partner. Darcie was right. The judge wrote a suicide note, then shot himself. There was no evidence that someone had physically forced him to write the note or put a gun to his head. "I don't know. It's just a theory." He motioned to her for them to return to the living room, where they remained standing. Sasha addressed the family. "We're going to look into everything you've told us today." He looked at Charlie. "We will reach back out to you if we have more questions, Mr. Cummins."

"Thank you for listening to us, Detectives." Charlie looked at his mother, then stood up. "I can't tell you how much we all appreciate it. We're obviously convinced that Dad did not willingly commit suicide."

The two detectives finished saying their goodbyes and left the Cummins' home. As they drove back toward the station, they continued discussing the possibilities that the judge was not involved at all in the deaths of the men on their list. It seemed inconceivable that someone had somehow compelled him to take responsibility by writing a note and shooting himself, thereby taking the fall to divert attention away from others involved.

Darcie studied her partner as he drove. "I know you're noodling on something. What is it?"

Sasha smiled. "You know how someone can look at a problem that you're too close to, and from a different point of view, give you a completely different perspective that turns your whole world upside down?"

"Yeah."

"The Cummins family just did that. Something's not right, and we need to figure it out." He made a turn off Washington and headed south on Clinton. "Let's get some lunch."

37

Sasha decided to stop for lunch at his favorite restaurant and requested seats in a corner booth in the bar away from other patrons. The first time he'd taken Darcie to the place on East Grove Street in Bloomington and ordered the King Tenderloin, she'd thought it odd that he had ordered extra buns. She saw why he'd done so when their meals had arrived. The tenderloin had been pounded flat before being battered and fried. It was close to twelve inches in diameter and no more than a half-inch think. She could see why one hamburger bun wouldn't suffice. Somehow Sasha was always able to finish it. Since that first visit, Darcie always ordered the Mound of Beef on a French roll with a side of au jus.

After they ordered, Sasha told her they were going to have a "Just Practicing" discussion. He had a baseball cap Janet had made special for him with "Just Practicing" embossed on it, which sat on his desk at the station. There were two rules everyone had to follow while just practicing. First, you could say anything you wanted since you were just practicing, and second, no one could ridicule what you said. It was great for Darcie because she was still learning how to be a detective, and for anyone participating, it offered opportunities to suggest what could be considered an unconventional idea and have it openly discussed and debated without recrimination. Sometimes participants would include the federal or state alphabet soup agents from the FBI, IBI, or the DEA. Several had included the district attorney, judges, and even a few friends of her partner who were defense attorneys. As a young detective, she had learned a lot during these sessions.

After about ten minutes of them throwing out ideas, Darcie said, "I'm just practicing, but why don't we conduct another search of the Cummins' home on East Washington?" She paused for a few seconds. "A more robust and thorough search."

"To what end?" Sasha asked.

"You and I both looked around, and so did Becky, but I for one didn't go through the house like we did searching Ashley's room or the rest of Charlie Cummins's house." She paused for a moment. "I doubt you did, either. We were being respectful because the judge had committed suicide. I'm talking about tossing it like we would someone we were investigating for committing a crime. Maybe we missed something."

Sasha looked at his partner and smiled to himself thinking that she was becoming a really good detective. "I like the idea." Their food was delivered, and they continued discussing how they'd proceed as they ate. They agreed to call Charlie Cummins after they finished their lunch to ask if his mother would be okay with them returning to the home for a more thorough inspection.

Before making their call, they decided not to involve the CSI team. They could do a more thorough job on their own, and it would be less intrusive if it were just the two of them. They called Charlie, and he called his mother, who agreed to another search that afternoon.

They pulled into the driveway and parked next to Charlie's Mercedes, got out of their car, and walked up the sidewalk to the open front door. Charlie Cummins was standing there to greet them. His mother was behind him in the foyer. Charlie asked, "What are you looking for, Detectives?"

"We're not sure." Sasha looked at his partner. "Detective Lyman has a hunch that we may have missed something after listening to what you and your family told us this morning. We just wanted to take another look."

Charlie let them in. "Well, I think Mom and I are going to go over to the funeral home for a while to see Dad and leave the house to you."

"Sounds good, sir," Sasha said. "We can text you when we're done."

"That would be fine." Marjorie and Charlie Cummins put on their coats and walked out the front door, leaving the two detectives to begin their search of the house.

"Ready?" Darcie asked as she pulled on a pair of latex gloves.

Sasha glanced around the foyer, took his latex gloves from his jacket pocket and pulled them on, wondering what they were hoping to find. "Let's do it."

38

MARCH 5, 2013

I t was 9 p.m. when Charles Johns was spotted leaving the westside home of a friend. He'd been hiding out at the friend's home for several days. Police had gotten a tip earlier in the day that Johns had worn out his welcome and would be leaving soon. Undercover officers had discreetly followed Johns at a distance after he'd left the friend's house.

Once they had confirmation that officers had eyes on Johns, dispatch called and alerted Sasha that plainclothes officers had Big G under surveillance. Sasha and Janet were at home watching a men's basketball game between Northern Iowa and Illinois State University, his alma mater, that they'd recorded the previous Saturday, when his cell phone rang. The game wasn't that interesting; he already knew that his team had lost. "Tell them not to let him out of their sight," Sasha told dispatch. "I'll stay on the line with you to see where he's heading."

The senior detective was sitting silently, listening to the chatter between the surveillance teams and the dispatcher as they followed Johns. It took about five minutes for Johns to make the drive to his home, park, and go inside. "Now that he's inside," Sasha said, "make sure we've got the house totally covered twenty-four, seven." He listened to what the dispatcher had to say, then ended the call.

"Sounds like he resurfaced?" Janet asked.

"He went home. Now we just have to wait for someone to try to make a move on him." Sasha and Darcie had expected that Johns would either head to his house or maybe try to drive to Chicago. Either way, they were prepared as arrangements had been made with county, state, and federal law enforcement agencies to help keep Johns under surveillance if he should leave Bloomington. Now they just needed to be patient, sit back, and wait.

———

Timothy Darby and another plainclothes officer were parked in a vehicle disguised as a cable company repair van in the alley behind the house that Charles Johns had returned to hours earlier. There was just enough light from a streetlamp at the end of the alley to offer them a good view of the back of the house through the one-way glass installed on the side of the van. The two had been alerted earlier by the undercover team sitting in an unmarked car on a side street. They were catty-corner to where Johns had parked out front and could see the front door he had just entered.

A light was turned on inside the house. The two officers in the van could see Johns through a window, and he appeared to be standing in the kitchen over the sink. Darby let the officers in front know they had eyes on Johns. The surveillance teams were in place, allowing them to keep watch on all sides of the home.

It was almost midnight when the officers in front reported a man slowly walking back and forth on the sidewalk across the street from Johns's house. "What do you think this guy's up to?" Timothy Darby whispered to his partner, who just shook his head. Another team radioed reporting that a second man was now entering the alley from the east. "We see him," Darby replied softly.

The man in the alley stopped briefly and looked toward Johns's house, then continued down the alley toward the undercover van. The man turned before he reached their van and walked into Johns's backyard. He stopped under the shadow of a tree until the kitchen light went off, then walked onto the back steps of the house. Darby radioed dispatch, "The man at the back of the house may try to enter Johns's house through the back door."

Dispatch told Darby that Sasha Frank was on his way, and that if it appeared someone was breaking into Johns's house, they needed to stop them before they got inside. Johns was to be kept safe and unharmed at all costs.

Darby acknowledged the order and motioned to his partner that he was going to exit the side door of the van to take up a closer position. His partner followed him, taking a different path toward the back of the house.

Seconds later, the two detectives on watch out front alerted dispatch and the team watching at the back of the house that the man they had eyes on out front had walked across the street. The man was now attempting to hide behind bushes at the front of the house. Dispatch gave them the same order as Darby and his partner—protect Johns at all cost.

Darby was slowly approaching the man standing on the back steps of the house from the east while his partner was doing the same from the west. They both stopped when they got within twenty or so feet.

It appeared as though the man standing outside was attempting to pick the back door lock. Darby and his partner heard dispatch order the team out front to count down from thirty, then apprehend and arrest the man hiding in the bushes at the front of the house. Dispatch then ordered the team at the back to use the same countdown and arrest the man at the back door simultaneously.

When the countdown reached zero, the two teams quickly converged on both men with their guns drawn. Darby got to the man in back first and pushed him off the small porch and pinned him to the ground with his knee in the man's back. His partner quickly handcuffed him. The team at the front of the house had cornered their man hiding behind the bushes and had ordered him to lie spread-eagle on the ground, where they handcuffed him. Both men were found to be armed with 9mm automatic handguns and knives. They were also each carrying cell phones.

Sasha Frank was a few blocks from the scene when dispatch informed him that the two men had been arrested. The senior detective told dispatch to keep the two separated. He wanted to make sure they weren't able to communicate. When Sasha pulled up in front of Johns's house, additional uniformed officers and cruisers were already on scene and had taken up positions in the alley and the streets surrounding the block.

The senior detective got out of his vehicle as his partner pulled up and parked behind him. He stopped and waited for her. "I'll take the guy in front, and you take the guy out back."

"Sounds good," Darcie replied, heading behind the house.

Sasha walked up to the two plainclothes officers standing over the hand-cuffed man in the front yard. With a big smile, he asked, "What did you catch for me this evening?"

"Somebody's been messin' where they shouldn't have been, Detective," said one of the officers. Sasha laughed. "We took those off him." The other officer held up a 9mm and a large knife.

Sasha nodded. "I'm guessing he doesn't have a permit for that gun. Can you please put those into separate evidence bags and have one of the uni-forms get them over to CSI ASAP?" The officer holding the weapons nodded. "Okay. Let's get him up."

The two officers yanked the man to his feet. He was dressed in black, wearing boots, gloves, and a sock hat. Sasha pulled the flashlight from his jacket pocket, stepped up close, and shined the light in the man's face. "Out for a stroll this evening?"

Jaime closed his eyes and turned away from the light. He couldn't believe that he hadn't spotted the men who were obviously also watching the house waiting for Big G's return. Diego was going to be furious with him. He hoped Teo had managed to get away, but more likely, his accomplice was in hand-cuffs at the back of the house.

Usually Diego's lawyers would be able to get him out on bail, but this time it would be different. Jaime knew there was a chance that the police lab could find blood from the first man he'd killed on the knife that was now in an evidence bag. He had fired one gunshot at the man in the house they had set on fire. That gun had been put into another evidence bag. Teo had shot the man twice, and he was carrying that gun tonight. They hadn't planned on using their pistols then, but when he'd gone for his own gun, he'd given them no choice. Everything had gone wrong that night. The burner phone in his back pocket had the pictures he'd texted Diego of each of the dead men on the list. It was stupid not to have deleted them.

The man with the flashlight was holding his billfold. "I'm Senior Detective Sasha Frank. Mr. Guerra, you're under arrest." Sasha couldn't be sure that Guerra was even the man's name. He waited, but the man did not respond.

"I hate to bring up old news"—the detective was sure that the man had heard his rights many times—"but I'm going to read you your rights." Sasha recited the words everyone in law enforcement knew from memory, then asked if Jaime understood his rights. Jaime nodded.

"Would you like to answer some questions I have for you, Mr. Guerra?" Sasha asked.

He wasn't surprised that Jaime Guerra remained silent. Most people in his situation declined to talk and requested a lawyer. He saw Darcie at the corner of the house, and he walked over to her. "How's it going back here?"

Darcie told him of her interaction with Mateo Bacerac, a twenty-eight-year-old with a Chicago address who had also declined her offer to talk. She held up an evidence bag containing another 9mm. "Darby told me he took this off the guy." She held up a second bag holding a lockpick. "And he was using this on the back door."

"Nice." Sasha smiled, then looked over his shoulder to where his guy was standing and told her what little he knew of Jaime Guerra. He was the same age, also had a Chicago address, and was also carrying a gun, along with a big knife.

"I'm ready to have Bacerac transported back to the station," Darcie said.

"Maybe he'll get friendlier after we get a chance to have CSI run the weapon." Sasha looked over at his guy. "I'll ask him again nicely to see if he's changed his mind about talking." Darcie laughed. "I've got his phone, too. That should be interesting."

Jaime saw the detective walking toward him. He had already decided to at least talk with him to see how he might improve his and Teo's chances. He could always ask for a lawyer.

Sasha returned to the front of the house, and Jaime told him, "I don't need a lawyer . . . yet."

Sasha smiled to himself. This was an unexpected twist. He mentally cat-alogued what they had found on the two men and immediately thought that this man must be carrying something CSI would find incriminating. As he stood looking at Guerra, he could tell that his lack of response to the man's offer to talk was getting the desired effect.

English was not Jaime's first language, but he spoke it well enough that the detective had to have understood him. "Did you hear me, man? I don't need a lawyer. I will talk with you."

"Okay. Let's get out of the cold and head back to the station. We can talk there." Sasha would need to get Andy Simon and his CSI team working what they took off the two men. He asked the two officers to transport Jaime to the station.

As he watched them walk Guerra to a police cruiser parked in the street, Sasha got out his cell phone. His first call would be to Andy. He would need CSI to start work immediately. Next, he'd call the ME to tell her he may need her to check on possible evidence in the lab tonight. Then he'd give the district attorney a call to alert him that if the conversation with Guerra got interesting, he may need to come in to hear exactly what the man had to say. Sasha also planned on arresting Charles Johns as a person of interest and putting him in protective custody. Since he had resurfaced tonight and the two men from Chicago were making an attempt to eliminate him, the safest place for Johns would be in jail. His last call would be to Janet to let her know that it was going to be a long night and not to wait up for him. Or at least that was his hope.

39

I t was almost two o'clock in the afternoon, and neither Sasha nor Darcie had left the station since their return last night from Charles Johns's home. They had made a lot of progress in the interconnected murder investigations since the arrests of the two Chicago gang members.

Guerra waived his rights to an attorney and had his first conversation with the DA just after midnight. That initial discussion allowed the DA to gain an understanding of their involvement in the deaths of the men on the list of suspects in Ashley Cummins's murder. In return, Guerra wanted to understand from the DA what he would be willing to offer for his and his partner's cooperation in providing evidence and testimony against the key players who had hired them.

Sasha had also been present. Although the gang member was a stone-cold killer, the senior detective was begrudgingly impressed with Guerra's understanding of criminal law and his ability to negotiate with the DA on sentencing recommendations, the protection they'd receive in prison, and even which prison he and Bacerac would be assigned to. The DA had been working on gaining approval from the court on the sentencing guidelines the two would receive for their full cooperation. He hoped to have final sign-off from a judge shortly.

R.J. had called the senior detective just after lunch and had asked to meet at two o'clock. Sasha was waiting for the vice unit detective in the conference room he and Darcie had been using since Ashley Cummins's murder. R.J. walked into the room and sat down. He looked at the senior detective and said, "Thank you for meeting with me, Sasha."

"No problem, R.J." Sasha wasn't sure why R.J. had requested they meet, but he assumed the vice detective wanted an update. "What's up?"

"I need to get something off my chest that I've neglected to tell you." R.J. looked down at the table. "I messed up."

In Sasha's mind, R.J. had messed up a number of times since Ashley had been killed, but he wasn't one to bring up old news. "How so, R.J.?"

"You asked me if I had talked with anyone outside our immediate circle about the list." R.J. paused. "I told you I had not."

Sasha looked R.J. in the eyes and waited. He wasn't going to say a word before R.J. did.

"That wasn't true."

The senior detective leaned back in his chair and sighed. "Who did you tell, R.J.?"

"John Lewisman."

40

Darcie pulled into the Downtown Bloomington garage just after 1 p.m. and found a place to park. She looked over at Sasha. "Ready?"

Sasha was deep in thought and did not answer. In his mind, he was going over the events since he and Darcie had met with the Cummins family three days ago. The family had seen inconsistences in the CSI photos of the judge's desk that Sasha had given to Charlie. Those inconsistences had led the two detectives to conduct a second search of the Cummins' home and garage and the judge's car, where they had discovered a cell phone hidden in the trunk. The phone had the judge's fingerprints on it and contained enough details to bring many of their investigations to conclusion. Sasha and Darcie had made great progress over the last several days.

"Sasha." Darcie tapped the senior detective on the arm. "You ready?"

The senior detective looked up from his notes. "Sorry. Yes, I'm ready."

The detectives got out of the car and walked toward the elevator.

Sasha hit the down button that would take them to the lobby, where they would go through security before taking another elevator up a few floors for the interview.

The detectives flashed their badges and weapons as they went through the lobby security screening. Darcie walked into an open elevator with Sasha right behind her, and the two rode in silence up to the sixth floor.

When the elevator door opened, they walked down the hallway to the last office on the right. Fifteen minutes ago, Sasha had called a friend who officed on the same floor to confirm that the person they wanted to talk to had returned from lunch. They stopped at the office and found the door open. The man they wanted to speak to was sitting behind his desk. Sasha stepped into the office first. "Good afternoon."

John Lewisman looked up from his work. "Hi, Detective. Detectives." He looked down at the calendar sitting on his desk before asking, "Did we have a meeting scheduled?"

"No, we didn't, but we wanted to stop by and ask you some questions, if you have some free time." Sasha sat in one of the chairs in front of the desk. Darcie had followed him but remained standing to his side.

He leaned back in his chair. "Okay. What's up?"

"I'm sure you're aware of the spate of murders in the area since February 9th," Sasha said.

"Yes, I'm aware of some."

"There are details no one outside the police department knows about. Once we make an arrest and file charges, more details on the investigation will become public."

John leaned forward. "Okay. How can I help you?"

Sasha looked up at Darcie. "Why don't you sit down?" Darcie sat in the chair next to him. "We had been working the murders as separate investigations, but we've learned that the cases are intertwined."

"Intertwined?"

"Yes. The news media has written about"—Sasha looked at Darcie—"what is the current count? How many murders in Bloomington-Normal?"

"Six is the right number."

"Right. Six." Sasha looked across the desk. "The murders started with Ashley Cummins three and a half weeks ago."

"And you're looking for my help?"

"Well, we just wanted to talk with you about what we've learned so far. Ashley's death was the genesis of all the murders."

"I'm not following."

"I'll try to explain. We don't think any of the murders would have come about without Ashley's death." Sasha turned to Darcie. "Our investigation into her murder kept hitting walls." She nodded, then he turned back to John.

"When we hit walls, we find ways under, over, or through them to solve the case. It was frustrating for the two of us. I don't want to waste your time going over all the evidence we discovered, but you know evidence often bears no fruit."

John looked from Sasha to Darcie and nodded.

"Sometimes it does, though. In Ashley Cummins's murder investigation, we had a witness who saw three men outside her car at the time of her death, but the witness couldn't identify any of them. CSI didn't find any fingerprints that could lead us to suspects. The ME recovered a bullet from Ashley's body, and CSI found the spent cartridge in her car, but neither the bullet nor the cartridge were in the FBI's NIBIN database. See what I mean by hitting walls?"

"I guess."

"We came up with three strong suspects we thought could have been the men our witness saw outside Ashley's car. We interviewed all three, but since we didn't have any solid evidence tying them to the scene, they denied involvement. Without evidence to use as leverage against them, there was no incentive for them to cooperate." Sasha paused. "Two of the men are dead."

"That's unfortunate."

"Yes. William Green was found shot dead in the trunk of a burned-out car in Chicago, and Danny Williams was found drowned off the Florida coast. They were both drug dealers, and neither was a nice person. Sadly, Mr. Williams left a young daughter to be raised by his girlfriend, the kid's mother."

"I'm sorry to hear that." John looked back and forth between them. "That's unfortunate."

"Yes, it is. It was unfortunate for them as well as for Ashley's murder investigation. With a little more evidence to go on, we might have been able to leverage one of them to give up the others, but their untimely deaths ended any opportunity to discover their true involvement." Sasha looked at the man who showed no emotion staring back at him. "So it doesn't seem surprising to you that two of our suspects in her murder are dead?"

"I wouldn't know."

Sasha nodded. "It is unusual for a suspect in an investigation to be murdered, let alone two, killed twelve hundred miles apart. I have to tell you, it's one hell of a coincidence."

"It sounds like it." John leaned back in his chair.

"Yes. Then we have the murders of Adrian Wolenski and Marvin Milcen in Bloomington and Carleton Ward in Normal."

"I remember reading about Milcen. He died in the house fire with the two women, right?"

"Correct. Milcen was shot several times by two men before they fire-bombed the house. He was a drug dealer, too. A young woman and her friend in the attic apartment were unable to escape. The friend was the mother of two young children who had already lost their father. Dental records were needed to identify all three."

"I do recall reading about the mother."

"Yes. You might also remember reading about Wolenski. A victim of a brutal hit-and-run on the east side of the city a couple of weeks ago. He was run over multiple times and left for dead in the parking lot of his apartment complex. The coup de grâce was the crushing of his skull, killing him instantly. Like I said, brutal."

John leaned forward again. "Sounds like it. I don't recall reading about—who did you say—Wolenski?"

"Maybe you were out of town when that happened?" Sasha waited for a response. He did not get one and continued. "The first person killed after Ashley Cummins was Carleton Ward, a low-level drug dealer who lived in Normal. Normal PD detectives believe a rival killed him over drug turf. We're not sure that's right, as it's hard to imagine anyone would kill him for just his territory. Have you read about Mr. Ward?"

Looking at Sasha, John shook his head. "I don't think so."

"Someone slit his throat from ear to ear." The senior detective looked at Darcie. "I think they also slit his dog's throat, too."

Darcie glanced from Sasha to John. "That's right."

"On the street, Ward was known as Carlos Ward-Wallace. Does that name sound familiar?"

"No, it doesn't." John turned from Sasha and looked out his window before looking back. "I didn't read about a murder in Normal."

"So, those are some of the murders in Bloomington-Normal."

Darcie looked over at Sasha. "Don't forget the other two."

"Other two?" Sasha nodded, then looked across the desk at the man. "That's right. There are also two men missing." John did not react. "They disappeared right off the face of the Earth. One day they were around, and the next day gone. We can't find them anywhere."

"I'm not sure why you're here talking with me, Detective," John said.

"I thought you'd be interested in knowing all that's happened. It's bizarre, isn't it?" Sasha turned to Darcie. "Around mid-February, Leon Ross and Darren Redmond went missing."

John looked down at his desk and sighed heavily. "What are you doing here, Detective? What do you want from me?"

"I believe you know R.J. Carlson."

"Yes."

Darcie spoke up. "R.J. told us that he met with you on February 11th."

"We have drinks every Monday." John looked at his calendar. "The 11th was a Monday."

"Ergo, you had drinks." Sasha smiled. "He tells us he discussed the names we've mentioned to you this afternoon on the 11th."

"I had a fair amount to drink that night. I don't recall him mentioning any names, but I do remember him talking about a case he was working." John leaned back. "As I said, I had a lot to drink."

"R.J. said he had a lot to drink, too."

"We both did." He looked at Darcie and smiled.

Sasha changed his tack. "How many men have you defended over the years?"

"A lot. I've prosecuted a lot too. Why?"

"Did any of the names R.J. mentioned that night ring a bell?"

"I told you I don't recall any of the names. I was drinking."

"You're not drinking now." Sasha paused. "So, none of the names we mentioned ring a bell?"

"No."

"None?"

"I told you no." John shifted in his chair.

"Once we realized that the men on our list were being targeted, we tried finding the remaining men on the list." Sasha smiled and paused before continuing, "Just after midnight, early this past Wednesday morning, officers arrested two men as they attempted to kidnap and kill Charles Johns at his home." John's expression did not change. "Do you know the names Jaime Guerra or Mateo Bacerac?" Sasha was hoping to see a small tell that John acknowledged knowing the names, but he saw none.

"I'm not familiar with either of them."

"They're talking. Both are members of a Chicago gang led by a man named Reyna. It's an offshoot of a Mexican cartel. Do you know Reyna?"

"I'm not familiar with that name, either."

"Really?"

John started to stand. "Is that all, Detective?"

"Just a few more minutes, please."

He looked at his watch. "I've got a two o'clock meeting."

"We'll be done shortly. I promise." Sasha watched as John slowly sat back in his chair. "Thank you. I believe you when you say you don't know Bacerac or Guerra, but I don't believe you don't know Reyna."

John sat up straight in his chair. "You're mistaken, Detective."

"Odd. Reyna says he knows you." Sasha saw a slight change in John's expression.

"Then he's mistaken."

"I don't think so. Reyna says he's known you for quite a few years."

"Maybe he's heard about me, but I don't know a Diego Reyna."

"That's interesting. I didn't say his first name." Sasha let that sink in. "He says he met you when you were a public defender. You defended one of his gang members." Sasha looked at his notes. "Manuel Cabeza."

John stared across the desk at Sasha.

"Do you remember Mr. Cabeza?" Sasha waited, but there was no response. "Court records show that you defended him." Since arresting Guerra and

Bacerac, Sasha and Darcie had been looking for connections between Reyna and his gang to the Bloomington-Normal area. They discovered that almost ten years ago, when he was a public defender, John Lewisman successfully had the charges dropped for one of Reyna's gang members accused of attempted murder. Sasha was now going to lie to John about what Reyna and the arrested gang members were telling them. "Reyna said you two were like BFFs." Sasha waited a few seconds. "With Guerra and Bacerac talking, Reyna cut a deal. We know everything."

"You know everything?" John leaned further back in his chair and looked at the two detectives across from him. "You know everything. I don't even know what that means." He was quickly going through his options. John couldn't be sure whether Diego had talked with the detectives or what he might have told them. If the other two were in custody, police would have quickly established their affiliation with Diego. If Diego knew the two were in custody, why hadn't he given him a heads-up? Did the two cave during inter-rogation, giving up Diego? Doubtful, but he couldn't be sure.

"Bacerac and Guerra are in custody." Sasha leaned back in his chair, appearing confident and at ease. "We already know Reyna didn't kill any-one himself, but he is responsible for having everyone killed. Everyone except Ashley Cummins."

"I wouldn't know."

"The two in custody decided to cooperate with the DA when he took the death penalty off the table."

As though he was playing a game of chess against worthy opponents, and on the clock, John sat considering his next move. "I don't know the two men you've got in custody, but you're correct. I do know Diego Reyna. It's been years, and I didn't initially recall his name. My caseload as a public defender was much heavier than as a prosecutor. I'd forgotten his associa-tion with my client."

Sasha smiled to himself. Admitting he knew Diego Reyna was the first volley that scored a hit. "Reyna says you contacted him recently."

"That's not true."

"Reyna says you wanted people killed."

"That's not true either." John knew he needed to keep his emotions in check.

"What was in it for Reyna to kill off all these people for you?"

"For me?" John said firmly. "You're wrong, Detective."

"I don't think so. What was the quid pro quo for Reyna?"

Growing impatient, John stood up and said, "I've got an appointment soon."

Sasha wanted to escalate the building tension in the room. What he and Darcie had learned as fact, and what he planned on suggesting they knew, would be critical to further rattling John and putting him off balance. Whether he believed Sasha or not would make all the difference. "We know Reyna was behind the death of William Green. Chicago PD discovered his bullet-riddled body inside the trunk of a burned-out shell of a stolen car on the South Side. A bold statement by Reyna, especially considering the car and body were found on a rival gang's turf. A 'we're taking over, and there's nothing you can do about it' kind of statement."

"As I already told you—"

"He was one of our prime suspects in Ashley Cummins's murder." Sasha paused. "Remember?"

"That may be a fact, but I still don't know him, Detective."

Sasha liked that John used the word "fact." "Another fact is that R.J. Carlson told you the names of the men on our list of suspects. With so many of them now missing or dead, you are the only person outside a select group in the department aware of those names. That certainly makes you a person of interest."

"Are you suggesting I need a lawyer?"

"Only you would know that." Sasha paused. "Right now, I believe you have information that will provide us further clarity and help us solve every one of these murders. Why don't you tell us what you know?"

"If I thought I knew something that would help you, I'd tell you, Detective. This is getting tiresome. I think we're done here."

"Well, we're finding it interesting talking with Jaime Guerra and Mateo

Bacerac." Sasha leaned forward. "Let's talk more about them. Remember we talked about the two men involved with Milcen's death? And the two girls."

John sighed. "Yes."

"The first 911 caller who reported gunshots and the fire identified a picture out of the photo array we showed him yesterday morning." Sasha paused. "We included mug shots of Guerra and Bacerac in the two six-packs. He immediately picked out who he originally told detectives was the 'big guy' on the back stairs. It was Bacerac. Having a witness identify him was the main reason the big guy decided to talk." That was a lie. He paused again. "We also have the guns the two used to kill Milcen." That was partly based on fact. CSI had confirmed the gun carried by Guerra had fired the bullet the ME had removed during Milcen's autopsy, and the man who'd fired the gun had admitted that he and Bacerac were the ones who had killed the man.

"I don't know either the big guy or the small guy, Detective." That was true. John hadn't met either Guerra or Bacerac, but he knew which was which. So they were talking to save their skins. John's mind was whirling. He needed to stick to stating facts and not get caught in lies.

Sasha smiled. "Well, we've discussed the coincidences of you being the only person outside the investigation knowing about our suspect list and your connection to Diego Reyna." The senior detective glanced at Darcie. "With your acknowledgment of a relationship with Reyna, we can now further connect the dots from you to Guerra and Bacerac." Sasha waited for John to reply. He'd learned early in his career that his best offensive play was to remain silent.

"That's obviously a stretch, Detective."

"I disagree. Again, I know we're talking about coincidences, but they're adding up."

"I've got a two o'clock meeting."

"Don't worry. Darcie will let your assistant know we're running a bit late and will finish up soon."

John stood up. "No. We're finished now."

Sasha and Darcie stayed seated. "Not yet. I understand this is running longer than you'd like, but I must insist we keep going." Sasha looked at Darcie.

"Could you please let John's assistant know our meeting is running long?" Darcie nodded, stood, and left the office.

John sat back down. "What more do you want from me?"

"I think we were going to talk more about coincidences." Sasha thought now would be a good time to bring up the judge. "Let's wait for Darcie to return."

Darcie walked back into the office and sat down. She looked at Sasha, then to John. "We're good. Did I miss anything?"

"No. We waited for you. Now, where were we?"

"I think you were going to talk about Judge Cummins." She looked at John. "His family believes the judge was coerced into committing suicide."

Sasha nodded. "Yes. Not everyone knows the judge left a suicide note."

"Word got out, Detective."

"Probably. We believed the judge willingly wrote the suicide note to take responsibility for the murders. Honestly, everyone but his family did." Sasha looked for a reaction from John but saw none. "As a father, I can see how he could have been capable of seeking revenge for Ashley's death." The senior detective paused. "I'm sure you can, too."

John nodded but said nothing.

"The family also doesn't believe that the judge would know someone like Reyna. Someone with the capability of having people killed here in Bloomington, let alone ordering the deaths of people in Chicago and Miami." The senior detective paused again. "More importantly, because of his religious beliefs, they find him incapable of taking his own life."

John shifted in his chair.

"You were friends with the judge?"

"I've been a public defender and prosecutor in this area for years. Every lawyer knows the judge."

"That's another fact. But the judge's wife told us that he'd gotten together with you many times since Ashley's death. She said the two of you having coffee together was—" Sasha looked down at his notes. "She said it was *unusual*."

"As you know, my daughter was a murder victim. The judge wanted to know how to deal with such a loss. I had a sympathetic ear."

Sasha looked at John and thought that was a quick, plausible explanation. Almost practiced. Sasha decided to push harder. "Perhaps, but we don't think that's the only reason you were meeting. Ultimately, you used the judge as a fall guy."

"A fall guy? I don't follow."

"The judge was coerced into killing himself. His family saw inconsistencies in the photos CSI had taken, subtle messages that the judge did not willingly kill himself." Sasha paused as he prepared to tell John what the family had seen. "You knew the judge was left-handed?"

"Yes."

"The judge used his right hand to hold the revolver. That seems odd. He also left the note and pen positioned opposite from the way he would have naturally left them on the desk." Sasha placed a sheet of paper on John's desk and recreated what the judge had done when he'd left the note. "See what I mean? The judge went out of his way to leave a clue that he was coerced. The family saw it, but everyone else missed it."

John looked at Sasha. "So you're suggesting the judge committing suicide somehow incriminates me in all this?"

"If the judge was involved, as his note clearly states, he'd need someone like you who knew someone like Reyna to carry out the killings. You would also have a hatred of men like those on our list. Men preying on the vulnerable, destroying their lives with drugs, and destroying the lives of their families as collateral damage."

"This is all pure fabrication, Detective."

"No, John, it's not." Sasha paused a few seconds, waiting to see if John would say something. He didn't. "You recall my mentioning Guerra?"

John fidgeted in his chair. "Yes."

"Let me lay it out for you again." Sasha looked down at his notes. "You got the names on our list from R.J. You reached out to your contact, Reyna, to carry out the vigilante justice you had so desperately wanted, revenge for your daughter's death. After your initial meeting with the judge, you felt sorry for him for the pain that he was experiencing. The pain you understood so well. The pain he was feeling after losing his only granddaughter to drug dealers."

John lowered his head, then looked up at Sasha. "Ridiculous. I really don't know why you're here. Now you're just making things up."

"You and Reyna planned out the revenge killings. After two innocent women died in the fire, you and Reyna decided you needed a fall guy. The judge was a perfect patsy." Sasha paused again and leaned forward in his chair. "You and Reyna decided to set him up, forcing him to write a note confessing he was solely responsible for all the killings and to shoot himself."

John shifted in his chair again. Based on what the senior detective was laying out, he now believed Diego and his men were in police custody. Did they cut a deal as Sasha had said, leaving him out to dry? Up to this point, John was holding out hope that all this was smoke and mirrors. After learning the men on their suspect list had been killed or were missing, police might have been shadowing the last man Diego's thugs were looking for. If they had arrested them as they attempted to kidnap Johns, the two could be singing like canaries. Was it plausible, he wondered? He hadn't spoken with Diego for several days, so it was a distinct possibility.

"Do you remember having coffee downtown on February 28th, the morning after the house fire killed Milcen, Jenna Jameson, and Kelly Moran?" He could see he was rattling John. "You and Judge Harvey Cummins were arguing." There it was. Sasha had just seen it in his eyes. "What were you two arguing about?"

"We weren't arguing."

"Yes, you were. Everyone in the restaurant heard you. Why were you arguing?"

John sat in silence, assessing his options. It was clear R.J. had told them he had passed along the list of potential suspects over drinks. It was apparent the detectives had learned a great deal from Diego and his men. How should he answer the senior detective? Time was running out for him. "As I mentioned, I had a sympathetic ear. He was angry about his granddaughter's death."

"So you're suggesting that the judge was upset that morning about Ashley's murder? Blanche Collins told us that she heard the judge say something to you loudly about a *tragic accident*."

"I don't recall that."

"Blanche is positive that the judge said it."

"Then she misheard."

"I don't think so, John. Blanche also told us the judge said something about one of them having two small children." Sasha looked at his notes, then he looked back at John. "Why was the judge talking about Kelly Moran?"

John was trying to maintain his calm. "I have no idea why Blanche would say these things."

"Waitstaff working in bars and restaurants overhear things all the time. There is no expectation of privacy." Sasha leaned forward. "Blanche is a credible witness. You may be surprised to hear that after the judge died, she memorialized what she heard of your conversation since she felt it was a little odd." The senior detective paused. "Blanche also told us that she overheard the judge telling you, 'That wasn't supposed to happen.' What wasn't supposed to happen?"

John sat back in his chair. Blanche had overheard more than he'd thought. His back had been facing the front of the restaurant, so he hadn't seen Blanche coming and going. "I can tell you what I know."

Sasha leaned back in the chair. "We're listening."

"Harvey was frustrated that you hadn't arrested Ashley's killer. He wasn't a patient man, and he wanted retribution. When I told Harvey that R.J. had asked whether I had defended or prosecuted any of the names on the list of suspects in Ashley's murder, he asked for the names, knowing the names provided what he called *a unique opportunity*."

"A unique opportunity?"

"Revenge for Ashley. With the police not finding her killers, the judge asked if I knew of anyone that could give him justice. I told him about Diego Reyna and gave the judge a way to contact him. That was all I did."

Sasha glanced at Darcie. "It sounds like you were heavily involved."

"I had no idea what Harvey would do or how he'd decide to proceed."

"So, you're telling us that the judge contacted a man he didn't know, orchestrated a plan of revenge with a Chicago gang leader, and then when the plan went awry, committed suicide?" Sasha paused. "I don't believe you."

"That's what happened."

"I'll tell you what I think happened. R.J. inexcusably passed along the list of suspects to you. You took the names to the judge, and the two of you concocted a plan to avenge the killing of Ashley and your daughter. You enlisted Diego Reyna. I don't know why Reyna agreed to help you, but we will find that out. When two innocents died, the judge had second thoughts and expressed to you he wanted to confess his involvement. Neither you nor Reyna could allow that to happen, so the judge was forced to write a suicide note and shoot himself." Sasha shook his head. "A foolproof plan. What you didn't expect was that the judge would leave clues for his family to let them know he hadn't willingly committed suicide."

"You're wrong, Detective."

Sasha eyed John. He had admitted discussing with the judge the list of names and contact information for Diego Reyna. Those two acts alone made him a co-conspirator in the deaths of many, including the judge. With Guerra telling them that he'd gotten the judge to kill himself by threatening the lives of his family, the DA could ultimately charge John with the deaths of nine people. The two detectives hadn't shared that divers had found the two missing men in a lake south of Odell this morning.

Sasha was sure that John was the instigator in all that had transpired. In Sasha's mind, with the judge dead, John was left holding the bag as the mastermind in the plot.

Darcie received a text. She looked at her phone and showed the picture to Sasha. The senior detective was looking at a picture of a box of burner phones in the trunk of John's car, which was parked in the same garage where they had just parked. Sasha grinned. He believed he now had damning evidence to arrest John for his deliberate duplicity in exacting revenge for his daughter's death and Ashley's murder.

"Hey, John. We just found your stash of burner phones. I'll bet a dollar that one of those phones is going to tie you to the one we found hidden in the judge's car." Sasha believed that with a little more work, they'd be able to tie the two men from Chicago's phones to Reyna and ultimately back to John. With Guerra and Bacerac in custody and talking, the die was cast. "Guerra and Bacerac are providing details of their involvement, as I said, and the DA offered them leniency to get them to tell us all they know." Sasha shook his head. "When facing the death penalty, life in prison is always a better option. You of all people should know it's surprising what little you have to offer to get someone to cooperate when they're cornered."

John looked across the desk at Sasha. With Harvey dead and Guerra and Bacerac under arrest, the senior detective was correct. John understood there would be sufficient evidence to charge him with conspiracy. It was very likely that one of Diego's men had cut a deal as the senior detective had suggested. With the two gang members in custody and facing charges, police and prosecutors would be able to keep them under lock and key without any opportunity for bail. There would be no chance for him to get out on bail, either, or Diego, if he was indeed under arrest as the detectives had suggested. He knew investigators would continue to look for additional evidence to tie the four of them to the murders. If Harvey had left incriminating evidence for police to find, John would indeed be left holding the bag. He knew he had few options left. "I'm going to want to talk with my lawyer now, Detective."

Sasha stood. "Certainly, John."

"I'd also appreciate you asking my assistant to call the DA. It's time to put an end to all of this."

Darcie stood up, turned, and walked down the hall to talk with John Lewisman's assistant, as he'd requested.

"This tragedy started and ended with the death of a Cummins," Sasha said, "with a lot of death in between. I'm sorry you were a part of this tragedy, John."

"You're wrong, Detective. It actually started with my daughter's death." John bowed his head. "It's no one's fault but my own. It was time for revenge. The judge and I traded our souls for it." John shook his head. "Because of my daughter's brutal murder, I became a willing participant. I'm just sorry that the two young women died. Harvey was right. That wasn't supposed to happen."

"Why did the judge have to die?"

"He gave us no choice."

Sasha stared at the prosecutor and shook his head. "He gave you no choice?"

"When we left the restaurant that morning, it was clear he wasn't going to see the plan through. The two girls dying in the fire changed everything. I was concerned that he was going to go to the chief and tell him everything we'd done." John paused. "I called Reyna to let him know what the judge had said, and he went crazy when he heard. He threatened to kill the judge, his family, and me and mine. I tried to explain to Reyna that I thought Harvey could be convinced to take the heat for everyone, but that wasn't enough. He said Harvey had to die."

The senior detective looked at John incredulously. "So you went along with that?"

"My choice was to go along with Harvey dying or face Reyna's wrath on all of us." John lowered his head. "I made the only choice I could. I rationalized that having the judge dead would save the lives of both our families."

"And you," Sasha said. "So that's why you forced the judge to shoot himself?"

John looked at Sasha quizzically. "You want more details than you already have?"

Sasha nodded. "I want the unvarnished version of what happened directly from you."

John nodded. "Guerra and Bacerac entered Harvey's home through the garage. Marjorie was with her daughters in Chicago for the weekend, so I knew he would be alone. They found him in his library, and Guerra gave him the simple choice." John sat down and leaned back in his chair. "Harvey was told that he had to write the note taking responsibility for the killings of the suspects in his granddaughter's murder and shoot himself, or they'd kill him and Marjorie and all of his family."

"Reyna would have done that?"

"No question. Reyna is an animal, and Guerra and Bacerac can be very compelling. Harvey wrote the note as"—John stopped and laid his head back—"as I instructed them to have him write it. The words he wrote were my words." John laughed to himself. "And he did write them. But leaving the note and pen on the desk the way he did and using his right hand to shoot himself—" John paused again. "Harvey got the last laugh, didn't he?"

"The judge was going to die anyway." Sasha shook his head. "I guess he didn't want to die without sending a message."

"What do you mean, he was going to die anyway?"

"The judge had stage IV stomach and pancreatic cancer. He only had a few weeks to live."

John was dumbfounded. "I didn't know that. That explains why he was adamant we move so quickly. He wanted pictures of each man killed. He wanted to see them paying the price for taking his granddaughter from his family."

Sasha stepped forward. "Are there pictures of the men on the phones we found in your car?"

"Yes. Guerra and Bacerac took pictures of each man they killed. Diego sent them to me, and I sent them to Harvey. You'll also find a picture of Williams taken in Florida." John stood up again. "I will give everything to you, Sasha." He looked at the detective. "It sounds like you already have most of it. I purchased all the burner phones we used to communicate with each other and with Diego as well."

The senior detective walked around the desk. "We should go now, John." Sasha stood next to the prosecutor and read him his Miranda rights.

"I'm sorry the two young women died."

As the three walked down the long hallway to the elevator, the senior detective smiled to himself. While getting John to fully admit to his participation in all that had taken place, Sasha had presented facts, misrepresented some facts, made false claims of evidence they had uncovered, and bluffed his way through the meeting with the prosecutor. He thought his father, a retired FBI agent, would be proud of his work on all the investigations tied to Ashley Cummins's murder. Although the investigation had started out slowly, what they'd found would result in solving multiple cases and getting multiple convictions.

He knew that if Kelly Moran and Jenna Jameson hadn't died in the house fire, he and Darcie may have never been able to solve any of the murders.

Sasha hoped they would be able to solve Ashley Cummins's murder. The deliberate duplicity of the judge and John had made that more difficult, but not impossible.

After he and Darcie arrived at the station and booked John Lewisman for conspiracy to commit murder—the first charge they would level against him—Sasha would call Charlie Cummins and ask to meet with him and his family. He would be able to tell them that the judge hadn't committed suicide but was as guilty as John Lewisman and everyone else.

EPILOGUE

In the months following the arrests of John Lewisman, Diego Reyna, Jaime Guerra, and Mateo Bacerac, Sasha and Darcie continued investigating the string of murders that had begun with Ashley Cummins. In an effort to gain leniency from the DA, the four men provided specific details of each murder.

Charlie Cummins and his mother met John Lewisman in the county jail, and John told them what Guerra and Bacerac had done to coerce the judge to shoot himself. John was able to relieve at least some of the pain the family was feeling.

Sasha had been considering retiring, but as the cases against the four men were wrapping up, Sasha received a fortuitous call from Damien Murphy, the Chicago Police detective who had reached out to him and Darcie. He updated them on some new information about the gun used in the killing of the Chicago gang member he'd been investigating, the same gun used to kill Ashley Cummins. It had been found in the possession of a man named Aaron Slater. Slater was arrested during a drug sting operation on the city's South Side. One of the other gang members arrested during the sting flipped on Slater and told police that he was one of the shooters involved in the February 21st murder of three men in the Chatham neighborhood. Slater had provided information to police that had ultimately led them to a Chicago gang leader named Rattler, who in turn provided information on a gun Charles Johns had traded him the day Ashley had been murdered.

Sasha had believed two of the three men Jasmine Warren had seen outside Ashley Cummins's white convertible had paid the ultimate price for her death, but he had been unable to prove it. Now, with the gun used to kill Ashley tied directly to him, Charles Johns confessed to killing her that cold night, and he provided all the details of what had taken place at the corner of Lee and Oakland that led to her death.

After talking with Janet, Sasha decided that now wasn't the time to retire. Janet would still be working, and he wasn't someone who could stop and do nothing. Being a senior detective defined him, and Sasha decided to put off retirement. He liked his new partner, Darcie Lyman, and he hoped that she would stay working with him for a while longer before moving to the Rockies.

Deliberate Duplicity

David Rohlfing

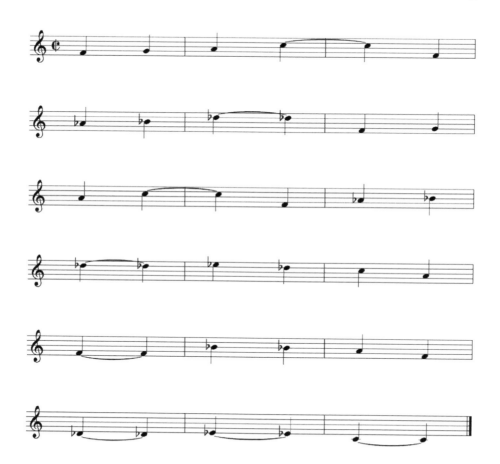

© 2020

AUTHOR Q&A

Q: This is your second book in the Detective Sasha Frank Mystery Series. What was your inspiration for this mystery? Did you draw any ideas or inspiration from *Deliberate Duplicity*?

A: *Cold Consequences* was written as a prequel to *Deliberate Duplicity*. The inspiration for this book was the uptick in drug-related crimes and murders in the twin cities of Bloomington-Normal over the past few years. In this book, I provided additional background information on various characters that appear in *Deliberate Duplicity* and those who will be continuing characters in the Detective Sasha Frank Mystery Series.

Q: *Cold Consequences* takes place about five years before *Deliberate Duplicity*. Which did you have the idea for first? How do you feel this prequel gives readers better insight into Sasha Frank's character?

A: During the writing of my first book, I enjoyed writing about the main character, so I decided that I should write a series of books featuring Senior Detective Sasha Frank. I did not have the series laid out in my mind when I first started, but while writing *Deliberate Duplicity*, I began thinking about what would be required to develop recurring characters and what *Cold Consequences* could be about. I provided a great deal of background about Sasha and other characters in the first book with the series in mind. In this second book, I tried to provide readers with more insight into what drives Sasha in his pursuit of justice for those killed. Justice is an overriding mindset for Sasha.

Q: In several chapters, you switch the perspective from Sasha Frank to either a victim or a criminal. Were these chapters easier or more challenging to write? You could have written the entirety of the book from Sasha Frank's perspective, so what motivated you to switch perspectives?

A: As both a reader and writer of books, I believe that giving the perspective of other key characters makes the story more interesting and not so one dimensional. By giving additional perspectives from those committing the murders, and those of the victims, readers are given an understanding of personal motivations for the crimes from various characters and not just from Sasha Frank. I think giving the reader other takes on what is happening in the book makes the story more interesting and believable.

Q: You often reference the severity of the opioid epidemic and prescription drug abuse in your novel. Why did you decide to write about this issue? What message did you want to send with this book?

A: Drug abuse is not a new phenomenon. Opioids are in the news quite often. They cause immense destruction to the greater community—not only to the person addicted to the drug. Those who spiral into drug addiction often find themselves unable or unwilling to find or ask for help. The ease of availability of opioids for those seeking relief of chronic pain, or in some instances the desire to escape the stresses of daily life, makes the opioid epidemic one of the most important health issues of our time. As a society, we need to find solutions to help all of those impacted by the dire consequences of drug abuse.

Q: It seems as if every chapter in this book brought on a new layer of mystery or new bit of essential information to Sasha Frank's investigation. Which chapter did you enjoy writing the most? Which did you have the most trouble with?

A: It is difficult to point to a single chapter in providing an answer to the first question. I enjoy writing, and each chapter adds depth to the story. I find myself continually returning to earlier chapters to add details as the story unfolds. My writing style is to not outline the book but rather to develop the storyline as I write. This style goes against everything that I have read about how to write a book, but it is what works best for me. In answering the second question, writing a chapter featuring details of a gruesome murder are always difficult. Family and friends are amazed that the ideas for the Detective Sasha Frank Mystery Series exist in my mind.

Q: The relationships between the gangs in *Cold Consequences*, namely between Rattler's and Reyna's gangs, is interesting and well-written. What was your process for researching gang dynamics in Chicago? Did you find out anything you didn't expect?

A: Although I grew up and now live in Central Illinois, I have spent a great deal of time over the years in countless large cities around the globe. Gangs are a part of everyday life in most cities, and you can't escape the daily barrage of news stories about the destruction gangs bring to the most vulnerable among us. That is especially true for Chicago, where I lived for fifteen years in the River North area of downtown Chicago. I witnessed the fast rise in gang activity and violence in the city, so writing about it wasn't difficult.

Q: The pivotal moment in *Cold Consequences* is, arguably, when you reveal that the gruesome string of murders is the result of vigilante justice. What inspired you to write this twist? Was this your intent when you set out to write this book, or did it come to you later?

A: Seeking revenge is a basic human instinct. The innate desire to mete out vengeance, especially when those responsible seem to be going unpunished, is what drives the characters in *Cold Consequences* to seek revenge for the deaths of their loved ones. With the police unable to find those responsible for Ashley's murder, they see no other choice but to seek justice on their own. The fact that people bearing no responsibility for her murder are also killed means nothing to them, as they seek their own justice.

Q: Once the investigation is complete, it turns out that many characters were somehow complicit in this string of murders. Who did you feel was the true antagonist? Was it hard to write this character?

A: There are multiple antagonists in the book, so it is difficult to point to just one, but I would prefer readers determine who they see as the main antagonist. It is hard to step into a character who embodies such evil.

Q: Do you have a favorite character in this novel? A least favorite? Why? Was there any direct inspiration for either of these characters and their traits?

A: Sasha is, of course, my favorite character as I find a lot of myself in him. Various characters who commit the killings in the book are evil people and are my least favorite; they have no redeeming value, but each of them is key to telling the story. Developing those characters is difficult as it is hard to delve into their minds and imagine being them.

Q: You've mentioned before that you relate to Sasha Frank as a character. Do you find this helps or hinders you as you write and develop him? Do you often access your own opinions and motivations to help you understand Sasha Frank better and write his reactions?

A: Yes, I think it is easier to write about Sasha for that reason. Some of my life experiences, how I interact with others, my view of life, and how I deal with issues are, in some part, embodied in Sasha's character.

Q: The characters in *Cold Consequences* are dynamic and layered, with complex backstories and desires. What's your process for creating characters like these?

A: As I mentioned earlier, I continually go back and add details to characters as I write to make them more interesting to me; I hope readers of the series will find them more interesting as well. As I write, I think about how and why various characters react to the events as they develop in the story. I attempt to develop characters as complex as the story. Those are the types of books I like to read.

Q: *Cold Consequences* is truly an immersive and complex journey. What was your writing process like? Did you set a schedule and a strict time to write? What was the most challenging part of the process for you, and how did you overcome it?

A: I tend to write during the late fall and winter, typically writing for four to six hours a day. While writing, I often wake up in the middle of the night when an idea for the book comes to mind, so I get up and write to ensure that I don't lose the idea. I do not have a strict routine and often walk away from the book for several days to help refocus on what I have written, how it can be improved, and what comes next in the story.

Q: As readers, we watch Detective Sasha Frank unravel the mystery of Ashley Cummins's death and the murders that follow, but as the author, what was your process for creating the mystery and the crime?

A: The idea for the second book in the series came from a desire to write about the ongoing opioid crisis and how drug abuse can cause unintended consequences, which can therefore affect countless people besides the person using them.

Q: The writing in this book conveys a lot of knowledge about police and detective work. How did you research for this novel? Did your research and research process change between writing *Deliberate Duplicity* and *Cold Consequences*?

A: I used the same methodology in writing *Cold Consequences* as I did in writing *Deliberate Duplicity*. Through reading and watching both fictional and real-life police and crime books, movies, and television shows, I think we have all been immersed in and absorb many of the tactics used by the police to solve crimes. I use all that I have learned over the years and occasionally check online on any issue that I don't grasp.

Q: What advice would you give aspiring authors? Did you have any specific experiences while writing this novel that would help them?

A: I think I am too early in my writing career to really offer advice to others. I know what works for me and that is that if you want to write a first novel, find a genre that speaks to you and just start writing it. Finding someone close to you that you trust, who can offer you honest feedback on what you are writing, is critical. For me, that is my wife. Whoever that someone is in your life needs to find what you are writing interesting, of course.

Q: In the epilogue, we see Detective Sasha Frank make the decision to stay on the force. What can you say about your plans for future Detective Sasha Frank mysteries?

A: I am in the process of writing the third book in the series, and it will be no surprise to know that Sasha hasn't retired and is investigating another murder.

My plan is to have it ready to be published in the first half of 2022. I have ideas for several other books featuring Detective Sasha Frank, so don't expect to see him retiring anytime soon.

QUESTIONS FOR DISCUSSION

1. Detective Sasha Frank is often adamant about respecting and caring for the humans behind the crimes in this book. How do you think this impacted his investigation?

2. In *Cold Consequences*, the public places a fair amount of pressure on Sasha Frank, especially the mayor and Ashley's grandfather, who even goes so far as involve himself in the investigation by planning the deaths of those involved. What was your opinion on this? How do you feel about the public's opinion on active investigations?

3. In the book, Darcie states that Ashley put herself in the position to be murdered. Do you agree with Darcie? Why or why not?

4. Which moments did you feel were the most defining for the investigation? For Sasha Frank?

5. Many characters in *Cold Consequences* have some sort of secret that motivates them throughout the novel. Did you ever suspect that any of these characters had secrets? How do you feel these hidden motivations moved the plot of the novel along?

6. What was your reaction to discovering that the gruesome string of murders was the work of Ashley Cummins's grandfather and a lawyer? Did you expect it? How did this revelation make you feel about these two characters' acts of vigilante justice? Do you think John and Harvey were justified in their actions? Why or why not?

7. After Harvey Cummins's suicide, it is revealed that he had late-stage cancer. How much do you think this influenced his decision to seek out justice himself for his granddaughter's murder? Do you think this justifies his decisions? Why or why not?

8. How do you think this investigation impacted Sasha Frank? Do you think it changed him or influenced how he worked in *Deliberate Duplicity*?

9. In *Cold Consequences*, nearly every character was somehow complicit in the series of murders. Which character do you feel was most at fault? Which character do you think was the biggest victim?

10. Did you enjoy when the perspective shifted in several chapters to that of the victim or the criminal? How did it impact your reading of the book? Did you find it made you sympathize with the characters more or less?

11. Which do you think was the bigger motivator for John Lewisman to reach out to Diego Reyna—to lower crime and get these people in jail, to help Harvey Cummins, or to get revenge for his daughter's murder? Why?

12. Throughout *Cold Consequences*, the initial crime quickly spirals into a diabolical plot that spreads far beyond its original reach. What signs did you catch earlier in the book that there was more going on?

13. The author often makes references to the severity of the opioid epidemic in America and the challenges people face. Where did you find these references in the book? How do you think they impacted your reading? Did it make the book more real and personal for you?

14. What emotion was the primary motivator for Sasha Frank? Harvey Cummins? John Lewisman? Diego Reyna?

15. Which character did you like the most and why? Who did you most dislike?

16. Ashley Cummins is portrayed as an innocent woman whose murder led to a spiraling series of events. Do you feel like she was innocent? Or do you, like Darcie, feel as if she put herself in the position to get murdered?

17. What role did you feel Janet played in the story? How did she contribute to your perspective of Sasha's character? Did you appreciate what she brought to the story? Why or why not?

18. Through the perspectives of the antagonists in the story, as readers, we remain relatively close to the truth as we watch Sasha try to figure everything out. Did you enjoy this departure from typical mystery novels? Why or why not?

19. In your opinion, what was the main theme or message of this novel? What message did you take away from it?

ABOUT THE AUTHOR

Over the past year and a half, while we all experienced the COVID-19 pandemic, David wrote his second book featuring Senior Detective Sasha Frank. Although travel has always been an important part of his life, he spent most of his time in Illinois during the pandemic. He's looking forward to spending more time with family and friends. David continues to live in Illinois with his wife.

He is currently working on the third novel in the Detective Sasha Frank Mystery Series. Please visit his website at www.davidrohlfing.com, where you can sign up to receive updates on the release of future books.

Made in the USA
Columbia, SC
04 September 2021